P9-DTB-413

Nell's head rested against his shoulder and his arm went gently about her. His hand turned her chin gently upward.

"Not—yet, please." Nell slid strategically so his lips hit her temple.

"Forgive me," he said quietly. "For a moment I forgot myself." Instantly Alexi was correct, straightening up, drawing Nell's hand to his lips, breathing deeply in and out, the picture of a man mastering passion, prepared to wait forever for the favor of the one woman in the world.

Was it possible this man planned to kill her stepson and marry her?

SATAN'S COAST

ELSIE LEE

A DELL BOOK

Published by
Dell Publishing Co., Inc.
1 Dag Hammarskjold Plaza
New York, New York 10017

Copyright © 1969 by Elsie Lee

All rights reserved. No part of this book may be reproduced or transmitted in any form or by any means, electronic or mechanical, including photocopying, recording or by any information storage and retrieval system, without the written permission of the Publisher, except where permitted by law.

Dell ® TM 681510, Dell Publishing Co., Inc.

ISBN: 0-440-17827-4

Printed in the United States of America
First Dell printing—November 1978

SATAN'S COAST

CHAPTER I

It is not easy to be a second wife, particularly when the first one died of alcoholism, and your husband has only gained custody of his son by vicious court battles. If, furthermore, that husband is fifteen years your senior, and you love him deeply, you do not ask questions or raise subjects he prefers not to discuss.

So I knew little of Costa Demonio, except that I had inherited the place—and apparently not too much else, aside from the guardianship of Bart's son. I remembered Bart's reaction when *he* inherited by his great-uncle's death. The letter arrived one Saturday morning, shortly after our marriage. "That's strange," he murmured frowning. "There doesn't seem to be anything but the property. What the hell was he living on?"

"What did you say, darling?"

He tossed the letter aside. "Dom Sansao Valentim—I told you he died a while back?"

"So you did. Does that make you Dom Bartolomeu?"

"Not really. Americans don't use titles." He took a forkful of omelet and eyed the letter again. "I don't understand it. Here's the list of assets from the agents in Caldarém, and there's nothing but a couple of thousand dollars and Costa Demonio."

"What's that?"

"It's a castle—but not in Spain." He snorted sardonically. "It has one foot in the sea, and the rest of it will shortly tumble after."

"Still—a castle!" I was impressed. "Not everybody has one, darling. Shall we go and look at it?"

"No," Bart said with finality. "I've already seen it."

Now I was about to see it too—but not with Bart beside me. I stared drearily from the plane window into a gray sky of scudding clouds, wondering if we'd be able to see the coast of Portugal when we reached it. Beside me, my stepson, Christopher Valentim, slept soundly with the imperviousness to discomfort of a healthy fifteen-year-old. Beyond was the spare figure of Mariana, dozing correctly upright as befitted a servant who ought (she felt) to sit in the rear, except that the plane was full, and Bart had made a point of getting three seats together when he'd bought the tickets months ago.

Why, after leaving everything to an agent for five years, had my husband suddenly decided to take us to Costa Demonio? "It's time Chris saw the ancestral cradle; he's old enough for Europe now. We'll take a look, drive up through Portugal, cut across Spain to France . . . give the boy a taste of travel."

But even at the time, perhaps because of the extreme casualness of his voice, I'd thought Bart had some reason unknown to me. He had no desire to go, so it must have been something he *had* to do as owner of the castle. Yet, why *now?* He went to Lisbon on business at least once a year, sometimes oftener. If it were repairs, he could have whipped down by plane any time, but from the folder in his study file I knew he hadn't He didn't even know Revalhao, the Caldarém agent; the man was the son of the deceased Sansao's local attorney. I'd gone over and over it in my mind, but there was no clue—only my sixth sense.

It might be pure fancy. From chance words I knew Costa Demonio was concerned in Bart's discovery of Cecily's fatal weakness. Something had happened there the summer after Christopher's birth, something that superseded all the happy early memories, caused a complete breach with his great-uncle, and left a lasting scar. I had no clue to that either. I would never know now; Bart would never answer the questions I hadn't asked. He'd died two months back, following his annual date with the trout. Traditionally he held a stag week at the Adirondack cabin from April first. This time he had quite literally caught his death of cold, and my principal emotion was still incredulity.

NOBODY dies of pneumonia these days!

But Bart had, and suddenly I was Humpty Dumpty, surrounded by pieces of life without knowing where they belonged—although I was going to have to find out in a big fat hurry because Bart had left everything unconditionally to me.

I could tell Mr. Anderson wasn't happy about that when I walked into the law office, but I'm used to that reaction. It is not, after all, my fault that my ancestors gave me Celtic blue eyes, a mop of natural ash blonde curls, and a bone structure that causes photographers to swoon in ecstasy. I also have an IQ of 142 thanks to my mother, who may not look like much but who is a pioneer in computer programming. The resultant anachronism delighted Bart. "Who could *believe* that feather-witted exterior cloaks a steel-trap mentality worthy of Keynes!"

By the time I left his office, Mr. Anderson did, and it was the greatest relief to him. He gave me Xerox copies of everything to study at my leisure.

"What for? There isn't going to be enough, no matter what I do." But I took the manila envelope and tottered home, where Mariana opened the door. "Don't bother about dinner," I said wearily. "Bring me a sandwich, or some cheese and crackers . . . anything. I have to go over some things."

Her eyes widened slightly, but she only said, "Yes, senhora."

I went into Bart's study, spread out the papers, and looked at them again . . . but the end probuct was the same: not enough.

There was education money in a trust fund for Chris, set up as part of Bart's gaining custody; I hadn't to worry about that, thank goodness, aside from proper disbursement. There was some insurance, a modest stock portfolio, the apartment and cars could be sold, everything else was land and Bart's share in Valentim & Company. With luck, I'd have about four hundred a month, which would be luxury to lots of people, but was inadequate in my case.

The X-factor was Chris.

In the first moments of shock, we'd clung together wordlessly. Somehow we had gotten through the formalities of funeral and cemetery too numb for conversation, but Chris appeared to take it for granted he'd be with me.

But Cecily Drummonds' family were rich as Croesus, and Chris was their only grandson. They could and would provide every indulgence for him—which was exactly why Bart had fought them for custody. He said they'd ruined Cecily, he'd see them in hell before they got their hands on Chris. He would rely on me to hang onto Chris at all costs. But I didn't doubt that the Drummonds would be into court the instant they learned of Bart's death. At fifteen, any judge would allow Chris to decide with whom he wished to live.

I thought he'd choose me—but unless I could provide clothes, walkabout money, vacation bed and board, the Drummonds could make a good case for a change of guardian. On four hundred a month, with Chris growing out of his clothes twice a year, I couldn't do it without using capital, or selling land before it reached its eventual price.

The sickening thing was that I *could* manage it easily, but my hands were tied by the damned Drummonds. I had only to go back to work for a few years. I thought I'd even welcome being busy to occupy my mind. But my profession was (what else?) a highly paid photographers' model, and I could just imagine what the Drummonds' lawyer would insinuate about that! Yet if I used capital now, five years hence I might be past such work and unable to replace the money.

"Dinner, senhora." Mariana set a tray before me.

"I don't want anything, really."

She stood over me. "Eat!"

Automatically I picked up the spoon, began the cup of bouillon. It was borne in on me that from the moment of Bart's death there had been a subtle change in Mariana. She had always been polite, always accepted my orders; she was Portuguese, and she went with the family—first Bart's father, and after his death she moved on to Bart. With a horrid jolt, I realized Mariana had now moved on to Chris, or would expect to do so. But if I couldn't think how to pay my own bills, what on earth was I to do with her?

She was naturalized, so she could get another job; really well-trained maids are always in demand. But I had a fatalistic hunch she wouldn't leave, no matter what I said, and that would mean an apartment with three bedrooms. Silently, I wrestled with this unexpected problem, eating mechanically until I reached the demitasse, and Mariana took away the tray. "Thank you, Mariana. It was delicious."

"*De nada, senhora.*"

She came back shortly with a liqueur glass, "Curaçao, senhora." Then she simply stood, respectful but authoritative, a gaunt-faced middle-aged woman in conventional black evening uniform with organdy apron and crisp cap on her silver-fox hair. Her black eyes met mine. "I have dismissed Clara, senhora. There is no need for her at the moment."

"No. I cannot afford you either, Mariana," I looked at her directly, but she only nodded.

"Do not be disturbed, senhora. Together we can arrange everything," her voice was matter of fact. "First the apartment: I learned there is a smaller one on the third floor, and there are many requests for a penthouse."

I shook my head. "We can't afford a cooperative. We can't afford anything, Mariana," I said despairingly. "Oh, it's not poverty, there's really enough, but not right now. I don't know what's best to do, and I *can't* make a mistake, or those awful people might try to take Mr. Chris away from us."

"Not," said Mariana, "if he is living in a castle, senhora." I stared at her blankly, and she smiled. "Why not? It is what was planned by Senhor Bart. It removes us from America at little cost for the summer, allows time for further plans, and," she finished gazing innocently into space, "creates difficulties for legal matters."

"I suppose so, but could we really live there?" I scrabbled among the papers from Anderson, drew out the figures on Costa Demonio. "You see? Twenty bedrooms in the living section—and if there's more than one bath I'll be surprised! Even now, when the Algarve is fashionable, the agent can't rent it for more than a week or two each year."

Mariana studied the sheets, frowning. "Three farms rented, nearly eight hundred acres. I had not thought it so large," she murmured absently. "No matter about the old section, Dom Sansao's was comfortable, with old-fashioned furnishings perhaps, but with all modern conveniences. How can there be nothing more than money for taxes and a few repairs? What has become of the orchards, the vineyard, the livestock? Tchk, my father grows old!"

"Your father?"

"Huberto—he was Dom Sansao's personal servant. He is still caretaker," she said surprised. "You did not know? But yes, I am from Ponto Lucido. I was sent to Senhor Bart's father; my sister Luisa was with Senhor Rafael's mother; Juliana went to California." She eyed the figures again. "There was *always* money from the estate," she stated firmly, "apart from Dom Sansao's personal income, which was well known to be vast."

"Well known to whom? He must have spent it, Mariana. There was only a few thousand left when he died."

"I do not believe it," she said flatly. "He was wealthy, senhora. To the day of his death there was never the least economy, so much I know from my father. Always there was money! If it was not in banks, it is somewhere in Costa Demonio."

"Senhor Bart was surprised, too," I recalled, "but why would Dom Sansao have hidden his money?"

"Old men are strange." She shrugged. "Even my father does not believe in banks, although he has lived everywhere in the world when Dom Sansao was ambassador."

"I never knew that!"

"But yes, he was very important! My father was always with him from the time they were young men. There was the blood tie," she remarked calmly. "They had the same grandfather."

I gulped. "I didn't know. Senhor Bart never told me anything about Costa Demonio or his great-uncle."

"That was not right. He should not have held the bitterness so long." She laid aside the papers. "So: it is agreed? We go to Costa Demonio and see for ourselves, senhora?"

It sounded sensible. I had the tickets, and here we were on the plane. I was more than willing to leave New York after the exhaustion of the past six weeks. I didn't care what shape the castle was in, so long as there was a bed on which to fall flat and sleep forever. I didn't care that Mariana had master-minded the entire safari from the first moment. I could never have done it alone. Via the elevator, our apartment was so sooner offered than sold, which was nice for the exchequer but required total clearance. Any woman knows that what can be accumulated in five years is incredible.

All was behind me now; everything was packed or discarded, stored or shipped to Costa Demonio, and I was moving like a zombie, too tired either to close or fully open my eyes. Still, I'd gotten safely away with Chris, with Mr. Anderson's loud approval. Once in Portugal, I could collapse until the smoke cleared.

I looked around at the boy tilted back in his seat—a carbon copy of Bart. Involuntarily my eyes blurred; it was pleasure and pain together. He was going to be one of the tall Valentims—or so Bart had said. "We're of two sorts, Nell. The tall ones come from Plantagenet peccadillos of John o'Gaunt, the short ones go farther back to the Moorish occupation. But we all have black hair and eyes, the deep chin dimple, and we're all quite definitely gents," he'd grinned broadly. "We prefer blondes."

Bart had been a tall Valentim, and already Chris had only two inches to grow to equal his father. He was pure Valentim, and almost heartbreakingly beautiful in this fledgling period of beardlessness and uncertain voice that was basso profundo when least expected. If there were anything of his mother in him, it was inside. That was what Bart had mistrusted, but after these past weeks, I thought Chris had inherited more than just looks from his father.

He opened his eyes suddenly and smiled at me. "How we doin'?"

"About another hour, I think. They're bringing out breakfast trays."

Actually it was rather longer than an hour, and even longer before we finally cleared the formalities, but at last we were out of Portela Aeroport, headed for Lisbon proper. I had thought vaguely of sight-seeing, depending on trains for Caldarém, but between indifferent sleep and the gray skies, the prospect did not allure.

Even Chris was a bit damped by the weather. "I thought Portugal was sunny," he complained. "This is like Long Island in early June."

"I think it's the same latitude—or perhaps it's just an off day; I suppose they have them, like any other place. Anyway, Caldarém is bound to be warmer; it's nearly to Africa," I said, trying to be cheerful. We had, or course, just missed the good express train.

Everyone was so regretful, that I felt they'd have held it for us if they'd known we were coming! If only la senhora had told the air hostess, who would have informed officials, who would instantly have expedited . . . for there was ample time, *comprendido?* Now there would be only the afternoon baggage train, taking twice as long besides stopping and starting with grave discomfort, *que lamentável!*

Why did not la senhora spend the night in Lisbon at a *pousada*, the ultimate in comfort, state-owned and hence the ultimate in low cost? Excellent food, superb beds, a sound sleep, and la senhora would take tomorrow's good train, refreshed and able to enjoy the scenery, which was also the ultimate—only equalled by the scenery going north, *é coisa sabida?*

I looked uncertainly at Chris and Mariana. "I'm for going straight through," he said firmly. "You're so beat already, a few hours more won't matter, Nell—and at least you could sleep till you wake, instead of having to catch a train."

"Yes, I think I'd feel better just to get away from this dismal bleakness into the sun. We're sure to run out of the storm when we're farther south."

Unfortunately that was where the storm was. We were scarcely out of Lisbon before the dark clouds produced first a drizzle, which increased to rain, and eventually became a steady downpour streaming over the train windows. By the time we pulled into Caldarém and stopped with a bigger jerk than any of the previous ones, I felt bruised from top to bottom, and my head was splitting. We crawled painfully down the steps, and were instantly wet to the skin before we could get across the platform.

There was nobody to meet us. It figured. It was all of a piece with the rest of this damnable trip. Anderson had written Senhor Revalhao of Bart's death, requesting figures for inheritance tax. I had written the man myself, saying I would arrive with Senhor Valentim's son, and giving the date and the flight number. From Lisbon this morning I'd wired we were taking this train, having missed the express.

But no one stepped forward in the waiting room, nor had any car been left for us as I'd asked. How were we to reach Costa Demonio which was still twenty-five miles away? Thank heavens for Mariana, who could at least speak Portuguese! I wanted to linger briefly on the chance someone would turn up, but she shook her head.

"No, there is no delay; it is the siesta. All is shut until eighteen hours—that is six o'clock. No use to telephone; there will be no one to answer."

I groaned with exasperation, but I knew she was right. The daily afternoon closings, the random weekdays off so that you never know what will be open where or when . . . it all depends on how the local populace feels. These are standard hazards in Europe. Even in major cities, they're forever shutting shop in order to prop their feet up—and then they wonder why we do so much better at living than they! "Is there a restaurant or hotel, some place to wait?"

It was called the Navegador, naturally. In the Algarve nearly everything recalls Prince Henry, unless it's Vasco da Gama or Magellan. They could have called it Satan's Hideaway for all of me. With an impulse for self-preservation, I said we'd take the luggage with us. The checkroom wasn't open anyway, and maybe the bags would have been undisturbed if stacked in a corner, but I wanted to have no further dependance on Sunny Portugal.

"You've got a good point!" Chris grinned, calmly piling everything into the porter's cart. "Mariana, distract the *chefe's* attention, will you?"

We trudged along one square to the right, two squares to the left, as directed by Mariana, and were finally inside the hotel. Amazingly it was quite modern, with a Hilton-type bar parlor that was deserted aside from a somnolent bartender and one customer on the end stool. They stared at us with deep disapproval as I slid into a corner banquette and hauled Mariana down beside me. "Get me some water, for heaven's sake!" I rooted in my handbag, and mercifully there was some aspirin.

Chris swaggered toward the bar with a very creditable copy of his father's roar: "*Agua, faça favor, y aguardente—pronto!*"

"*Sim, sim, senhor.*" The bartender snapped to attention, scurried about, and instantly produced glasses, bottle, tray, and obsequious service, while Chris flumped into the chair opposite me.

"Well, I'm glad you know the word for water," I remarked, "but ought you know *brandy* in your first vocabulary?"

"Of course," he grinned cockily. "How else could I take care of my women?"

For a while it appeared we weren't going any farther. Mariana duly telephoned Revalhao; he was out of town. He'd left no instructions. Yes, my telegram had arrived, but as nobody'd ever heard of me, they had thought it must be a mistake! Furthermore, since the boss was away, nobody but a clerk had returned from siesta. The rain, *comprendido?*

"To be expected, senhora," Mariana said grimly, "but the porter says no one will drive a hired car in this weather. I tried to reach my father, but there is no answer. They think the lines must be down."

"Well, that's that. Have they rooms here?"

"Only two, senhora."

"Well, we'll have to double up, Mariana." I was resigned to outrageous fate and the discomfort of that filthy train trip for nothing.

Chris was not adjusted to Europe; he wouldn't give up. He thumbed through the tourist dictionary and tackled the bartender. "*Desejo aluguer un automóvel—esta dever possivel!*" he said firmly.

The man spoke some English. Cautiously he admitted that autos existed in Caldarém, some which might be hired. Where did the senhor wish to go?

"Costa Demonio."

That registered! The bartender spluttered in happy amazement, and the solitary customer jerked around to stare at Chris. "Costa Demonio? Who are you?" he demanded curtly. "There's no *pousada* there, where d'you mean to stay?"

"We own the castle," Chris replied. "I am Christopher Valentim—and who are you—sir?"

Wow, I felt proud of Chris! Bart couldn't have done a better snub.

The man was obviously English, and by his accent he was both "U" and London-bred. He peered sharply through the dim lighting of the bar parlor. "You're a Valentim," he conceded, flicking a glance toward Mariana and me, "but which one, and what are you doing here?"

"I'm *trying* to get my mother and our maid to Costa Demonio," Chris said, "and what's it to you—sir?"

"But this is Senhor Lord, who rents Quinta Choupo on the estate of the castle, *é coisa sabida?*" The bartender was quivering with excitement. "*Au, que fortuna!* No need to hire a car, Senhor Lord can drive you on his return today. Only a little moment before the car is brought from the garage as commanded. *Muito bém.* All arranges itself, no?"

From Mr. Lord's expression, I saw it was far from arranged to his taste, but he could scarcely get out of it. Reluctantly he descended from the stool and came to our table, with Chris at his elbow. "Mrs. Valentim? I am Damon Lord. I don't understand any of this."

"Why do you have to?" I raised my eyebrows. Seen face to face, he wasn't bad looking, a bit like Richard Burton, in fact, but not quite so rugged and considerably older.

Slowly he pulled out the chair beside Chris and sat down, regarding me unsmilingly. He had eyes of such an incredibly light blue that they seemed nearly colorless. "I don't *have* to know," he agreed, "but since Dom Sansao's death, I've kept a friendly eye on the estate. I am—merely surprised. I understood the castle now belonged to an American grand-nephew whose wife died many years ago. It seems natural to wonder," his tone was odiously polite! "at the appearance of another claimant."

"I never heard of you before either, Mr. Lord," I said evenly. "I don't know why Senhor Revalhao didn't tell you we were expected, particularly if—as you imply—you've been doing his work for him. And why he didn't tell you that Dom Bartolomeu Valentim, my husband, died of pneumonia two months ago." I shrugged, staring coldly at the shock in his pale eyes. "But since Revalhao made none of the arrangements I requested, perhaps he didn't believe we existed, in spite of the notification from my husband's lawyer."

There was a long pause. "Sorry," Damon Lord said gruffly. "I didn't know, of course—not that I'd have reason to. I never met your husband, but Dom Sansao often spoke of him. You have my deepest sympathy, particularly if you expected Revalhao to do anything." His lips curled. "He's far too busy making money out of the tourist beaches around Da Rocha to worry about a derelict castle. I never understood why your husband let the place go so completely, and I'm afraid you'll be disappointed when you see it. In any case, you'll scarcely care to go out there tonight."

"Why not? If you can make it, so can we—unless you object to passengers?"

"No, no," he said more gently, "but I'm afraid

you can't be comfortable even for the night, Mrs. Valentim. The place is a barracks, you know, and it will be hellish damp; we've had a prolonged spell of rain. If Revalhao ignored your arrival in Caldarem, he wouldn't have arranged for food, or fresh rooms in the castle. I'm not ever sure the electric plant is working. Really, I would advise you to stay here," he said persuasively, "and come out by daylight, when you are rested."

I looked at him doubtfully. He'd certainly made it sound unattractive, but Mariana said quietly, "Huberto will have everything ready for us, senhora, unless you are too tired?"

"Huberto?" Damon Lord said sharply.

"My father. I have written him to expect us."

"I see," he said slowly. "I have been away for some weeks, and only returned at the start of the storm. . . ." His voice trailed away, then firmed again. "Well, I would not depend—that is, I doubt he's been able to come up from Ponto Lucido any day this past week, and he would certainly not expect you to brave this rain. Today has been worst of all."

"He will have managed somehow," Mariana stated.

I could see by his tightened lips that Mr. Lord was thoroughly annoyed by her stubbornness, but if Mariana said Huberto had the place ready, it would be so. And the thought of sleeping in my own bed with no more traveling tomorrow was irresistible. After all, what concern was it of Damon Lord's? "I think we'll chance it, then, Mr. Lord."

For a moment I thought he meant flatly to refuse, but finally he snorted ungraciously, "Oh, if you insist!" He stood up impatiently. "If you've the usual female mountain of luggage, it'll have to wait until tomorrow. I haven't room for it." Without waiting for an answer, he stalked away to the lobby.

"Of all the . . ." Chris exploded. "Who does that bastard think he is?"

"Language!" I warned automatically, gliding along the banquette until I could stand. "Mariana, please pay the bill? I don't understand the money yet. Come along, Chris—and mind your manners."

I needed the advice for myself. We were all loaded into the car, which proved to be a luxurious Mercedes 600 with all the room in the world for our bags, and there we sat for a solid fifteen minutes, while the rain sheeted over the car! All the tiny warmth created by the brandy was gone, and I was shivering like a discothèque patron. Where in hell was the man? If he was in the Gent's, he might have had the decency to give us all equal time! I half wondered if the porter had put us in the right car; perhaps we ought to be waiting somewhere else? Peering anxiously into the lobby, I saw Mr. Lord coming out of a telephone booth, walking swiftly toward us and frowning intently.

Typical English masculine rudeness, I fumed to myself. Why not say he had to make a call, let us wait in the lobby? I felt a mean satisfaction that whatever he'd learned wasn't happy, I hoped he'd just lost all his money or his wife had eloped with a postman! He made no explanation, merely slid under the wheel with a curt nod to the porter closing the door. In a series of nervous motions, he'd started the motor, released the brake. We were moving forward.

If the train trip had been uncomfortable, these last twenty-five miles were ghastly. Whether he was the world's lousiest driver, or deliberately working off bad temper, he hurled us around curves, up and down hills, the length of the coast. The storm was horrendous; God knows how he could see through the cataract on the windshield. The road was equally bad, full of jolting potholes and side-slips of mud. I thought we'd plunge over the edge into the sea at any moment. It was not possible to get any idea of the terrain. Sometimes we were directly over the water, attested to by sheets of spray flung up and over the car. Sometimes there must have been a stretch of beach because there was only the sound of breakers.

"Is the road always this bad?"

"More or less," he grunted. "I told you we've had rain for ten days."

That was the extent of our conversation. Chris and Mariana sat silently in the rear seat, luggage piled about them. I sat silently on the front seat, mostly with closed eyes. I think I had never fully realized the finality of Bart's death until that dreadful trip. Rocking from side to side, bumping up and down, I had no tears, but inside I was crying to match the storm. Dear God, why did I have to cope alone with a stepson who required careful handling, a maid I probably couldn't afford to keep, a tenant who was taciturn to the point of filthy rudeness? *Oh, Bart, BART, where are you? Why did you leave me with nothing?* I hadn't even a child of my own. That had been the secret plan for this summer: we'd try for a baby to replace the one I'd aborted inadvertently two years past after six months of tender fecundity.

"Here we are," Mr. Lord's voice was sardonic. "Here's your castle, Mrs. Valentim."

I opened my eyes and leaned forward, trying to see something—anything—through the torrents of water beating on the car. Dimly I distinguished buildings ahead of us as we swung around a curve, jolted into a rutted drive. There was no light, no sign of life anywhere. We seemed to be skirting a headland, and without warning the sky was split with lightning in every direction, against which weird round towers and pointed turrets leaped into lurid relief. Simultaneously, a tremendous curtain of spume sprang up from the sea beyond and below. Involuntarily I gasped and shrank back back against the seat.

"Yes, it's aptly named . . . Devil's Coast," he said softly. "And it's not much better by sunlight."

"I wonder you care to live here, in that case."

"Oh, I don't. Quinta Choupo is a mile farther inland, altogether a different matter, completely protected from gales and sea." He braked the car and peered intently at the shadowy building. "As I thought: Huberto isn't here. Not surprising he couldn't manage in the face of this wind. I hope the electricity is working; it sometimes fails in a bad storm." His voice was odiously cheerful, pleased that his initial prognosis of discomfort seemed in a way to be vindicated.

"Oh, I'm certain we'll contrive, now we're here.

Mariana knows her way about, and I can probably get things fixed up tomorrow."

"Hah, you'll find the place practically floating after this storm! A pity your vacation is ruined. How long had you meant to stay?"

"All summer." I stared blindly into the rain, half faint with horror while lightning seemed to dance about the crenels like a set piece for Independence Day.

"You aren't planning to *live* here, surely?"

"Why not? Dom Sansao did."

"He was a man. It's out of the question for a woman."

I scarcely heard him. Mariana was already out of the car, vanishing between towering shrubs. It was her idea to come here, but she hadn't seen the place in years. Was it really so tumbledown as Damon Lord implied? If we couldn't stay here at least for the summer, what was I to do? I hadn't the cash for Bart's original tour plans, to stay in hotels and eat in restaurants . . . and what would I do with Mariana? But if we went back to New York at once, it would be even more expensive until I found an apartment. Could I get a summer cottage on Long Island or Cape Cod? By now, anything decent would be rented. Everything had been predicated on our staying at Costa Demonio rent-free until time for Chris's return to school. But this man seemed certain it was a stupid female idea.

In the lightning flashes, I could identify a path, a heavy wooden door. *Did I even have a key?* That would be the final humiliation: to find we couldn't get in! I gritted my teeth in fury, and made a mental note to discharge Revalhao tomorrow morning—after I cancelled the lease to Quinta-whatsit. But apparently one didn't bother to lock castles, or perhaps Mariana had her own key, because suddenly there were lights: two immense carriage lanterns at the entrance, a chandelier within the hall, glimmers springing up in rooms to left and right.

"Well, the generator's working," Mr. Lord commented dryly.

"You sound disappointed, Mr. Lord."

"I am," he said with a sudden grin that utterly changed his face. "It'd be better if you had the full dose at once, Mrs. Valentim. Costa Demonio without lights, heat, water pump, or cook stove is indescribably dismal. Ponto Lucido isn't a metropolis, you know. There's one store that is post office, gas pump, and a few basic supplies, but there aren't any repairmen."

"If the castle conveniences break down so regularly, how did Dom Sansao cope?"

"He was Dom Sansao. You are not." He let it lie there, lighting a cigarette and lounging over the wheel, staring moodily at the rain above the headlights. I could hear Mariana and Chris unloading baggage, but he made no offer to help. Finally she opened the door beside me.

"If you will hold my arm, senhora. The stones are slippery."

"Yes, thank you, Mariana. And thank you for the lift, Mr. Lord."

"Good night. I'll see you tomorrow."

"Not," I said sweetly, "if I see you first." I crawled out of the car and stomped through the puddles, hanging onto Mariana and sternly ignoring the deep chuckle dying away behind me. Concentrating on keeping my balance and hardly protected by the umbrella she'd found, I didn't look back until we reached the hall—when all I could see was vanishing taillights. To say that I was less than gruntled is putting it mildly. As Chris had said, who the hell did that British bastard think he was?

I abandoned Damon Lord in favor of dry shoes unearthed by Mariana from one of my bags. Chris was already dashing from one room to another, bright-eyed with anticipation for tomorrow. "It's not half bad, Nell! There's a huge suite for you, I took the bags up. And another suite looks like it was made up for me at the other end of the hall. The place looks like Grand Central Station, but there's lights everywhere, plenty of heat. Why'd that guy sound so gloomy? What's it to him if we stay here?"

"Haven't the foggiest, sweetie," I said wearily. "Did you change your shoes, dry your feet? Sorry if I'm overprotective, but I'm understandably anxious about wet feet these days."

He looked at me sadly. "Yeah, it'd be better if we weren't alone . . . but we'll make out, Nell. You'll see!"

Everything was perfect: a glass of superb sherry before the fire; a dinner that was mostly out of tins but was tasty when Mariana got through with it; a warm bath at ten-thirty when I went upstairs to find everything neatly unpacked; a tiny fire in the bedroom grate; a gigantic Victorian bed that would have matched Bart but engulfed me in an expanse of loneliness. . . .

I am one who needs moving air in order to sleep. Dubiously I inspected the windows behind close-drawn draperies. The storm was past, the wind had gone, leaving a steady rain in its wake. I opened the casement an inch, and to my surprise the air was sweetly soft, damp, certainly, but with that good fresh smell of new-washed greenery. It might have been any early summer evening anywhere. The sea had subsided to a lulling murmur in the background. Insensibly my spirits rose, and I pushed the window another six inches, leaning out to judge the slant of rain. It seemed to be coming straight down without enough wind to blow it into the room. I was turning away when my eye caught flickering lights bobbing up and down. Somebody was out there in a boat, although it wasn't the time or climate I'd have chosen for a water trip. It was a large cruiser, though, based on the distance between running lights fore and aft. There must be a good-sized harbor to handle her. I watched idly until she'd vanished, beating up to my right and obscured by a headland.

Did Costa Demonio have a landing, perhaps a boat of some sort? Was there a beach? Was the coast safe for swimming? What about fishing? Tomorrow. I yawned comfortably, crawling into bed.

My last conscious thoughts were questions: Why had Damon Lord tried to put us off, discourage us from staying? Was he trying to avoid some discomfort, some disillusion about Costa Demonio—or did he have some other special reason to wish the house unoccupied?

CHAPTER II

The storm was miraculously gone as if it had never been! The sky was clear blue, dotted with puffy little clouds; the air was deliciously perfumed, mostly rose, with a dash of clove pinks and orange blossoms. From each of the three windows in my room there was an incredible view.

To the right was the road and a curving entrance drive that must lead to our front door. Mr. Lord had let us walk through the rain from the outer road last night, but I conceded that a car would be disastrously scratched in forcing it through the overgrown shrubbery. Beyond the road was a stretch of land that was mostly an orchard. Olives, I thought, and looking ready for discard, although you can't tell the age of an olive tree by its appearance; they grow weird when quite young. Flowers and vines rioted about in between and ended abruptly to resume in the distance. That must be the harbor, or was it a river?

Straight ahead of the window I'd opened last night I had a breathtaking expanse of sea. We weren't as close as it had seemed when the storm lashed the waves into spray. There was a sizable garden, once formal but now badly overgrown, and even from the second story I couldn't see shoreline nor guess how high we were. The water looked doubtful for swimming, let alone boating. It was apparently a cove filled with grotesque rocky humps tossed about at random. You'd need to be a very knowledgeable seaman to negotiate a passage in these waters! Whoever had brought in the cruiser must have been a native; even the harbor entrance held hazardous outcrops.

Finally, to the left was the real castle, and it was definitely old! Out on the headland was a round tower topped with crenels and merlons, the architecture learned by the Crusaders from the Saracens. Behind it was a square stone building. Other sections were connected to it by stairways and arched galleries with Moorish iron grilles. They rambled backward, up and down and sideways at an angle, until they apparently joined the modern part in which I stood. There were four definite divisions, as though various Valentims through the centuries had built whatever was the last word at the time, and each section possessed some sort of excrescence. There was a square tower with a complex of buildings jutting out with mathematical precision. Next, two funny little round things flanked an immense archway that seemed to lead into an interior courtyard; this section was built at a completely different angle, so that it looked as though it were turning its back on its ancestors! Peeping over its shoulder was a pointed turret reminiscent of New Schwanstein, and finally came an immense bulbous affair that was either a mosque or an astronomical observatory.

I stared at the overall effect, torn between awe and guffaw. Good heavens, it was straight out of Otranto—Hollywood combined with LSD. Sid Grauman would faint in chagrin, and if Hearst hadn't died, he'd have bought it at once. I couldn't think of anyone else who'd want it, including me! Mr. Lord was right that the place was a barracks. I had never visualized *anything* like this. Was it habitable . . . furnished? It was absurd to wonder if there was plumbing or electricity!

Chris's voice floated up, talking eagerly, and suddenly he came around from the front garden, accompanied by an elderly man. "Hi! Did you sleep well?" I called.

"Sacked out as soon as I hit the bed! Hurry up, Nell. You won't believe this place!" his voice was cracking with excitement. "Oh, this is Huberto. He didn't think we could get here because of the storm. That's why he didn't stay when we hadn't shown by afternoon."

"*Bem dia,* Huberto." I smiled.

It wasn't returned. He looked up impassively, ducked his head curtly, and plodded steadily along the weedy path to disappear at the rear of the house. I could hear the click of a gate latch while Chris was plunging in the other direction, yelling, "Mariana. She's up. She'll be down in a minute." I stood there, thoroughly disconcerted. There was no doubt Huberto didn't want me here either. But why not? Peasant distrust of foreigners? Perhaps he thought I'd upset his routine, expect him to do more work?

When I opened my bedroom door, I thought he

might have a point! I'd been too weary to notice last night, but now I looked wide-eyed at a broad corridor extending approximately a quarter mile straight ahead. It was lined with closed doors on both sides, except for the central staircase hall with its curving steps. And everything was neat, no trace of dust on the carved handrails or wooden floors darkened by age. The prisms of the superb antique chandelier were not exactly sparkling, but neither were they dull from five years' neglect.

It was the same everywhere. An immense formal salon with impressive double doors lay underneath my bedroom suite. The room we'd used last night was a smaller sitting room full of books and comfortable informal furniture. To the rear of the hall was a dining room, with an immense banquet table, surrounded by ornate high-backed chairs. But nowhere was there dust! With a jolt, I realized this was the so-called "living section," and it was obviously the size of a country club. If Huberto had been keeping it in shape single-handed, I certainly had no fault to find!

"We don't use this," Chris said behind me. "There's a small dining room over there. I haven't quite got the layout yet. Some of the doors are locked, but Huberto has keys."

I followed obediently through a door to the left, down a short hall, and into a charming breakfast room flooded with sunshine streaming through French windows opened onto a flagged terrace. "Oh, how lovely!"

"It's the greatest," he agreed, eyeing the breakfast tray Mariana was bringing in. "Any more of those eggs and sausages, Mariana? Or a stray bun? It's been a long time since my breakfast."

"When one rises at six, eleven is a space," she agreed austerely. "Yes, there are pancakes—if you can wait so long. Good morning, senhora."

"Good morning, Mariana. Does it feel good to be home again and see your father?"

"Yes . . . but the condition of the house is shocking!" she stated. "All, but *all*, must be cleaned. It is a task to last all summer. Why could he not have got some women from the village to assist for a week each spring? No man understands these things, and to say that Dom Sansao did not like women in the house is not to the point. He was only a man too."

I laughed at her indignant voice, but if Mariana had greeted her father with an immediate condemnation of his housekeeping, it explained Huberto's lack of enthusiasm for Senhora Valentim. "Don't be too hard on him. The place may lack a woman's touch, but after New York soot, it's perfection."

She sniffed contemptuously. "Perhaps, but it is not good enough for Costa Demonio."

"You're not going to spend all the time cleaning, are you?" Chris protested when she'd gone. "Gosh, there's so much to see, Nell! How 'bout that whacking great thing out back?"

"Purely psychedelic! No sugar cube would conjure up anything to match it," I agreed, "but I wish I could pack it into a sugar cube and dissolve it in a teacup at will. How many rooms are there?"

"I don't know, I saved that for us to explore together. But we have chickens, ducks, geese, goats, lambs," he ticked off on his fingers. "There's a cow, and a pregnant pig."

"A sow in farrow," I said automatically. "I didn't know there was any livestock."

"There's everything! We grow our own vegetables and fruits; I picked the oranges for your juice! And did you know you can eat ripe lemons, they're delicious! There's a vineyard somewhere, and olive trees. We can make our own wine and oil." His voice was cracking again, and he finished triumphantly, "There's a jeep and an old pickup truck. And guess what: we don't have to hire a car! Old Sansao's is still here. It's a Rolls. What d'you think of that?"

"I think it'll need a new battery after five years, but if there's a garage anywhere, we should be able to get it rolling," I said impressed. "Wow, that would be a major break! Does Huberto speak English then?"

"After a fashion, but he says his French is better, so you won't have any trouble."

"That's a help."

I drank fresh orange juice like none I'd ever tasted before. I ate double-yolked eggs tenderly fried in butter and flanked with country-smoked ham, while Chris demolished a stack of pancakes. My mind was working as busily as my alimentary canal. Mariana had been surprised there was no money from the estate, she'd said Costa Demonio always did better than make ends meet, and what had become of gardens, orchards, livestock? Now we were here, so (apparently) was everything else—but if Huberto maintained it, what became of the produce? Did Huberto sell and pocket the money? Perhaps that was Bart's arrangement in lieu of salary.

It would have to be investigated tactfully; I'd have to go through the files I'd brought from Bart's study. Insensibly I was optimistic. Far too much space for one woman—but suppose I chose a few rooms and closed off the rest? Then: if the car could be made to run; if I learned a bit of Portuguese; if Mariana stayed with me (absurd! she'd no intention of leaving her Valentims); if I could have enough farm produce for my needs (and a couple of women do not eat that much); and I did have about four hundred American dollars a month—why couldn't I hold up here very comfortably until Chris was through school? Only three years before college.

I wouldn't be entertaining formally, needing a wardrobe . . . and at my rough glance, there was enough gardening to keep me from boredom, to say nothing of helping Mariana clean the place. I finished the last bite of toast and poured another cup of coffee with a short sigh of decision.

"Did the sum come out straight?" Chris asked slyly. "You're wearing the witchery expression."

I laughed. "Yes, it's adding up nicely."

"Good! Can we explore as soon as you finish?" He rapidly crammed pancakes into his mouth, mopping up the syrup.

"Huberto? *Que acqui?*" I heard light footsteps on the patio flags . . . a shadow across the table . . . I looked up and suppressed a scream. For a split second the man facing me was Bart! I closed my eyes tightly, then opened them. He was a small Valentim. Nevertheless, he was unmistakably part of the clan. I was accustomed to seeing Bart every time I looked at Chris; to face an adult replica unexpectedly gave me a nasty turn. Somehow I'd never thought there were any relatives still here.

"*Desculpe,*" he bowed briskly and rattled off some Portuguese.

"I'm sorry, I don't understand."

"Ah, forgive me. I am Alexandre Valentim, cousin to the owner. I said that I did not know Costa Demonio had been rented, and in fact there must have been some mistake, senhora, for the usual tenants will arrive the end of this week." His English was slow and careful; his rueful smile was charming. "Oh, it is really too stupid of the agent to have made such an error!"

"I'm not sure he did. It appears my letter went astray. We're not tenants, you see. I am Eleanor Valentim, and this is Christopher, Bart's son."

If he'd been surprised to find people in the dining room, he was stunned when Chris scrambled to his feet, hastily wiping his mouth before turning around. "Christopher?" he murmured, stepping forward hesitantly to extend his hand. "Yes, that is so. But the last I saw, you were a babe in arms. It is—more years than I realized."

"Fifteen," Chris said. "How d'you do, sir?"

"Oh, we must not be so formal! I am Alexi to my cousin, surely!" He turned to me, "Eleanor? I thought—but it is so many years." He sighed. "One forgets. Forgive me, please?"

"Oh, Nell is my stepmother. I expect you knew my mother, Cecily," Chris said. "She died ten years ago."

I was feeling more and more peculiar over this. Damon Lord might not have known of Bart's remarriage or death; he was only a tenant. But why didn't Alexi know? All the other Valentims did, and there were plenty of them—lots I hadn't even met in California and Brazil. There was a family in London, another group around Paris, and some descendants of Dom Sansao's sister in Lisbon; they were named Alenda and one was the Lisbon agent for Valentim & Company. It was a hot-tempered, highly individual family that could fight internally but was instantly a clan when the chips were down. I'd had condolence letters from all over the world; all the American Valentims had inundated me with solicitude, offers of help, and loudly approved our trip to Costa Demonio. But nobody—not one single person—had ever mentioned a Valentim living in Portugal.

Did this Alexandre even know Bart was dead?

He didn't! It was the worst shock of all. He went ashen gray and literally staggered, catching the back of a chair for support. "No! How can this be? Bart has died, and I did not know," he murmured, half to himself.

"I can't understand it," I agreed helplessly. "I didn't know there were any relatives still here, or I'd have written—but Senhor Revalhao knew, he had to send data for the probate. Why didn't he tell everyone?"

Alexi shook his head silently and sank heavily into the chair without waiting to be asked, his black eyes fixed on me—just as Bart used to wait courteously for me to explain something . . . like why we had to go to the opening of the opera with Aunt Agnes. "I know she's deaf and will fall asleep right after the overture, darling," I said each time. "But she does so love to be asked. And at her age where else would she have a chance to wear those filthy diamonds?"

"You see, we'd meant to come abroad and take Chris touring this summer. All the arrangements were made, so I decided to carry them out," I told Alexi, unburdening myself as I'd have explained to Bart. "I wrote Revalhao, saying we'd arrive yesterday. I suppose the letter was lost, although there was a return address, it never came back. But when we got to Caldarém– in all that dreadful storm—nobody expected us.

"Except Huberto. Mariana'd written him, and he'd got the place ready, although he didn't think we could get here through the rain . . . and we could not have if we hadn't run into Damon Lord last night at the Navegador. But it was all news to him, too. In fact, for a while he didn't believe us," I finished. "He was for leaving us at the hotel, to find our own way out here today!"

Alexi laughed mechanically, but I sensed increased surprise, as well as faint displeasure."Damon? He is returned them," he murmured fingering his chin. "One had not known that."

"He did say he'd been away," I remembered. "I think he said he got back at the beginning of the storm. Who is he?"

"An Englishman who's lived here for many years, I believe he was injured in the war," Alexi said. "He and Dom Sansao were very close friends. They were two woman haters together, you understand? And I must admit," his black eyes twinkled mischievously, "Dom Sansao will be spinning in the crypt that you should be here, Nell. In his last years, my grandfather would not permit a woman to be seen at Costa Demonio."

"Your *grandfather*?"

Alexi nodded calmly. "You wonder I did not inherit? No, no, Bart was always selected. Even after the breach, or perhaps because of it, my grandfather never considered altering the inheritance. I did not exist for him, you know. And so," he smiled at Chris, "you are now Dom Christopher! How long do you plan to stay?"

"All summer," Chris said, while I wondered what breach? Why did he not exist for Dom Sansao? Before I could frame a question, Mariana came in to clear the table. Her eyes widened at sight of our visitor, and I thought she wasn't best pleased to see him.

"Alexi! What are you doing here?"

"Staying at Casa Castanha. How are you, Mariana?"

Mariana raised her eyebrows slightly, but applied herself at once to the question of village help. "Huberto says he knows of no one," she sniffed. "Who is with you?"

"Rosalia, with Anita to assist."

"*Bem, bem,* I will do them the honor of a visit this afternoon," she announced regally. "You would like to discuss menus, senhora, or leave to me the first days?"

"You do them, please." Her use of Alexi's name wasn't lost on me, nor her casual, almost cavalier treatment of him. When she'd gone, he stood up.

"I must go. I came only because I saw light last

night and wondered who should use the master chamber," he smiled easily, "but may I return to guide you about? Perhaps in an hour? I do urge you," his face went serious, "not to venture into the older sections alone! Ocassionally an entire passageway falls in without warning. Some of the stairs are crumbling. The whole place is a labyrinth in which it would be easy to lose yourself."

"Huberto said he'd take us whenever you're ready," Chris looked at me tentatively.

"Oh, no doubt he knows it better than I," Alexi conceded, "but I should count it a privilege to conduct my cousins—if you could bear to wait until I conclude my business."

"Of course," I decided, "if you can spare the time, Alexi?"

"I can, and I would, even if I could not." He eyed me with a flattering twinkle exactly like Bart's. Involuntarily I chuckled, and he laughed. "*Até a vista,*" he clapped Chris lightly on the shoulder and went away through the French windows. Shortly there was a revved motor . . . then silence.

"Well," I said to Chris, "what d'you think?"

"I dunno, I don't get it," he returned frankly. "Dad told me a lot about the castle and family history, you know. We were practically pirates around the time of the Crusades, and Valentims went on the Navigator's voyages; that's when we got the title. It's all in old history books, but it was still a smuggler's paradise, even when dad was a boy."

"Good heavens!"

"Oh, *we* went straight after the first Bartolomeu brought back the loot from Brazil," Chris grinned, "but there was a big operation during the Thirties. Dad said half of Ponto Lucido lived by smuggling, and the other half helped. Not us, of course. Officially we didn't know a thing."

"Good heavens!" I said again, fascinated by this unexpected vignette of my husband's youth and his son's calm autocratic *we!*

"Yeah, it must have been exciting," Chris agreed, "but it was only that sort of thing he told me, like lying out on the bluff at night and watching government cutters overhaul smugglers' boats. I never heard of this Alexi. Maybe dad didn't know he was living here now, or why wouldn't he have asked Alexi to take charge? The thing I really don't get is why Revalhao never told a soul that dad was dead. You'd think he'd have passed it along to somebody as an item. There can't be that much going on in Caldarém, by the looks of the place. And Huberto knew; why didn't he tell anyone?"

"I don't know," I said slowly, because it suddenly struck me: Alexi had certainly not expected to find the owners at Costa Demonio. And if he was only checking on lights last night, it must have been he on the cruiser I'd seen. But recalling his dramatic reaction to the statement of Bart's death, I thought now that he *had* known. There was aflicker in the dark eyes . . . Yet why should Alexi pretend to be ignorant?

I stood up and piled the remaining dishes together neatly. "Lend a hand, kiddie. We don't have Clara any longer, and Mariana can't do everything alone."

* * *

It was much more than an hour before Alexi returned, but I was too lost in exploration to notice. Chris went off to ask Huberto about getting the car in shape. Mariana was engaged in organizing pots, pans, and pantry supplies to her satisfaction—it was no moment for family gossip. I left her to it and started a tour of the house, growing more and more wide-eyed. Had people ever really lived like this?

The main salon resembled a country club lounge in size. There were two others, only slightly smaller, one of which I thought was probably a morning room. I studied it with deep interest; you read about morning rooms in Edwardian novels, but I never actually saw one before. The furnishings were French, very light and airy, painted and gilded woods. The window draperies were heavy silk, patterned with rosebuds, and elegantly pulled aside from the jalousies by gilded ropes. The six shallow drawers of the escritoire held six piles of monogrammed writing paper, and a china tray holding six tiny pots, each flowered to indicate the color of ink. There were still faint traces of violet, blue, rose, green, dull orange and black—for condolence notes! An elaborate sealing wax equipage contained bits and pieces in every conceivable shade. I couldn't find a die; perhaps Valentim ladies had signet rings?

It was a charming room, it would suit me perfectly, although it must originally have been designed for a brunette who would look well against cool celadon with touches of rose and gold. The pictures were a clutch of Bouchers and Watteaus that I could have done without—I am not fond of milkmaids—but undeniably they were the right finishing touch here. I adopted this room for me, and spent some time repositioning the chaise longue, the reading chair, the desk, to suit modern ideas for lighting. When I'd got it in shape, I could look from the chaise longue through the opened jalousies and would see greenery and a glimpse of the castle. A small lamp for the desk, a floor lamp beside the reading chair, and we'd be in business.

I exhaled deeply in satisfaction and restrained myself from immediately investigating the greenery. Time enough to enhance the view later. I'd better see the rest of the rooms first.

There was a gaming complex. A room of tables, some sized for bridge and others, all covered with green felt; one oblong held a roulette wheel tidily swathed in muslin. Cabinets contained monumental stacks of poker chips, hundreds of packs of playing cards (some hadn't even been opened—oh, joy! I am a solitaire fiend), boxes of ivory dice, even a Baccarat shoe and a birdcage! An adjoining room contained two billiard tables, an immense closetfull of glasses, empty decanters and wine coolers.

I toyed frivolously with inviting a syndicate from Las Vegas. Why not write Princess Grace to ask her husband how to operate a casino? Surely she'd be happy to assist a fellow American, and he *must* know; Monte Carlo has been going since before E. Phillips Oppenheim, and I never heard the Grimaldis went broke.

By now, I'd found so many rooms I was going

in circles, and the only help was to leave every door open from the main salon (two fireplaces, six upholstered davenports, two grand pianos), to a library stuffed with books floor to ceiling, a genteel game room suited to ladies (bridge tables, fancy scorepads and tallies, boards for checkers and backgammon, enchanting mother of pearl counters for cribbage—and a closetfull of teacups), on to a music room that contained two more pianos, a harp in a soft flannel sheathe, a closetfull of very old crumbly sheet music, and another closetfull of neatly cased violins, cellos, various horns and guitars (don't let Chris find those, or life will be hell!). Beyond the large dining room was a ballroom, with spindly gilded chairs lined about the walls and another piano (how Steinway must have loved the Valentims!)

Twice I was totally lost, once in a cloakroom with racks for a hundred coats, and once just before I erupted into the kitchen where Mariana was still involved with her organization. "You are enjoying yourself, senhora?" she inquired kindly.

"Very much—except that the place is bigger than a hotel."

She looked at me sharply. "Exactly! That is why one wonders . . ."

"What?" I asked absently, opening a door and discovering a utilitarian estate office that led directly out a cobbled stableyard. I could see Chris prancing about an imposing ancient limousine. An unknown young man was polishing the top while Huberto stood majestically to one side. *Everyone works but father.* But there was no doubt Chris was creating goodwill. Huberto was actually smiling!

"Why is it not possible to rent at least some of the rooms?" Mariana was saying.

"Hmmmm? Oh, I'm not surprised now. There's so much space, it's depressing," I said. "Who is the young man working outside?"

"Jorge Pintos from Ponto Lucido. He helps Huberto for the heavy jobs." She nipped up the stepladder with a pile of pans. "Inspect the bedrooms, senhora. I will be with you shortly."

So I found my way through the breakfast parlor and the sitting room, but the doors on either side of the fireplace were locked. It had to be Dom Sansao's private study, but looking about it was obvious he'd also used this room rather than the huge formal salons. There was an old, but good-quality, gramaphone with several shelves of records. Pipes sat neatly in a handsome rack atop a humidor. A large canterbury was empty but must have been used for magazines and newspapers. And there was still another grand piano, with Bach's First Partita on the rack. I looked away hastily; that was one of Bart's particular favorites. He'd played it beautifully . . . he had a superb touch for anything by Bach.

Upstairs I was beginning to feel tired. Room after room, all were completely furnished, faintly airless but entirely tidy; eight bathrooms were distributed about; a large room had shelves stacked with linens. At the end of a transverse hall that led back to the old castle was a child's playroom; the cabinets and closets were filled with old-fashioned jigsaw puzzles, Old Maid, Parcheesi and tiddley-winks. What fun! I thought happily. Chris is as big a nut for puzzles as I am, and there looked to be enough here to keep us occupied for a year!

Every window produced a view, either a vignette of the castle or a glimpse of the sea. Sometimes one looked out over various gardens that must once have been delightful, particularly the topiary, although you could no longer determine the original shapes. It would take a dozen gardeners to clean up the place, but if Chris helped and I really put my back into it, we could probably clean up the worst during the summer.

He was in the opposite suite from mine. Automatically I made his bed and straightened the bath towels, which is something no male however personally tidy seems capable of doing. For a teenager, Chris is amazingly neat; what was unpacked was put away, but he hadn't unpacked more than he needed to dress this morning! I finished the job; self-discipline is not expectable at such moments. From the window I could see they'd run the Rolls out to the cobbled yard, and it was a behemoth. I'd need a complicated arrangement of pillows in order to see over the steering wheel. Also, undoubtedly Chris would insist on driving. What about insurance and an operator's license?

Going methodically from dressing room to armoire to chest, I became convinced that this—not my rooms—was Dom Sansao's personal suite. Little things: clothes hangers meant for male coats and trousers, mirror lighted for shaving, draperies, coverlet, furniture design subtly austere. When I discovered the lefthand bedside table contained a bar assemblage of glasses and empty decanters, I was certain. There was no such private stock in my bedroom.

No, this was definitely the master's chamber—and very logically: Dom Sansao could see his fields, stock, kitchen garden, vineyard, the road from Ponto Lucido; he could see the practical part of his domain and direct its progress—the hell with pretty views of the gardens and the sea! I had a frivolous mental picture of the old man standing at the window, yelling directions to minions in stables, garage, laundry drying yard. Whether a tall or short Valentim, he'd have had Bart's deep Bull of Bashan roar. They *all* did; Chris was getting there fast.

Except Alexandre, whose face was Valentim but whose voice was a silky tenor . . . and why didn't he know which was his grandfather's suite? Remembering Mariana's calm reference to a blood tie between Huberto and Dom Sansao, and her casual treatment of Alexi this morning, I felt positive he was illegitimate, which would explain why Bart never mentioned him, didn't ask him to look after the place.

Voices floated up through the open window accompanied by a clip-clop of horse's hooves on the cobbles. Damon Lord was trotting into the stableyard on a handsome chestnut mare. I drew back to watch as he swung himself down. The ease of his manner, the respectful bows from Jorge and Huberto and Chris's happy greeting, all were obscurely infuriating—particularly Chris's actions; I have rarely been more annoyed with my stepson.

In two seconds he'd forgotten yesterday's rudeness and was practically wagging his tail!

I had to admit Mr. Lord was better by daylight. He looked even more like Richard Burton, which is not bad if you like that heavy-lidded, sleepy smiling, sultry-charming type. Riding kit suited him; he'd a good figure with shoulders proportioned for lean flanks. To Chris, who adores horses, Damon Lord would be irresistible—especially if (as now) he made the least push to engage the boy's interest. They were walking about the chestnut, Chris questioning eagerly, Mr. Lord answering with a smile, and I was conscious of a slight stiffness that was not exactly a limp but a *carefulness* in placing his right foot.

If there were equines about, Chris would acquire the use of one somehow and be tagging after Mr. Lord every spare minute, I thought irritably. Still, aside from my personal umbrage, what had I against the man? He was evidently persona grata to the servants, had been a friend of Dom Sansao . . . Damon Lord could be extremely useful to me, if he were kindly disposed. He spoke the language, knew the lay of the land; he'd made a first move by coming to see how we did. I'd more to lose than gain by standing on my dignity.

I pushed the window fully open and called, "Good morning."

He looked up at me, and for a moment his face was oddly still. Then he strolled forward smiling. "Good morning. I hope you slept well?"

"Luxuriously, thanks."

Chris pointed toward the mare. "Nell, look!

Isn't she a beauty? And guess what: we have horses! Stop puttering and c'm on out."

Damon Lord's face was amused. "Please do," he coaxed. "Let Chris do his own unpacking."

I capitulated with a laugh. "Be right down."

Chris had returned to car polishing, but Damon Lord was lounging on the stone coping, chatting to Huberto. He got up courteously at the sight of me. Huberto ducked his head and abruptly started off, but before he could vanish, I said, "Huberto, *plusieurs des portes sont renfermées*. May I have the keys, please?"

"*Sim, sim*," he muttered, and turned his back on my outstretched hand.

"Mr. Lord, why does Huberto dislike me?"

"I'm not aware he does. He's a rather taciturn chap by nature, and he isn't used to taking orders from a woman, but I'm sure you'll find him very satisfactory."

"So am I. I only hope his distate for females won't cause him to resign."

He looked at me curiously. "It won't. In fact, if you tried to discharge him, he wouldn't leave."

"Mariana won't either," I said absently, "although she knows I can't afford—" I stopped abruptly; my finances were no concern of his.

Mr. Lord changed the subject tactfully. "I called to express my apologies for the apparent lack of welcome last evening."

"Don't mention it, we all have our off moments," I said politely.

"I'm grateful for your feminine understanding of masculine frustration," he sighed. "I coped with that storm to attend a crucial business conference, only to find the vital person hadn't arrived."

"How maddening! But I am happy to know it was not I who gave you an Excedrin headache."

"A *what?*"

"Oh, never mind; it's not important," I said with a grin.

"Are you ever frustrated?" he asked.

"Not long enough for it to be very unpleasant," I confided innocently.

His lips twitched, and he chuckled so infectiously that I laughed with him. "Friends?" he asked persuasively. "I was in a foul temper over that trip for nothing. It was all I needed to have to chauffeur a bunch of strangers—but I shouldn't have taken it out on you."

"No," I agreed with a smile. "I can't imagine how your wife puts up with you."

His face went cold as though wiped with a wet sponge. "I have no wife."

Before I could think of anything to say, Chris clattered up to us. "Car's nearly ready. Huberto always keeps it in running order; he had Jorge tune her up last week. It only wasn't polished because of the storm. As soon's it's finished we can go look at our horses. Did Mr. Lord tell you?"

"Not yet." I looked at him inquiringly, but he was still stiff.

"Dom Sansao sent them to me when he became ill, because Huberto couldn't exercise them properly," he said curtly. "I breed horses; we balanced stabling out of the get. When Dom Sansao died, Revalhao said your husband was satisfied with the arrangement, if it suited me—and it did, the Valentim stock is superb."

"Still, five years? Ought we to take anything back?"

He nodded more easily. "I've had more than enough foals, I always ear-marked a few to return. If I can keep Dom Sansao's stallion, I shall be in your debt."

"We've a three-year-old, a yearling and two mares—one's in foal!" Chris gloated. "We better leave her at Quinta Choupo; I don't know enough about foaling yet, but we can take the others as soon as the stalls are cleaned."

"But," I felt disconcerted, "hold on, sweetie! Who'll take care of them? What about feed?"

"Oh, I can manage," Chris said confidently. "Huberto and Jorge will help; they can't exercise, but we'll do that, Nell."

There'd be a lot more to it, and I expect my face looked appalled. Damon Lord shot a shrewd glance at me and suggested, smoothly, "You'd better check the condition of harness, Chris." When the boy had gone, "By the way, I hope you won't think me officious, but I tried to get through to Revalhao this morning. He wasn't there, he never is; I told you that. He leaves Costa Demonio to a clerk, who has been sick for the past month, and it appears it is no one's responsibility to take over his work."

"That figures—not that I know what to do about it, but thanks for finding out."

"You're welcome." He hesitated, drawing out cigarettes, offering one to me and lighting them. "I don't want to interfere," he said slowly, studying the toe of his boot, "but it's evident there are unsuspected problems, Mrs. Valentim. That is, unanticipated by you, and unknown to me, although I should have thought . . . however, that's neither here nor there. I'm afraid I was rudely blunt last night, but I repeat today: I urge you to reconsider staying here." His strange pale eyes met mine squarely. "You understand neither the language nor the people. Even if you did, there is no one suitable for social intercourse in the locality. Your stepson will command respect as a Valentim, but he is still a school boy. I am not exaggerating when I say Costa Demonio actually is dangerous, unless one knows it well. There are often coastal landslides, many parts of the cliffs are only loose shale. The water is full of submerged rocks, not very good for swimming and even worse for small boats, which is all you have," he interpolated, "and I'm not sure either of them is usable."

"I wondered about a harbor," I murmured. "I saw quite a large cruiser coming in when I went to bed last night."

His eyes sharpened suddenly. "What time?"

"About eleven. It must have been Alexandre Valentim," I began, and stopped, almost frightened by the sudden grimness in his face.

"Go on."

"He showed up this morning while we were at breakfast," I said obediently, "said he'd seen a light last night, and thought the house was rented. He came to check because it wasn't supposed to be yet. There are some other regular tenants, he said. Anyway, we were all equally dumbfounded. We'd never heard of him, and he'd never heard of me, although he said he'd seen Chris as a baby. And Alexi said the place was terribly dangerous, too. He's coming back shortly to take us around."

"Well, well, that's an unexpected development," Damon Lord murmured, narrowing his eyes.

"Mr. Lord," I asked impulsively, "exactly who is he?"

"He's the child of Dom Sansao's only son and the daughter of a Ponto Lucido smuggler," he returned after a moment. "And he may or may not be legally entitled to call himself a Valentim. His father lived a very wild life; he was killed in a smuggler's fight years ago. Alexi was living in Lisbon, but they kept his mother's old home here. After Dom Sansao's death, Alexandre moved back by slow degrees. He is now the *commisário* for the locality."

"Oh?"

"Yes," he said sardonically, "that's what I meant when I said you didn't understand the people here, Mrs. Valentim." He stood up, frowning thoughtfully. "At the risk of impertinence, I wouldn't encourage any social contact. Neither Dom Sansao nor your husband would approve."

"Why would Bart object? Apparently they knew each other fairly well. Alexi even knew Cecily."

"That's why," he said tersely. "In some way, Alexi caused the breech between your husband and his great-uncle–and, no, I don't know how; I was away that summer, but I'll tell you this: it was your husband who held to it. Dom Sansao tried to patch things up; he admitted he was at fault. He *missed* your husband, regretted the estrangement to the day of his death. Furthermore," Damon Lord added evenly, "Dom Sansao always said it was deliberate mischief-making by Alexandre."

My expression must have shown my confusion, and perhaps I really looked the dumb blonde.

"I'm sure I've no wish to influence your judgment," Mr. Lord's voice held an acid impatience. "Do as seems best to you; I'm certain you will, Mrs. Valentim." He sketched a salute with his riding crop and walked away to swing up to his saddle. He'd trotted out of the yard before I could find my voice.

"Hey! I wanted to ask for saddle soap!" Chris was aggrieved.

"Call him later," I said absently. The sun was too strong now, so I started for the house, when Huberto emerged with a heavy key ring. He walked deliberately past me to Chris and ceremoniously bowed.

"*Chaves mestras,* Dom Christo."

Chris took the keys blankly. "Oh—thanks, Huberto. Here, Nell, catch." Casually he tossed them to me, but I was already wiser.

"*Obrigado,* Christo," I said politely and continued into the house.

Of course, only Chris and I knew he was not the Dom. He didn't own Costa Demonio; I did. What, I wondered, did that make me? Was I a Domesse? No. After riffling through the tourist dictionary, I was apparently Dona Eleanor Valentim.

All the same, I thought we wouldn't mention that fact. Damon Lord had said last night, "He was Dom Sansao, you are not." Let everyone think Chris was Dom Christo, if it was the way to get things done. Chris wouldn't mind—and in the last analysis, Costa Demonio was his heritage. If he wanted it, I would deed it to him when he was twenty-one—but was I going to be able to keep it that long?

"Nell, Alexi's here."

We went all over the home grounds and along the cliff tops, with Alexi pointing out danger spots—of which there appeared to be so many that I began to feel we'd be confined to quarters. Occasionally we got a view of the shore, and I could believe it wouldn't make for good swimming, although it was fascinating: the rugged outcrops thrusting into the water in a series of coves with sandy beaches.

"Yes, I can see they're useless except for paddling, but isn't there any place to swim?"

"A beach on the farther side of the castle," he nodded. "I'll show you the path, but please do not try to get down these cliffs, Nell. There may seem to be paths, but only for a mountain goat, and it is easy to cause a landslide. I beg of you: do *not* attempt them—and do not go closer to the edge than we are walking. Here there is rock beneath the soil. It may not be very scenic, but it is safe." He smiled, "Come, let us go through the castle—but prepare yourself for desolation!"

I could see for myself the place was a ruin, but aside from crumbling balustrades and a few cracks in stairstones, I couldn't feel a need for undue caution—not that I yearned to spend much time among those cold empty rooms. No matter how hot the sun, nor how many tapestries and rugs there had originally been, I doubted anyone could ever have avoided chilblains.

The cellars were even worse. Alexi was reluctant to take us down, but Chris insisted. "Let's see it all, while we're here. It can't be *that* dangerous, or the main floor would have caved in. Come on, Nell, I brought a flashlight."

Perforce Alexi led the way, and when we reached the bottom of the stairway, I could see why he was anxious about our wandering around. The place was a perfect rabbit warren of cubicles and passages. It would be easy to lose your way, although there was a certain amount of light from barred windows high in the walls. Here and there doors were warped shut as in the upstairs sections, swollen by years of disuse, but one at the bottom of the steps opened easily onto the farthest seaside end.

As Chris flashed his torch about, I thought for a second that the Valentims must have had a private zoo. Then, with a shudder, I realized for what the row after row of iron cages with heavily barred doors were used. Despite the dim light from windows overgrown with shrubbery, despite a free flow of chill air—these were cages for humans! "Ugh! Come away, Chris, do! It's horrible!"

"Yeah, I guess this was where they kept the slaves."

"*Slaves? Oh, no?*" I cried anguished. "We weren't blackbirders, were we? Oh, Chris!"

"No, no, it was long before . . . Moors, I think." He pushed me hastily toward the stairs. "And we didn't sell people, just collected ransoms. I've forgotten exactly, but it's all in a book dad gave me."

"História Doméstico de Valentims," Alexi agreed "written by my great-grandfather. I hope you have kept it, Christo, although there will be a copy in the library here."

"Yes, of course I have it," Chris was pushing me up to the entrance. "Don't worry, Nell; I *know* it wasn't Africans."

"It would be centuries before, when the Moors were expelled," Alexi murmured, while I was inhaling deeply. "But it is good news that you have your copy, Chris! Mine has been lost, you can imagine how I felt? But since you have Bart's, perhaps you would be gracious enough to let me have my grandfather's? You will not need two, after all."

"Well, as a matter of fact, mine is—is stored in New York with our books," Chris returned, "so if there's one here, I'd sort of like to look it over. I mean, it's old stuff to you, but I'd kind of like to see what's described."

"Of course," Alexi smiled. "But, when you have your own again, you will not need the extra. Well," he turned to me, "are you tired, Nell, or shall we finish the tour?"

"Is there anything more to see? So far it's a disappointment," I said at random because I had a distinct memory of a small volume on Chris's bedside table. It was bound in green leather with the family crest stamped on it in gold. "Haven't we a ghost or a priest's hole—no, those are England—but what about a secret passage?"

"I'm afraid not," he said regretfully. "Costa Demonio is really a very dull castle, with nothing but drafty halls and icy cold rooms. You have not seen it all, but the rest is only more of the same. Shall we look at the beach?"

We went through what must have been the original kitchens, with immense fireplaces and rusty iron spits coming out on the other side of the castle. This was altogether different. The great headland protected the cove completely, there was a firm-packed earth path to a wooden staircase, leading down to delicious soft white sand. There were two cabanas in rather indifferent condition. "Tchk." Alexi tightened his lips. "Huberto has let them go entirely. It is to be expected; he grows old and does no more than he must, I'm afraid."

"Why maintain beach cabanas when there is no one to bathe?"

"Because it is his duty," Alexi said surprised.

"I don't see it," I returned, watching Chris strip to jockey shorts and dash into the water. "He's kept the house neat, maintains some livestock and gardens. What more could you want?"

He gave me that indulgent, intelligent-male-for-weak-little-woman smile. "Nell, *cara prima*," he said caressingly, "you spoke of staying here—I'm certain you see now that it is impractical, but I must speak frankly, even if it does not please you. Otherwise I would betray my childhood tie to Bart, you understand?"

I nodded, silently waiting.

"It is this: Costa Demonio might be made to provide an income," he said slowly, "with a younger, more energetic, estate man. Jorge Pintos is not sufficiently experienced—but there is Diniz Blendo, and I think there's a young Estevao working out near Faró . . . no matter, the point is that I could find you someone to get the *most* out of the land, and this is no reflection on Huberto," he added quickly. "You are right he has done well merely to keep things going, but he is over seventy, Nell! It is time for him to retire."

"Perhaps. Not so much for my sake as for his own; he's certainly entitled to sit in the sun and prop his feet up. The thing is, I can't afford a pension."

Alexi spluttered with laughter. "My dear Nell, if you need money Huberto will lend it to you! One does not know how much he may be worth, only that my grandfather provided for him long ago, and there is whatever Huberto has accumulated since," he shook his head cynically. "He has had a free hand with Costa Demonio for more than five years, but I doubt that Bart ever saw a penny.

"Nor will you. Not that Huberto is dishonest, he is simply old, but how can you maintain Costa Demonio without money for repairs, and these will become a large item!"

"I expect so," I said troubled. "Actually, if the place carries itself, or if we could rent for more than a few weeks at a time . . . although I can see it's hard; there's too much space. But the alternative is to sell, and I think that would be even harder."

He looked perfectly thunderstruck. "Chris is not of an age to make such a decision! In any case, you will never find a buyer at a decent price. Repairs would be astronomical, let alone any modernization of the old castle. This is not even the fashionable section of the Algarve that might attract a wealthy socialite," he said quickly. "No, no, far better to try for more rentals. I will speak to Revalhao personally."

"You won't get him; he's never there," I remarked. "Mr. Lord rang through this morning to find out why nobody met us yesterday, and it seems Costa Demonio is so unimportant that it's left to an elderly clerk who's been out sick for weeks, and *he* is so unimportant that nobody takes over his work."

"Damon has visited you this morning?"

"To apologize for apparent rudeness and return Dom Sansao's horses—which are more of a problem than a blessing—but it was kind of him to call Revalhao. At least I know the man's useless, even if I don't know what to do about it."

"I see," Alexi murmured. "I had the impression that Bart did not care, so long as the place made its taxes. One supposed he merely held it for Chris, but now . . . I will reach Revalhao, never fear!"

"I expect a local *commisário* can manage it."

Alexi laughed, but his face was oddly sharp. "Of course! It is my duty to know who is where—and Manuel Revalhao will be in Praia de Rocha, where he hopes to make a profit from certain shrewd investments in cabana properties." He hesitated, looking at me soberly. "Forgive me the impertinence, Nell, but from what you say . . . that is, this is a . . . a most unexpected development, that you should be here, that money should be necessary in any way, let alone require you to withdraw from your normal world and retire to . . ." He fingered his chin, murmuring half to himself. "It was thought Bart inherited everything unconditionally. Perhaps it was changed . . . or there was a need for capital expansion. One would not think *all* would be . . . but, however, a sudden death can tangle affairs, take time to settle advantageously. What I wish to say," he stated with sudden decisiveness, "is that the situation appears different from what I had supposed—and it is my *right* to assist, Nell. Bart would expect this.

"Let me explain: I was born illegitimate. It was why Dom Sansao disinherited my father. Later my parents married, I can prove a right to the name, but, frankly, it amuses my mother and myself to allow the world to guess." He chuckled wickedly, and I couldn't help laughing with him. Bart would have done the same: Valentim arrogance; the hell with people and what they think.

"When I was nine, we met," he said, staring at the sea. "It was on this beach, early one morning. We knew only that we were both Valentims: the face is unmistakable always. He was two years older than I. How I admired him! So tall, so straight, there was nothing he couldn't do."

Nothing, I agreed silently, tears dimming my eyes.

"Very soon it was discovered that we met every day. It was instantly forbidden—by my father as well as Dom Sansao. Do you know what Bart said?" Alexi smiled faintly. "A servant reported that he had said, 'Fight your own battles, *tio.* They are one thing I refuse to inherit.' "

Yes, that would be Bart, and I'd bet old Sansao respected him for it. "What did you tell your father?"

"I was not so courageous," he admitted ruefully. "I said, '*Sim, sim, pai,*' and ran away when his back was turned. You see, I was still a little boy and small for my age. My mother knew—mothers always do—but she thought it good for me to know an American cousin so that I would learn beyond the small village, and I think perhaps she hoped that in time . . ." his face was dark, tight lipped, "but it was not to be."

"What happened—or would you rather not talk about it?"

"Oh, after a few summers, my father—died, and my mother took me to Lisbon; there was the war." He shrugged. "We lost touch, but," he smiled at me brilliantly, "I have never forgotten Bart, nor what he did for me, Nell. That is why I demand the right to help you."

I felt touched by his concern. "It's not really desperate. I'll admit I don't quite see my way, and perhaps I can't stay here permanently, but there are other factors, Alexi. I—that is—I shall definitely stay until Chris returns to school." I could see this wasn't the answer he wanted, but Chris was coming across the sand, using his T-shirt for a towel with all the insouciance of youth . . . and who was to wash it? Did we have a laundry? "Gosh, it's wonderful, Nell. Couldn't you take off the top layer and have a dip?"

"No, I couldn't," I said firmly. "And don't twist that shirt too violently, sweetie! That's one of the cheap ones." I smiled.

"Yeah, so it is," he said guiltily. "I forgot."

"Don't!" I advised tersely. "There's no Sears Roebuck in Caldarém."

"Why don't we send for a catalog?"

"Because we have indoor plumbing. Come along, silly!" We went up the steps, giggling companionably, and by Alexi's expression we'd lost him. "Sorry, we are being American," I apologized. "Have you ever been there?"

"No, our export business isn't in the class with Valentim," he said lightly. "We're quite small, principally wine for England."

"Oh? What sort? Do you have your own vineyards?" I asked, to keep the conversation going.

"A few nearby. Mostly we distribute for Madeira and Oporto, but we've recently made a connection in Cadiz that we think will increase our affairs markedly," he said with modest pride.

"How exciting! Sherry, Malaga, Alicante, malvoisie, what?"

"You know wines!" He raised his eyebrows. "No, it is a muscatel. I will bring a bottle for your opinion. We think it outstanding."

"There's a vineyard here?" I asked, following him through an arched passage like a breezeway to the gardens behind the house.

"There was, but I doubt if there is anything left of it now." He sighed. "I will gladly look, but I imagine it should be pulled up and new sets made. If you think of trying it, I would enjoy helping you get started. Frankly, Huberto could not physically handle this. Jorge does not know enough; you would need Diniz Belendo or the Estavao boy."

"I see. Well, that is the sort of thing I must consider, Alexi. I wouldn't suppose the vineyards could make more than a basic supply for Costa

Demonio, and I don't know that it's practical to convert any of the other acreage into grapes." I could tell he was startled by my briskness, but I was conscious of my weariness and was longing to sit down quietly.

We came out at the edge of the topiary garden, and I took a last look at the sea. It's true I can climb mountains—small ones. I could, and would, do anything Bart wanted to do, but I'm a water baby at heart; left to myself, I can sit happily contemplating a mill pond, or the trickle running through a culvert. The bore at St. Johns, or Niagara Falls, the Mississippi and Big Sur create a positive ecstasy in me, and I have always secretly yearned for the cataracts of the Nile. So the sea swirling at the foot of the cliffs, springing up about the cove rocks, was one of the greatest lures to retaining my castle.

I stood looking across the water and was suddenly aware of a peculiar turbulence far out, centered between the headlands—not easy to see in the strong sunlight, but it appeared to be a circle in the ocean, quite divorced from the surrounding ripples—like a top spinning lazily by itself. "What's that?"

"What is what?" Alexi peered in bewilderment as I pointed.

"That—that circular thing in the water."

He straightened up and faced me with a faint smile. "That?" he said curiously. "You do not know? That is Demonio."

CHAPTER III

It was a whirlpool. It was nearly as big as the one in the Hebrides, and fully as dangerous. It lay neatly across the entrance to the cove and was a complete protection for the castle because the other side of its headland was sheer rock, impossible to scale.

"Why do you think the ancestors selected this spot? It is impregnable! Once caught by the eddy, only the strongest modern power boat can pull free, and then only in the first few turns," Alexi said. "For a small boat, it is hopeless. Oh, yes, there have been disasters even in Ponto Lucido, when a sudden squall drives a fishing smack into Demonio, to circle inward until it overturns and is sucked downward."

"How far out does it extend?" I asked shakily.

"Far enough that it is on all mariner's maps. Coastal seamen give us a wide berth, I assure you."

"So will I! You must be a very experienced captain to pass safely in the dark. That was you last night, wasn't it?"

"Probably. I returned from Cadiz, thinking the storm would precede me, but it did not move so fast as I expected. There was a stretch of rough water, but I know my way from long experience." He smiled. "I must go to Lisbon for a few days, but when I return I will take you out to look at Demonio."

I wasn't too sure I cared for any closer acquaintance. Between crumbling cliffs, a derelict castle with a cellar of slave dungeons, horses to feed, a vineyard to uproot and everybody urging me to leave, I felt the last thing I needed was a whirlpool on the back doorstep.

Chris had gone ahead for dry clothes, and we strolled slowly toward the house. "Thank you so much for showing us around, Alexi."

"*De nada!* Now you will know what to avoid, and while I am away you will think seriously, please?" He took my hand gently. "Bart would be sick at heart that you find yourself in this position—and for nothing but money, since that is easiest of all to resolve!

"One cannot picture you in these surroundings, my dear cousin. You are the essence of sophistication, the milieu of opera, ballet, taxis, a penthouse—the life you had with Bart," he said earnestly. "It is gallant for you to abandon your past way of life, but it is not right. You must realize something from Costa Demonio. Suppose I rent it from you on a yearly basis?"

"But what on earth would you do with it?" I asked bewildered.

"Rent, perhaps, or keep it in order for Christo." He shrugged. "I would certainly get more from the land, but what does it matter? I am a bachelor; I can well afford it. I would offer simply to give what is needed to enable you to live as Bart would wish, but I think you would not accept," he said quietly. "Here is a solution: I shall be allowed to help Bart's son, and the money will come from Costa Demonio. Please think about this?"

"Yes, but I told you there are other considerations. In any case, thank you, Alexi."

"*De nada!* One small thing." He stroked my hand absently. "I do not presume to advise you on behavior, Nell, but you are a stranger here. I cannot fail to say what you might not see quickly enough to avoid an entanglement. It is this: Beware of developing an acquaintance with Damon Lord. The friendliness from landlord to tenant, yes. But the association between my grandfather and this man does not guarantee his suitability for either Christo or my cousin's wife. That is all. I know nothing more is needed, *cara prima.*"

He kissed my hand gracefully and went around to the stableyard for his car. It was a sporty little black job, I thought vaguely that it was a Ferrari, and if he could afford that, he probably could afford to rent the castle for nothing but to help Bart's wife. Chris came dashing out of the house, there was a short interchange, and then he was piling into the car. "Horses!" he called through cupped hands.

"Hey!" I yelled, but the car was already heading for Quinta Choupo. *Oh, damn,* I thought resignedly. But if there were horses, we were going to have them. I would have to refigure everything, but if worst came to worst I could rent to Alexi next fall.

The house was cool and breezy, the rooms

shaded by jalousies. There was no sign of Mariana; three o'clock, she was either engaged in a siesta or had gone out majestically for a state visit to Ponto Lucido. A good moment to investigate kitchen and pantries.

It appeared Costa Demonio never threw anything away. There was a gigantic iron range, with boxes of wood and coal, a kerosene contraption, and a fairly modern electric stove. The refrigerator was frost-free; Dom Sansao must have bought it shortly before he died, as well as a separate deep-freeze cabinet that appeared well stocked with neat packages. An elderly fridge stood in the butler's pantry, containing a few bottles of wine and making ice like crazy.

I found a laundry behind the kitchen: old-fashioned set of tubs, but a modern machine flanked by a dryer. In the corner was an iron stove suitable for washboilers, and a huge closet revealed three, together with shelves full of irons. They were all shapes and sizes, including a peculiar thing resembling curling tongs. I stared at it blankly, and my mind dredged up "goffering iron." Good heavens, could it really be that old?

Still, I looked more carefully. Some irons had a chamber to hold hot coals, others were sharply pointed, there was one oblong stick that defeated me until I noticed a hat block on the next shelf. All the irons were fancily embossed, decorated on top and handles (A New York decorator would buy them with cries of rapture; they'd be converted to lamps and planted with philodendron.) I shuddered. Along with Demonio, I didn't need sixty-eight old irons.

When I came to a storage room for china and glass, I was really thinking. Complete sets of Meissen, early beige Wedgewood, Limoges: plates separated by flannel; cups wrapped in flannel bags. If you broke it all out at once there would have been enough for two hundred people. I couldn't see a crack or a chip anywhere. In a separate closet were oddments: five Spode plates, a Crown Derby teapot, two Lowestoft tureens, six goblets of one pattern and three of another, but definitely old Waterford.

When I found a vermeil centerpiece, I heaved a deep sigh of relief. Consult Chris out of courtesy—he wouldn't give a damn—and the sale of some of these goodies would certainly bridge the gap. It would take time, I was unclear how one went about selling such things: Christie or Sotheby, where a commission made it worthwhile to get the maximum?

I found my way to the morning room and sank onto the chaise longue with a sigh. Photograph a few samples, and they might think it promising enough to send an expert to appraise—but if I stripped Costa Demonio, what would I do with the residue? One lure for a purchaser would be furnishings included. Still, there was so much of everything that a few paintings or tables would never be missed. My mind went back to Alexi's offer, and I was as surprised as I was grateful. It was very Valentim, though; Bart would have done the same if positions were reversed . . . or would he?

I debated: I didn't need a hand-out, but I felt I could have taken it from Alexi now. His was the only partial welcome we'd had, and I did understand his urging me not to stay. Given anything that looks like me, the reaction was expectable, particularly to a European man unused to American competency.

All the same, I had a hunch Bart wouldn't like me to accept financial aid from Alexi. Bart could have offered; he was the Dom. I couldn't accept; I was la Dona. Damon said Sansao blamed Alexi for the family breach, which might or might not be true. I didn't doubt the old man had fulminated in typical Valentim thunder, but there were no details. Ironic that both men had warned me against the other! Damon gave Sansao as a reason; Alexi had delicately pointed to my position—and of course he was entirely right. Even traveling in sophisticated tourism, the American widow is suspect, and Ponto Lucido was a very small town. If I meant to live here, however temporarily, decorum was essential.

Actually, Alexi was a bit of luck. He belonged here, he was my husband's relative and never mind which side of the blanket. His approval would cause no social speculation, create sponsorship for the stranger. I'd got over my first shock at his resemblance to Bart. But the time Alexi left I was amazingly comfortable with him, as though I could consult him about anything. His English was slow, but fairly fluent; he couldn't follow slang or our humor, but those are always the hardest things. Even when I'd learned some Portuguese, it would be a long while before I'd know when to laugh—and Damon didn't really understand me any better than Alexi. He could just speak English more quickly.

He was right about unsuspected problems, though. Petrol for a Rolls? I'd meant to rent a VW or Citroen, sacrifice speed to economy. Stabling for horses? I might manage one for Chris, but *three?* All these dozens of rooms, Mariana already wanting extra help. Jorge and Huberto outside, who paid them and how much? Even if I hadn't been literally too busy to think in New York, I could never have envisioned Costa Demonio. Vaguely I'd pictured a rambling Edwardian horror like the summer house next to my grandmother's house in old Sands Point, but instead I was saddled with a mansion designed for banquets, balls, and formal weekend parties of thirty to forty people.

Could it even be turned into a summer hotel? I realized Mariana had had this in the back of her mind, but she hadn't seen the place for years. She'd remember it as it was, with a dozen gardeners and stable boys, six chambermaids. It would take all of that to clean up the grounds, fix beach houses, prepare and serve meals, make beds—meaning outlay before income, and I was already tight for cash. It would take weeks of correspondence before I could finalize the sale of anything; I saw that now. True that I could probably manage on my income, but I didn't have it yet because I'd invested everything; it's be a few months before dividends arrived regularly. I was six thousand miles away from immediate check-up, if they didn't.

Face it, I told myself miserably, *you bolted for what looked like a hole, and now you've fallen in!*

For a split second this morning I'd thought I

might turn to Damon Lord as an old friend of Dom Sansao's. He obviously knew all local ramifications; it was thoughtful of him to call Revalhao, to have kept the stable for us, but quite clear he wanted no involvement. I suppose on looks alone he thought I was a Dora Copperfield, who'd forever be running to him for help. Well, I wouldn't. He could go right on being a misogynist; I wouldn't need him now that Alexi had turned up. By the time he got back from Lisbon I ought to have a clearer idea of the exact position here.

Meanwhile, I had about a thousand bucks. Chris would need wardrobe replacements and walkabout money for school, there might be some leeway in the trust fund to cover that . . . write Anderson. Could I persuade Damon Lord to take back the horses when Chris left? I might sell the Rolls against a small cheap car. Could I get any sort of loan against the Vermont property when I was out of the country? Where was I to get cash if needed—and I began to think it would be.

I could always burn the bridges, return the air tickets for Mariana and myself. That would really upset Damon Lord, I thought viciously. He was so busy trying to get rid of me, so incredulous that I had a money problem. Alexi had been startled too; he'd thought it was just that Bart had tied everything up in some business venture, but I knew Bart hadn't had anything. Come to think of it, I was startled myself. Mariana'd said there was never the least economy; the condition of the house attested to it. Dom Sansao might have had a smaller staff in his declining years when he no longer entertained largely, but he *must* have had more than Huberto. Where had the money come from? Was Mariana right that it was hidden somewhere?

It could be in a safe in the study.

I had to try nearly half the keys on the ring before I found the right one and stepped through the door to the left of the sitting room fireplace. Opposite was a curve of shuttered French windows. I went through the dimness to unlatch, thrust open, and turned to catch my breath.

The room was a perfectly proportioned oval, similar to a Boston Bullfinch salon. A huge marble fireplace backed the one in the sitting room. Great wingbacks in worn cordovan stood to either side with their matching footstools. Between the windows were shelves of books floor to ceiling. There was an immense mahogany table-desk at one end; the high-backed armchair behind it resembled a throne.

Above the mantel was an oil portrait, unmistakably Valentim: a man with white tips feathering the black curls at his temples, sitting ramrod straight with a closed expression. It could have been Bart; occasionally he had that same locked-away face. I'd sometimes had a key to Bart, but I doubted anyone had ever had a key to Dom Sansao. I hauled over a footstool, got up to peer at the signature: Augustus John, 1924.

John? Had Dom Sansao been ambassador to London?Bracing myself on the mantel, I pulled the portrait gently from the wall, but there was nothing behind it. Not expectable; even a tall Valentim would need more than the single library step stool to reach. I straightened the portrait and got down to the floor. Would Dom Sansao have liked me? Had he liked Cecily that long ago summer? I wondered suddenly why he was a woman hater. I couldn't remember hearing of a great-aunt, but surely there'd been children aside from Alexi's father. Bart had mentioned dozens of cousins in childhood summers. Perhaps it was not hatred, but melancholy for the loss of an adored wife.

I would allocate the study to Chris. He was nearly big enough physically for the furnishings, and he'd adore having a lair of his own, while I used the morning room. Now where was Dom Sansao's hidey-hole? I inspected the shelves, but there was no space unaccounted for. The desk yielded pens, pencils, engraved stationery, a few rubber bands and postage stamps—and something rattled at the rear of one drawer. It was a key of heavy iron with a tremendous fancy handle, far too big to fit the desk.

The key to the castle? I looked at it carefully and thought not; it wasn't big enough, sturdy enough, for a door. What, then, would it fit?

With redoubled determination I toured the study. A few floor cabinets beneath the shelves held boxes of paper and carbon, which implied a typewriter and files. It finally occurred to me that, although the study was oval, the sitting room walls beyond were straight. How dumb can you be? There was no attempt at concealment, I simply hadn't noticed two door handles in the curved panelling; the key opened them. Behind the left door was an elderly royal on a rolling stand, a metal cabinet stuffed with neat but dusty folders.

Behind the other door was a narrow staircase. It led to Chris's dressing room. The upper door was locked, but the study key opened it.

I went methodically from chests to cabinets to closets, peered behind pictures, pressed panelling . . . with no result. But the key argued something somewhere—a strong room in the old castle? Dom Sansao didn't look the sort to go paddling along a drafty stone corridor to get money for the milk bill! I didn't doubt there might be a strong room in the older sections, there might even be valuables—if we could find it—but cash would be closer to hand.

Slowly I came down the private stairs (how Chris would love them!) pressing every inch of the panelling, and getting madder by the moment. Damn old Sansao! I was nearly ready to cuss Bart for leaving no instructions, expecting me to cope in a blind fog. Suddenly, I heard a sound. Hastily I thrust the key into my pocket and went into the study.

Huberto stood in one of the opened windows, glaring at me. "*Qu'est-ce-que vous faites ici, madame?*" he demanded in strongly accented French. "This room is for the Dom; it is forbidden that women enter." He took a threatening step forward, his hands working nervously as though he were itching to strangle me.

I don't know where I got the guts, but I managed to face him, to shut the door behind me and say calmly, "*Quel dommage.* Dom Christo will not agree. You were present when he gave me the keys? *Je suis sa régente; naturellement j' ai ouvri ses chambres.*"

"These rooms are to be *locked!*" he repeated harshly. "The key is for Dom Christo, to be kept on his watch chain."

"I'm afraid he doesn't have one, he's only fifteen," I tried placating. "And if I gave him the key, he'd only lose it."

"Then return it to me," he held out his hand imperiously. "If I had known . . . I did not dream Dom Barto's son would know so little as to give *you* the keys! Return it at once, if you please."

"Well, no, I think I won't," I said apologetically. "The study will be open hereafter, Huberto. We do not care for locked doors."

"That is America; you should have stayed there, madame!" he broke in contemptuously. "At Costa Demonio there are traditions to be observed. Dom Christo must take his proper place, learn to respect himself, and what is due to his position."

"Nonsense!" I snorted, beginning to lose my temper: "He doesn't *have* a position—and how dare you suggest Dom Barto's son is a barbarian."

"How shall he become anything else, if all is left in your hands, madame—*if* that is true!"

"Oh, it's entirely true. Do not accuse me of lying!"

He hunched his shoulders. "*Incroyable, c'est tout,* that Dom Barto should fail to provide suitable supervision for his son—and already we see the result!" he stormed. "Dom Christo's *régente* knows no better than to permit him to receive Alexi Revalhao—not merely receive, but actually to accept that one as guide, to permit use of Christian names!" Huberto was almost choking with rage. "Bah, you know *nothing*, madame!"

He straightened his shoulders, glaring at me, and for the first time I could see the Valentim heritage, watered down, but definitely there in the grim set of his mouth. "*Enfin*, I am not yet too old to instruct Dom Barto's son," he said arrogantly. "Stay here, if you wish, but do not think to interfere, madame. I have my instructions from Dom Sansao, confirmed by Dom Barto." He started toward me with determination, and involuntarily I put the desk between us. "The keys, if you please, madame, since you cannot be trusted with them."

"No." I was icy calm with rage. "You may do as you choose with the land—although I shall wish to see Dom Barto's 'instructions'—but you will have *nothing* to say about the house. Dom Sansao's rules died with him. Dom Barto left everything to me because he did trust me. He would be very angry at your behavior." I could tell by a flicker of Huberto's eyes that I'd struck a nerve; I pressed the advantage, "He always meant to come here this summer—"

"For only a week. I have this in his own hand! A short visit, and now that he is dead, you wish to change his plans? I say no, and again *no!*" he thundered. "*Allez-vous en, madame.* Go back to America; leave Dom Christo to me; you can do no good here." He leaned suddenly over the desk, reaching for the key ring in my hand, and involuntarily I cried out, stepping back.

I'm not sure what would have happened next, whether we were going to sink to the indignity of my servant chasing me around the desk after the damned keys, because I was fighting mad by now, and I'd see Huberto in hell before he'd get them back! But a sudden shadow appeared in one of the windows. "*Que acontece?* What is wrong, Mrs. Valentim?" Damon Lord's deep voice cut across the room.

"Oh, thank heavens you're here!" I said fervently. "Will you *please* explain to Huberto that I will not have things locked up, Chris is too young to be given keys; he'd only lose them. Besides, it's nonsense. Bart wouldn't have stood for it for a moment."

Huberto burst into vehement Portuguese, his voice easily outroaring mine, while Mr. Lord listened impassively. Finally he held up a hand, and the old man was silent at once. "*Sim, sim,*" Mr. Lord added some incomprehensible words of his own, but apparently they were satisfactory. Huberto nodded, and stumped away without looking at me.

"Thank you," I said shakily, turning to lean my head against the back of the desk chair. "I didn't know there were any ground rules about the study, but the way Huberto talked! For a while I thought we were going to play dodg'em around the desk! But *I* am mistress here, Mr. Lord. Huberto actually implied—but make no mistake: *I* am Chris's guardian; *I* will decide what's to be done, and I don't care if Huberto is a relative or how long he's been here, he'll do what *I* tell him!"

"That," he remarked sardonically, "is what you think. I warned you there'd be unsuspected problems, Mrs. Valentim. Your husband could have given orders Huberto would obey without question. Even Chris could have issued a few decrees if you'd left it to him, but no, you have asserted yourself. How typically American!" He snorted. "Your women are all alike: headstrong little queens expecting your lightest whims to be granted, and the instant you're in over your heads, you bust into tears and bawl hysterically for a man to the rescue!

"Well, I must applaud you! Inside of a single day you've botched everything beyond recall, and don't look to me for help. If you've a grain of sense, you'll silently fold your tent and steal away—preferably by night," he said bitingly.

That did it. I straightened up and turned on him. "As you see, Mr. Lord, I am neither weeping nor hysterical, *nor* an Arab. I regret to have troubled you; it was merely that I thought Huberto might understand better in Portuguese." I moved out from behind the desk, planting my feet carefully one step at a time. "As for leaving, there was never any question of it.

"Once and for all, Mr. Lord: Chris *and* I *and* Mariana are staying for the entire summer, even," I gritted my teeth, "if Demonio freezes over! If I have to milk the cow and collect the eggs, feed the animals and play midwife to the sow—and don't think I don't know how because I do! My grandmother had a rather nice farm," I laughed lightly. "And if Chris has to pick the peas and beans, and help wash the dishes . . . once and for all: *we will be here!* It is not merely that I cannot afford to go elsewhere, Mr. Lord, but for certain private reasons that are, frankly," my voice was odiously condescending, "no concern of yours. I feel under no obligation to explain my husband's wishes to you."

"No, of course not," he said hurriedly, stepping backward.

I ignored him. I think I was superb; it's amazing what you can do when you are furious. "I'll admit to a certain curiosity over this unanimous determination to get rid of me," I observed sweetly. "First yourself, then Alexi, who may or may not be the family bastard, even if I never heard of him before, and finally Huberto, to say nothing of the Caldarém agent who carefully does nothing. *Why*, Mr. Lord? What is going on at Costa Demonio that makes it inopportune for the owners to arrive?"

His eyes widened blankly. "What an odd question."

"Isn't it?" I agreed cordially, holding myself erect by main force. "Perhaps you can answer it?"

"Here, I say," he protested, "my dear girl . . . you are overwrought." He came forward to grasp my arm and push me toward one of the big chairs. "Do please sit down, and let me get you a glass of wine." He plunged to one of the cabinets, brought out decanter and glass. "Here, you'll feel better directly, you're just overtired."

"Yes—yes, that is one way to put it," I agreed, fascinated by the understatement of the year. "In the past few weeks I've coped with lawyers and brokers, distributed the contents of a ten room apartment between storage, shipment abroad and the Salvation Army, packed and spent twenty-four hours to arrive in the middle of a minor hurricane. All I ask is to be allowed to crawl into bed and pull the covers over my head.

"I don't care what the rest of you do," I said with detachment. "I don't want to replace Huberto with a younger man, or replant the vineyard, or rent the place to Alexi. I don't want a stable, or a Rolls-Royce, or a social life, or people talking to me about the good old days. I don't want sixty-eight antique irons, or a vermeil centerpiece, or a damned whirlpool in the backyard. All I want is to have the doors and windows open whenever I get up, and to be LET ALONE." I snarled, finishing the wine at a reckless gulp. "It seems such a reasonable request."

"Entirely," he said, steadying the glass and refilling. "You poor child." He stuck a cigarette in my mouth and flicked his lighter. "It was inexcusably thoughtless of me. Forgive, please?" He sat down in the other chair and lifted his glass with a rueful smile. "Of course you're worn out plodding around all day, and I've added the last straw—but you do see it was nervous-making to hear you squeaking in here? Not that there are dastards about in general, but one never knows. And when I rush forward, it's to find you standing like a—a chipmunk at bay over nothing but those stupid keys!" He rumpled his hair and looked at me abjectly, "Sorry again, Nell—Mrs. Valentim," he corrected hastily. "Oh damn—but Chris, you know . . ."

The wine was delicious, very soothing to the nerves. "Oh, I don't care what you call me," I said wearily. "My name is really mud." His lips twitched slightly, but he said nothing while I had another sip of wine. "Perhaps sometime you'll tell me what all this locked-study business is," I said suddenly. "I'd already decided to give this room to Chris; I'd rather have the morning room anyway. Don't tell me now, I'm too tired. I suppose you brought over the horses, and I don't want to think about them either."

"You needn't. Chris can handle them."

I nodded. "He knows how to talk to them. All Valentims can, but it's only fair to warn you he'll be a Pythias."

"I don't mind." We sat silently for a moment while I crushed out my cigarette. "Impertinent of me, but what is this about renting to Alexandre Valentim?"

"He thinks Bart wouldn't like me to be so far from the madding crowd of Park Avenue, the sophisticated world for which I seem suited," I said drearily. "Perhaps he wouldn't; I don't know. Alexi's solution is to pay me enough rent to go back to the 'life that late I led'."

"Shall you accept?"

"No." I fumbled to set the wine glass on the table and pulled myself to the edge of the chair. Another five seconds and I'd have been fast asleep. "I think, if you'll excuse me, I will go to my room," I said groggily. "Thanks for the wine but it was a bad mistake, Damon . . . much too relaxing."

He chuckled, setting aside his own glass and helping me to my feet. "That's what was intended. You look better already."

"I look moribund, which I am." I forced my eyes open, heading for the sitting room door. "If Chris is a nuisance, send him home ruthlessly. Thanks again for coping." I hung onto the door jamb and something jogged my memory until I turned back and said, with fuzzy dignity, "I am no *chipmunk!*"

"No, I can see you aren't. That's the trouble."

Damon's face was expressionless. "Go to bed, Snow White, and I'll see you when you wake."

A sliver of light through a cautious crack of the door, "Nell?"

"Yes, sweetie. I'm mostly awake; come in."

"Gosh, we thought you were going to sleep forever. Are you all right?" Chris asked anxiously. "You're not sick or anything?"

"No, I'm not anything, hon—just tired. Be a love and hand me the pink robe, will you? Did you have dinner?"

"Yeah, we ate ages ago, but Mariana's got something for you."

"We?"

"Damon stayed to keep me company; we worked on saddle leathers, I didn't really know how to do them, but he showed me."

"Damon?"

"He said I could because we're sort of going to be partners," Chris caught himself and looked guilty. "I mean, it's just breeding and selling, but it's the chance of a lifetime!" His eyes sparkled with horse fever. "D'you know who Damon *is?* Only the best horse breeder in Portugal, that's who!"

"How exciting!" I slid into the robe, crawled from the bed, went back and forth to the bathroom, hearing snatches from Chris tagging after me, "Jorge says . . . Huberto says . . . Damon says . . ."

"Well, that's lovely, darling—but rather more than I wish to hear," I said finally. "D'you mind to shut up until I've had some dinner? Is he still down there because I don't feel like dressing."

"No, he left. Oh, gosh, I'm sorry," Chris said guiltily again. "I wasn't supposed to bother you about anything until you stop being tired, but I forgot—you always listen so well. Do you want to eat downstairs, or have a tray up here?"

"I'll go down. Mariana's tired, too. You both ought to be in bed."

I ate from a tray before a tiny fire in the sitting room, to the accompaniment of Chris's verbal spate, letting it go in one ear and out the other until he reached Alexi. "He doesn't know much about Costa Demonio, Nell, but there *is* a ghost—not frightening, just a girl walking along one of the galleries—and there's a secret room and a tunnel, too. Dad was going to show me, because the book isn't specific."

I roused at that. "I thought I saw it in your room. Why wouldn't you tell Alexi?"

"Because I don't think he ever had a copy, I don't know where he could have gotten it," Chris said awkwardly. "There weren't many; they only go to direct heirs. The master copy is always here, but the Dom has another until he chooses his heir. Sansao gave it to grandfather, and when he died Sansao gave it to dad." He frowned suddenly. "Hey, you ought to have it now. I forgot you really own the place, Nell."

"Pro tem—I'll deed it to you later if you want it. That's one of the things we have to think about: to sell or not to sell," I said. "And, meanwhile, don't—do NOT—tell anyone you aren't Dom Christo, understand?" I grinned at him wryly.

"This is feudal land, sweetie. The Dom is respected; an American widow is not, and I've problems enough without local disaffection."

"You mean they'll do more for me than you? Why?" he asked bewildered.

"A fair question, and I can explain, but not tonight, hon. Take it as read that its okay to fib tacitly, let everyone think you're the Sultan of Pajama?"

"Sure, if you say so, Nell."

But I could see he was puzzled, and when Mariana came to remove the tray, I knew she wasn't happy either. What had happened in Ponto Lucido? I stood up briskly. "Dinner was delicious, Mariana; thank you for waiting up, but that's all for today! Go to bed, and we'll talk tomorrow. Chris, I have a present for you, and then you go to bed too."

"A present?" he inquired alertly.

How did I know Damon Lord hadn't already initiated Chris into the study, that they hadn't sat there working on the saddle leathers? I just knew he hadn't, that he'd have left it for me because I said it was a present. "Yes, this way." I opened the door beside the fireplace, felt my way to a lamp, and saw at once that someone (it could only be Huberto asserting himself) had closed windows, latched shutters—which was all right. I shouldn't have left the room open to night winds. The wine glasses had been washed and returned to their cupboard, together with a filled decanter, and that was not all right. The past winter, Bart had permitted Chris one glass of table wine for major holidays. Nothing more as yet, nor did Chris complain—but there would be no decanters in this room. I closed the cupboard and said nothing, for tonight. Tomorrow I would issue the Order, and Huberto either obeyed, or I would lock *him* out.

"Come in, hon. This is *your* room."

Chris was thrilled to the point of reverence, unable to say anything but, "It's the *most!*" and, "Endsville!" with various other "in" phrases. He sat in the wingbacks, in the desk chair, looked in drawers and cabinets, hauled down books from top shelves . . . and everything fitted him already, but it would be better in about five years when he was physically more finished; there was still an endearing limp-spaghetti look at the nape of his neck.

I sat on one of the footstools, watching him range about excitedly and holding onto my guts. I was so glad I had pleased him. Chris treated me as if I were his real mother; I hoped I would always do right by him.

"All sorts of languages, Nell. I'm not sure what they are even. Could he read all these?"

"Probably, he was an ambassador. Your father spoke French, Spanish and Dutch."

Chris wasn't listening. "Hey, look!" It was an autographed first edition of *Nicholas Nickelby;* "Por Oliveiro, *com es melhores cumprimentos de Charles.*" He dropped it in my lap, went back to the shelves, "I think there's a complete set except in different bindings," he said finally. "Oliveiro was Sansao's father. Gee, d'you suppose we knew Charles Dickens?"

Again that identification of "we." "Probably. Is there any Thackeray?"

"I dunno . . . but what's this?"

It was an illuminated manuscript. The first page was decorated with angels and saintly monks, hands clasped and eyes fixed on heaven. *In principio creatit deus coelum et terrum . . .*

"In the beginning God created the heaven and the earth." Delicately I turned the pages, getting a word here or there from my rusty memory, but I had no doubt really. It was a Vulgate Bible, on vellum. The final page said "*Frater Johannes fecit MCCCCLXV.*" 1465?

I stared at it blankly while Chris was inspecting other shelves. "I don't see any Thackeray, but there are some more of those fancy manuscripts." He piled them on the footstool beside me and went on to the next section. "A lot of French stuff! Balzac, de Maupassant, Flaubert; it's all autographed for Oliverio . . . and this is for Sansao, *A la Recherche du Temps Perdu* by Marcel Proust."

"It doesn't rhyme with Juliet Prowse, hon, it's Proost," I said absently because what Chris called fancy manuscripts were—peculiar. That is, they were certainly incredibly valuable. But what were they doing here? Arabic, perhaps. But weren't the Moors gone by eleven or twelve hundred? Surely there would be no Hebrew book in the library of Costa Demonio—if there'd even been one. The Latin books were equally puzzling: the dates ranged around thirteen and fourteen hundred, but somehow I didn't think they were local. If there were family monks, wouldn't they be Fray Joao, not Frater Johannes or Brother Mark?

"Gosh, I can't keep my eyes open," Chris gave a mammoth yawn, thrusting the Proust back into place. "Let's look at the rest tomorrow? I'm for the sack. G'night, Nell." He hugged me with bone-crushing strength and turned to the stairs. "Hey, my own ladder—how 'bout that?"

"Make the most," I advised, "and don't let it go to your head because back at the ranch you'll be using the stairs like always."

"That," he said sadly, "is the way the Mercedes-Benz."

"Personally I'd rather roll with royce," I told him snappily because the M-B joke was a private in-thing for Bart and Chris, and, now that Bart was gone, it was time for something else, even if I had to make it up myself.

Feeble as it was, it did the trick. Chris pounded off up his stairs and vanished. "See ya, Nell."

I sat for a moment, looking at the manuscripts and feeling both anticipation and deep depression. Already I didn't know what to do with a vermeil centerpiece, but if my suspicion was right, that was the least of my problems. I got up and methodically put the books back into the shelves, glancing along from one to another.

There was no question that I was right. Dom Sansao's acquisitions stuck out like sore thumbs, so innocently thrust between the other volumes of the family library. From whom had he bought? How much had he paid? If I'd been tired before, this was total eclipse. I couldn't face it. I turned off the lights, closed the doors and went to bed.

So now I knew—maybe—what had become of Dom Sansao's vast wealth. I'd always thought Europeans went for portable investments: jewels, postage stamps or coin collections. Oh, God, he'd probably bought paintings, too! The house was stuffed with them—but which were Valentim heritage, which were bought for resale? It was the height of absurdity to weep because Costa Demonio probably contained a hundred thousand bucks of rare objets d'art—but what was I to *do* with them?

Bart would have known; he was older and wiser (one reason I loved him). He could always explain things I hadn't hit upon yet, so I'd know how to go on. A college degree is only a cornerstone; someone has to show you how to use what you know. Bart was good at that. In five years I'd learned to apply my mind, whether for dinner conversation or planning a charity ball, but Alexi was right: all I knew was how to be the wife of a prominent New York business man.

It would all have been so *easy* if Bart were here . . . but he would never be here again with a quiet suggestion to set me straight. I flumped over in that huge lonely bed and abandoned myself to the luxury of howling. Nobody would hear, for once I could really let go, pound the pillows, wring my hands, stamp back and forth kicking footstools, blow my nose and start keening all over again. I could throw things, *scream* . . .

CHAPTER IV

They say the night brings counsel. It doesn't. What it brings is the capacity to see problems more clearly—not what to do about them. Added to those manuscripts was the huge key that must fit a safe or strong room somewhere. If Huberto knew, he'd never tell *me;* would he tell Chris? I strongly doubted it! Would Damon have been sufficiently intimate with Dom Sansao to know anything of his financial affairs? Perhaps. I could imagine the old man displaying his latest purchase proudly because Damon had the intellect to appreciate.

I would die rather than ask him.

Alexi wouldn't know. He hadn't been received here, didn't know the living quarters even now, only the old castle. Huberto would never had let Alexi get a toe in the door, judging by his fury at my "receiving" Alexi. Better not tell Alexi anyway, he was the local *commisário* (and taxes we always have with us!). He might have to be official about inheritance of unsuspected valuables.

I crawled out of bed; my body was rested, but my mind was more tired than ever. There would have to be an inventory of the library, a list of the paintings, a determined search for the safe. Clues might exist in the dusty files, but they'd surely be in Portuguese. I could send them to Anderson for impersonal translation by a stranger in New York, not to reveal anything locally; it would take one hell of a lot of time. *Think about it later.*

On impulse I went down the hall to Chris's bedroom when I was dressed. It was impeccably tidy, completely done up for the day. When I found a full wine decanter in the bedside table, I knew Huberto had taken over. There would be no way to prevent his attendance on the Dom as befitted the traditions of dignity for Costa Demonio. In a way I didn't mind Huberto's being responsible for these rooms—that much less for Mariana to do. Vacation time, after all, let Chris be a little spoiled. But the standards suitable for an elderly Portuguese aristocrat just couldn't be applied to an American schoolboy.

I went down the stairs to the study, carrying the wine decanter, and set it temporarily in the cabinet. Damon Lord had known where to find it for me last night. He might be entertained by Chris some evening, I imagined. Going toward the hall, I noted the study was also already in perfect order, still shuttered, but every chair positioned, every ashtray clean. The doors were closed but not locked. Huberto either had no duplicate key, or knew better than to use it.

In the kitchen Mariana was looking grim. "There is a development, senhora," she stated. "*No one* in Ponto Lucido wishes to assist us!"

"What do you mean?" I asked after a moment. "Bring a cup for yourself, Mariana, and we'll talk while I breakfast."

* * *

I was right that if we'd thought to make Costa Demonio into a hotel, we couldn't. "I do not understand it, senhora, but it appears that no one wants money! *Também*, there is an attitude created by superstition that is even more incredible. My cousin Rosalia says there is a ghost, that one hears groans and strange noises even in daylight, and that lights are seen moving in the old castle at night. No one will venture inside; they are convinced falling stones will wall them alive in the passages! *Assim*, senhora, I have done you a disservice when all I thought was to be of help to Dom Christo," her face crumpled; she was nearly weeping.

"It seemed so simple that we should come here, rent the rooms which are in good order: ample linen, equipment for meals," she assured me, "but all was based on the help from Ponto Lucido, and now it appears this is not to be had, senhora. Of the entire village, only my father will stay after dark—not even Jorge Pintos. It is *nonsense!* There was *never* a ghost here! Ponto Lucido was proud to send the young people; they received such excellent training, *é costa sabida*," Mariana was speaking vehemently while I ate omelet and toast thoughtfully. It was making a pattern—but whose?

This was the reason the place couldn't be rented, of course: no servants. Had Bart known, was that why he was bringing us here this summer—to settle things on the spot? What had he planned? Whatever it was, he'd thought it would take only a week, and then we would continue the

European tour. *Now* it was different; I was here, and here I meant to stay no matter how many people dressed up in white sheets and clanked chains outside my bedroom door. I was convinced that all of this was a deliberate plan, and whoever was behind it was going to learn Nell Valentim was definitely no chipmunk!

Somebody didn't want Costa Demonio tenanted. Why?

I cut through Mariana's words. "Don't worry, I've a better solution: we will sell a few of the valuables! One set of china, perhaps a picture; that will be enough, and shortly I won't need anything extra."

"*Sell!*" she was aghast.

"Mariana, think!" I cajoled. "Costa Demonio will never again be used as it was. That way of life is gone forever: great balls and banquets, house-parties with dozens of servants. So: let us sell very quietly the extra sets of china and silver. We will not need to rent rooms. Between us, you and I will clean at our leisure . . . and when Ponto Lucido finds itself unnecessary to Costa Demonio, I think there may be a change.

"When it becomes obvious that Dom Christo is here, plans to continue the stables, expects service, I think he may take precedence over ghost stories, don't you?"

Oddly, I felt less tired at the thought of unmasking someone—whoever had started this fan-dance for whatever reason. Mariana hadn't thought that far. "Eh, *hábil—esperto*," she murmured, her lips curving with satisfaction. "We allow time for them to realize it is Dom Christo who is in charge here. I drop a word in Rosalia's ear to spread about. It is not after all necessary for any help; we shall do very well by ourselves—until the valet for Dom Christo arrives with his wife for chambermaid. There will also be the chauffeur's wife to take care of laundry—all to come from London, *naturalmente,* since no one is available locally."

I chuckled helplessly at her ghoulish glee, but, "Don't go overboard, Mariana," I warned. "A hint that Dom Christo is disturbed there have been consultations, *la senhora* has written London, you are uncertain, but it appears guests are expected, and Dom Christo has been overheard to say English servants are always best."

"*Sim, sim,*" she said, briskly clearing the table, "Leave it to me, senhora. You will see, they will be coming hat in hand. Meanwhile, what is to be sold?"

"I'll decide later, there's no hurry. I have to have time, or I might make a mistake."

"*Sim, sim,*" she said again sympathetically. "It has been too much; one does not know how you have endured it, so little as you are, senhora. Leave all to me. Walk about, go swimming, eat, sleep, perhaps a drive to Caldarém; I will take care of everything. Do not exert yourself."

That was easier said than done, although she was as good as her word, and supervised me like a kindly dragon. I saw nothing of Damon Lord, and so little of Chris that I said, "Have you taken up residence at Quinta Choupo?"

He grinned at me. "Damon says if I'll talk to the horses for a while, he can finish some paper work, and you can have some peace. You are getting rested, aren't you, Nell?" anxiously.

"Yes, sweetie, slow but sure. Don't worry."

Undeniably it was peaceful to eat alone, with no eager voice to require attention. I was more tired than I knew; I went to bed early and slept soundly—and I still needed a nap in the chaise longue every afternoon. In between, I pondered. Where was Dom Sansao's safe—not that I was too anxious to find what *else* I was going to have to get rid of somehow. I was certain it was somewhere in the study; leave it until I could handle it.

More important was: who was doing what that had scared the Ponto Lucidans—and my answer was Huberto. He was elderly, fanatically pro-Valentim and status quo, and Bart hadn't jacked him up by any show of interest. Huberto might have been all over the world with Sansao, but his mentality was still major domo. Yes, I thought it figured, he was "carrying on." Sansao wouldn't have liked strangers in his home, detested women in any capacity—Huberto had taken his own ways to rid Costa Demonio of females. I didn't doubt Damon Lord had approved, or that they would both like to be rid of *me* at all costs.

At leisure I reinspected the oddments for possible quick sale, taking the old typewriter into the morning room and making lists. Going methodically from room to room, I knew Sansao had bought paintings: Picasso, Klee, Roualt and similar; all hung unobtrusively among portraits that were probably Valentims. The Bouchers and Watteaus in the morning room were not copies; they might have hung there since they were painted—

but defiantly I decided to sell them, if they'd fetch anything. They weren't Family, like the Fragonard in the grand salon—and even if they were commissioned to finish off the morning room, I do not like milkmaids!

Christ didn't either. When I showed him the vermeil centerpiece, it was the *coup de grâce*. "Good God, Nell, we aren't going to use that? It takes my appetite away!"

"Mine, too, so d'you mind if we sell it?"

"You mean anyone would buy it?"

"People collect it. There's a lot in the White House."

"You're kidding! No wonder it's so hard to get a good Republican president. Who'd want the job if he had to look at this stuff? Sure, sell it. Sell anything you like, *minha mae*," he said casually. He was picking up Portuguese very rapidly from the stables at Quinta Choupo. I could only hope Damon Lord would supervise both language and accent; I didn't care whether or not *we* saw each other (which we hadn't), but the man was a gentleman and nothing could be better for Chris than an authoritative older man.

Huberto continued to care for Chris's rooms, his clothes and the study, although no one was really using it. The wine decanters sat in the cabinet—but one morning another was in Chris's bedside table. I removed it and laid in wait for Huberto. "There is not to be *any* wine or liquor in Dom Christo's room, Huberto," I stated. "*C'est absolument defendu á cause de sa mère*—and this is not just my whim, but Dom Barto's order."

He ducked his head, but his eyes were stricken. "Pardon, madame, I had forgotten. It will not happen again."

"Thank you—and thank you for caring for his rooms, even if he is not often in them."

"De nada," he grunted stumping away. "He is better where he is."

So much for a possible *entente cordiale.*

Jorge drove Mariana and myself to Caldarém. The Rolls ran like whipped cream, and, in the clear sunlight, the road was breathtaking. Obligingly, Jorge went slowly, while Mariana indicated points of interest; in between he put his foot on the accelerator and we were running the Grand Prix! Caldarém was a cunning little old town, with surprisingly modern shops; not too much English was spoken, but smiling patience *por la turista.* I found a newsstand section in the stationery shop and got a copy of every English and French magazine they had.

The instant I was identified as Senhora Valentim, the atmosphere changed subtly. I couldn't put my finger on it precisely. The friendliness was there with increased efforts to assist; patience became deep respect but was accompanied by a flicking glance that was more than curiosity about the American stepmother of the new Dom. I had a peculiar instinct that everyone knew something I didn't, like a bunch of bright-eyed children up to mischief and wondering how long before mommy found out.

Mommy could be equally naughty. "Mariana,

where is Revalhao's office— and you are to say exactly what I tell you!"

It took thirty minutes of utter confusion while I simply sat, regally. Costa Demonio was to be withdrawn from their rental lists; Senhora Valentim wished to see the cards as proof that the castle was crossed from every sheet. Eventually a terrified file clerk turned up a note in the dead file: Costa Demonio had been withdrawn four years past. "Mariana, ask to see the letter of authorization."

There wasn't one, merely a handwritten instruction on the bottom of Bart's original letter to Revalhao, telling him to manage the property by rental and to render accounts by December 1st each year. "Where are the accounts, the tax receipts? Whose handwriting is this?"

"Senhor Revalhao's," the clerk stuttered. There was a current folder containing the annual accounts. Someone assured us I didn't owe anyone anything; all was in order. Someone else naturally threw the whole mess onto Revalhao. "It is the head who would handle this matter of importance; we would not be permitted, senhora. But he is unfortunately away from the office this day."

By now I was beginning to enjoy myself. "Mariana, ask for the leases on farms and fields, and also the recent correspondence: the letter from Mr. Anderson asking the accounting for probate, Revalhao's reply, my letter asking for us to be met."

This produced even more frantic scrabbling in files and desks, but eventually everything was produced, including my envelopes—unopened.

Senhor Belendo was still out sick. "*É demais,* one hopes he soon recovers," I said politely, rising to my feet. "Meanwhile I will take these papers with me. Come, Mariana."

The staff was less than happy to part with Revalhao's files but unable to refuse. Majestically we departed, although what good would it do me? Everything would be in Portuguese. Perhaps Mariana could give me the gist, or I'd forward to Anderson for professional examination.

Driving back to Costa Demonio, I felt modestly pleased at having got away with the evidence, such as it was. Revalhao would be sorry he wasn't in Caldarém this morning, he'd be sorry he hadn't somehow covered himself over that withdrawal-from-rent notation. Who had given him the high sign, or was it his own idea to waste no time on an unproductive property? The more major question was: what was everyone up to?

I hadn't any real doubt. The smuggling ring had surfaced once more, and tenants at Costa Demonio would be apt to notice . . . something.

We had two motorboats: one putt-putt for dashing around the farther shore of the harbor to collect an emergency need from Ponto Lucido and one fairly large job suitable for fishing, with a motor strong enough for water skis. Both were seaworthy, and there was a usablc aquaplane. "How lovely, darling. Is there a usable chart for avoiding those damnable rocks?"

"Damon's going to show me; he knows these waters like the back of his hand."

I wasn't surprised when I saw his boat. It was a full yacht, completely dwarfing our little twiddlies and berthed at our mooring. "It used to be Sansao's. Damon bought her when Sansao got too old to handle her," Chris explained. "That's why there isn't a separate berth. But we don't mind, do we?"

"Of course not." But I wondered.

The harbor was much larger than any of the coves, it widened into an immense curve once past the mouth, was a good half mile across at the full. I'd known it must be big, if it could take Alexi's yacht, but Damon's was equally big, and there was certainly space enough for several more. In fact, I saw four—no, five—similar docks scattered around the shores, although ours was the most advantageous for easy exit and entrance between the outer rocks. A trim cruiser lay at the mooring next us; it was exactly like Roberto Valentim's in Long Island Sound, which slept six with two crew bunks and was a thirty-footer.

Damon's yacht was certainly fifty-feet long, extending regally into the mainstream of the harbor and far beyond that cruiser. She'd be uncomfortable in full ocean perhaps, but perfectly competent for long coastal work, with plenty of hold space, and the more ballast the better; a crew of four, sleeping in shifts, could manage her unless there were a yachting party. Somehow I didn't think she'd been used that way for some years, although perhaps Sansao was more vigorous in old age than I realized.

"Want to come aboard, or are you too tired?" Chris asked. "Damon's going to invite you formally next week, but he wouldn't mind if you feel like a look-see."

"I think I'll wait for the ticket," I said, looking at the spotless white paint—but unless I was much mistaken, there'd been another, longer, name under the fancy red and gold letters of *Thetis*. What had been her original registry? I thought perhaps I'd rather not know.

When I later came on a faded bill of sale in one of the dusty files dated ten years back, I was sure of it. Dom Sansao's yacht had been laid down to his own design at Clydebank in 1937, and christened *Pirata Blanca,* which means exactly what you think it does.

It was the nadir of my despondency, and commonsense came to the rescue. Everyone, including Bart, had been certain Dom Sansao was rich and had always been rich. His money couldn't have come from smuggling—not that I'd put anything past a Valentim. How could Sansao be smuggling when he was being Portuguese Ambassador somewhere?

The manuscripts might be stolen, but if so, why were they sitting openly on the study shelves . . . unless they were the reason the suite was always locked. It still didn't fit Smuggling, exactly, not that I know much about the gentlemen, but I had the impression one smuggled things like cigarettes, brandy, nylons, or guns—no, if it was guns, it was called running. Whatever it was, it was a full load, and how could you make a full load of illuminated manuscripts? Besides, Dom Sansao was too old for skipping under the noses of Revenuers; he'd be over ninety if he were still alive. The concept of an ex-Ambassador taking up smuggling in his seventies was *too* absurd.

I felt sufficiently cheered by this ratiocination to reqpuest Chris's assistance for a library catalog on the first evening he honored us for dinner. "Damon has a meeting in Caldarém, and we don't expect Allegra to foal for another week."

"Oh? Well, it's lovely to see you, darling, and since you're here you can give me a hand," I said politely, "unless you have horse-plans?"

He grinned at me endearingly. "You don't really mind. You're glad to be rid of me so you can roll with Royce!"

"No, I don't mind, so long as you surface often enough that I know you're still a boy and haven't turned into a Houyhnhnm."

"Gosh, you really do feel better. That sounded like you again!" Chris sighed with relief. "What's on the fire?"

"An inventory of the books in the study. If there's already a list, I haven't found it, but we ought to have one. Those autographed first editions are damn valuable, sweetie, and it'll go faster with you to haul down while I type."

"Do we *have* to sell those?" Chris sounded troubled.

"No, no, that's your private library, hon, but I have to know what's there for insurance—and there may be *some* things you won't want to keep," I said carefully. "If they've any value, we could sell, or give to the goodwill, and make room on the shelves."

It took two hours, and we were still not finished, but what remained were the low shelves I could easily reach. Chris had only a dim idea of money values, but my eyes literally bugged out!

Judging by the autographs, the Valentims had personally known every literary genius everywhere from about 1830 to 1930, and even before that they read. *Otranto, Frankenstein, La Nouvelle Heloise, Candide, Werther,* all of Jane Austen . . .

Name it and it was there. Dom Sansao had set every valuable family book in his study, these were not bought for investment. They were well worn, some had bookplates or signatures of long-gone Valentims—but Sansao had known what he had, had concentrated in this one room to cloak purchased goodies. In the midst of my catalog, the additions were unmistakable. Sly old man. Within these four study walls Dom Sansao had stored his wealth, expecting his heir to come at his death even if implacable before—and Bart would have understood, I knew that.

He'd treasured some books, a packet of letters (content dull but signatures authentic) directed to his father and grandfather. They were stored in New York, marked Property of Christopher Valentim, but at a glance, Bart would have known Dom Sansao's study was Golconda, his great-uncle's last effort for forgiveness . . . and all for nothing, I thought sadly. Bart hadn't come, his Valentim son didn't own anything, the whole package was in the lap of an American ex-model, who only knew it was valuable—not what to do with it.

Chris yawned widely. "I've had it, Nell. Could you finish?"

"Yes, but are you enough with it to say what you want to keep?"

He studied the lists silently. "How do *I* know?"

he asked suddenly. "Nell, you decide? I think I'd sort of like the Dickens—what a *bit* to use an autographed first edition for English *Lit*?"

"Yes, as well as all the others, whether or not you can read them yet. In time, you will. So: you leave it to me?"

"Why not? Dad did, and he was no fool," said my stepson succinctly. He suppressed another yawn and grinned at me. "Never think I don't know how lucky I am to have you, *minha mae!*" He hugged me briefly, "G'night. See ya."

"Good night, hon." I listened to him hauling up the stairs, shutting the upper door. It was—sweet to be called "my mother," and a new departure for Chris. In New York he always called me Nell, rather like introducing "my stepmother" to his school friends and their parents, "because you're not anyone's idea of a wicked old witch!" Our relationship had been unstrained from the beginning, the final touch to Bart's happiness, because I had made him happy, I knew that. But now, five years later, Chris might have gone either way, old enough to branch into independence of his father's widow. Instead, we seemed closer than before.

It was most encouraging, what I needed to give me strength to cope. I went back to the catalog and was finished in another hour. The very last book, at the end of the shelf nearest the desk, was the *História Doméstica de Valentims*. It was in three languages; Portuguese, French and English, privately printed in Paris in 1890. When I'd closed up for the night, I took it up to my bedroom, along with a glass of iced tea.

The book went from 1100 to 1890, and was principally useful for the documentation. Oliveiro Bartolomeu Valentim had the writing style of a pompous old goat, but he'd done a thorough job of research, noting where references to early Valentims could be found in old books, papers in archives. It was a pity he took himself so seriously. A dash of humor would have made a best-seller, the Valentims had all the ingredients.

A bunch of brigands is what they were! Oliveiro hadn't omitted anything, but you could tell by the bald recital of facts where he was ashamed of his ancestors, in contrast to the effulgence of pride in more respectable events. Oddly enough, he had no qualms about the ransom operation: it was only Moors, which apparently made it okay. There was even a list of who was put in those cages, and how much the Valentims were paid to let them out.

A special section was devoted to the castle: who built what and when with dates and costs. The titillating item was the secret passage. Oliveiro said it was built by the chap who made the first addition and was extremely useful for odd jobs of piracy. He didn't specify location, said it was a secret known only to the Dom and his heir, and gave the distinct impression it was abandoned when the Valentims went respectable, which was 1770 when they'd got enough loot out of Brazil to build the final section we were living in.

But Chris said Bart had known the passage, was going to show him. Would Huberto know? If Chris asked, Huberto would probably tell him—and make the boy take an oath not to tell me! Not that I cared, but the directions ought to be in *this* copy of the book because I realized it was the Dom's responsibility to continue it. There were pages of printed genealogy, but extended by handwritten entries. Sansao's marriage to Ofelia dos Martinhao in 1900, Alexandre born 1902, four subsequent daughters with their marriages and children; Bart's father, Bart himself and his marriage to Cecily, the birth of Chris, and innumerable neat entries for other branches of Valentims.

It was complete—but not entirely. The omissions and inclusions were significant. Huberto's father was there, with a star for illegitimacy (there were quite a lot of stars!), Huberto himself, his wife and children . . . but no death date for Ofelia or Cecily, no record of Alexi.

I put the book aside with a yawn. It couldn't be given to anyone, of course, even if Chris were amenable. It was the family bible, he'd have to carry on for as long as Costa Demonio belonged to us.

The luminous clock dial said 4:00, and I woke feeling thirsty. In the dark I padded sleepily to the bathroom. With my hand on the light pull through the window I caught a flicker in the castle cellars—or I thought I did. My eyes opened at once, intent on the old buildings, and suddenly there was another faint gleam farther along toward the sea. Then there was only blackness.

That was no ghost. Someone was prowling about with a flashlight. Who was it? where had he gone? I went as quickly as possible through the darkened bedroom, peering from the other windows, but there was no hint of motion. The man could have gone through the old kitchen and out the far side, down to the bathing beach. I continued to watch for a full half hour, but if he'd come by boat, he'd gone farther up the coast instead of turning for Ponto Lucido. No point to flinging on clothes and trotting over to investigate. I didn't know the place, I hadn't gone back since the tour with Alexi. If anyone were still there, I was only asking for the broken neck at the bottom of a stairway. *O que accidente horrivel!* when everyone had warned *la senhora* of the danger.

All the same, I was not about to play. Let them do their smuggling somewhere else, I decided grimly; I had enough problems. Just as I fell asleep I had a lovely luscious superb idea: *hah!* Tomorrow I would start putting spokes in wheels.

CHAPTER V

Never mind the phone bill, someone was going to be enraptured to have Costa Demonio for a photographic fashion layout, particularly if Eleanor Marchant was part of the package!

Someone else was going to be seriously inconvenienced by a dozen high-fashion models (who are always smarter than they look) capering about, to say nothing of a few photographers (who rarely look like anything, so they can't help being smarter than).

Exactly the right moment for winter-playclothes issues. With luck I'd latch onto a group already in Europe and happy to have a free vacation. If necessary, I'd pay expenses; let 'em think I wanted publicity for my castle. I sat up in bed and carefully went through the magazines I'd bought in Caldarém. I better start in New York where Eleanor Marchant could get through to anybody. I'd have to wait till afternoon for the time difference, but I could type the inventories, write letters, outline the plan to create a major "fubar," which is an unprintable Navy term beloved of Bart.

During siesta I'd take a look at the old castle,

see if I could find traces of our visitor. I can't say I relished the idea, remembering the maze of those cellars, but it was better to go alone. In daylight, I ought to be able to find my way—or why not try Ariadne's thread? There must be balls of string in Costa Demonio; God knows we had everything else you could think of.

That I did nothing as planned was due to the first bundle of mail from America, which arrived shortly after breakfast together with notice of the air freight arrival in Caldarém. "Tell Jorge to pick everything up when you go to market, Mariana," I tossed over the cards and settled to the letters. One was a note from mother. Another was from an apartment neighbor saying the new tenants were not in the Valentim league, and the cleaner had delivered my blue dinner dress which had been overlooked; she'd packed and airmailed; forget the money. Finally there was a bulky envelope from Valentim & Co.

Magazines, notices of meetings long past, requests for charities, general junk, I thought Miss Gorman might have handled instead of spending air postage for me to drop in a Portuguese wastebasket! There were three unopened envelopes. Two were from old college friends who had not heard the bad news; the third was only bad news for me.

"Dear Mr. Valentim,

With further reference to your letter of March 30, we have explored your suggestions and already feel certain your deductions are correct. We have been successful in laying a firm basis, and expect to be able to finalize the matter during your visit. We are deeply grateful for your cooperation, and await your contact as soon as possible after your arrival on June 10th."

The letter was signed Homeros Plakidon, Division 6, Interpol. It was dated Paris, May 29th, receipt stamped in the Valentim mail room on June 5, and why the hell did I only get it *now*? Because Bart's secretary was a stupid lazy bitch, who couldn't be bothered to send the office messenger up to the apartment with accumulated mail before I left so I'd have time to consult Mr. Anderson, inquire about previous correspondence, get in touch with Interpol before flitting off into the wild blue yonder. Damn the girl, Bart himself had said she was the worst he'd ever had! Mixed with my rage was a spinetingle of terror. If Interpol were concerned, the smuggling must be serious!

I thought fleetingly of the manuscripts and paintings . . . dismissed them. They'd all been here for nearly six years—or had Sansao masterminded a smuggling ring and Huberto carried it on? Possible, aside from his age; Damon Lord had the yacht, Jorge Pintos, and various stableboys to lend a hand. I'd buy that, I decided: Huberto with five undisturbed years, unlimited storage spots in the old castle, plenty of contacts in Ponto Lucido.

No wonder they didn't want anyone here, didn't want me *affiché* with Alexi, the *commisário!*

Yet if it were known in Caldarém, Alexi couldn't fail to be aware, could he? And, twice as dangerous, if his other grandpa headed the original Ponto Lucido smugglers, he'd know every in and out, every ruse. Although perhaps he didn't; now that I thought of it, he'd been a small boy when his father died and his mother took him to Lisbon. On the other hand, not likely anyone would tip off the *commisário*, and Alexi was constantly going back and forth to Lisbon or Cádiz. It was quite possible that he wasn't here enough to catch on, and, that because of his traveling, Interpol hadn't contacted him.

It would *have* to be Huberto, and/or Damon. Who else could scare away the locals?

Or Ponto Lucido itself? If there were smuggling, they were bound to be part of it. In my few contacts with the villagers I'd had nothing but smiling respect, even a few bobbing curtseys. Slowly I put together what I had: Caldarém knew what was up, but was not actively concerned, sitting back to enjoy the situation. Ponto Lucido *was* concerned, knew I was unaware, and hoped to be rid of me before I found out. Make *la senhora* so uncomfortable she will leave?

But I'd refused to be dislodged. The second line of attack was to make firm friends with Chris, hoping I would confide any puzzlement to the boy, who would innocently reveal it to Damon and Huberto. I laughed mirthlessly inside at their suspense, since nothing would emerge. It was the one thing I'd done right, saying nothing to Chris! All he could discuss was the library catalog and that I meant to keep nearly everything. Hah! Let them wonder. I hoped it'd give them ulcers!

Interpol first, I wrote Mr. Plakidon tersely but fully, outlining all my private deductions for what they were worth and asking for immediate instructions. Should I continue to stay at Costa Demonio, was there apt to be gun play, would my plan to invite a crew of photographers and models be safe, or a hindrace to the law? Answer requested SOONEST! Sealing the envelope, I thought fatalistically that this would be all the Drummonds needed: to have their grandson involved in a ring of international smugglers.. . .

I went with Jorge to Caldarém for the air freight and mailed my letter personally. The boxes were marked for ready reference, luckily; Jorge took them to appropriate rooms, leaving the smallest in my morning room—but there was nothing of Mr. Plakidon. Either Bart hadn't kept previous correspondence, or I had not realized its pertinence and had stored it in New York with the rest of his personal files.

Imperative to explore the castle cellar now, I filled time before siesta by typing neat copies of the library inventory and completing letters to my mother and Mr. Anderson. I sealed the envelopes not only with spit but with a few daubs of the fancy sealing wax, and secreted them in my handbag. Then I changed into denim pants and espadrilles. Armed with the flashlight and two large balls of twine bought in Caldarém, I was all set. . . .

"Nell? Let's try the runabout?" Chris called, eager-faced at the foot of the stairs. "You don't want a nap," he cajoled. "Bring a suit, and we'll swim."

Perforce I agreed—impossible to investigate the castle if Chris were at hand, but while I got sun glasses, shade hat, bikini thrust into tote bag, I admitted secretly that I was glad for the reprieve.

"There's no danger if we stay *in* the harbor. Damon says all the underwater rocks were blasted out during the war so supply boats could duck in here during the North African campaign. They left enough at the mouth to prevent a straight path for torpedoes." Chris helped me into the runabout, started up and out. "Don't worry, I've been around once with Damon. He said I couldn't take you until I proved I knew how." Chris grinned cockily, "Coo, 'e sounded just like me old man! 'Drown yerself, matey, but not yer pretty Nellie!"

"Tell yer what, matey," I said austerely, "that's not H'english!"

The harbor ran much farther inland than I'd realized. Immense shade trees completely hid the upper end from view; I'd never even know there was a bridge, thought the road merely skirted the shore—and when we passed under it before my amazed eyes lay an entire other stretch of water, with a dozen docks, all sorts of boats!

"Nearly every family has one; it's a fishing village, Nell," Chris remarked. "They go out before dawn, get back around noon, handle most of the catch before siesta and finish before dinner, or the next morning."

"Sounds like a long day!"

"I guess it used to be, but we built them a packing plant in 1953. Dad got it from American and set it up; we still get an escudo for each package, but Ponto Lucido owns the company. Now the men fish in the morning and are through for the day when they get home. The women do housework, and the kids go to school while the men are gone. Afternoons, the women pack, the kids work in the fields. The older people fill in to drive the shipment trucks to Caldarém, finish yesterday's catch, handle the stock, or bottle wine." Chris shrugged. "Everyone has a job that's scaled for what he can do physically, you know? Sounds sort of communistic, but Damon says it works very well. They share out the money on the basis of productivity, which gives the younger people more when they need it most, you see? For raising babies or getting settled in a home—but everything gets done, no sweat, and there's plenty of leisure."

Yes, indeedy; plenty of time to go smuggling! "Well, it sounds Utopian, hon. We should all have it so good. Tell me more of what Damon says."

Chris was turning the runabout, avoiding boats, heading back. When we were under the bridge and back to our mooring he said, "Why don't you like Damon, Nell?" There was a tone in his voice that argued *caution.*

"It's not dislike," I said after a moment. "I know he's a gentleman. I'm glad he'll take time to tell you things."

"So?" It was Bart's courteous voice, waiting for explanation.

"So I should have had notice of this question," I said lightly. "Degrading as it is, I think it comes under the heading of 'you'll understand when you're older.' There's no explaining adult reactions, Chris—and when it comes to that, he doesn't like me either." I hopped out to the dock, tied up the prow while Chris did the stern. "That path.

Could we go round it and bathe in the near cove? I haven't been this way before."

We swam, but there were too many submerged rocks. You couldn't get beyond them to free water. After we'd both scraped our legs and arms I said, "I've had it, let's go back—and I wish they'd blasted out some of these rocks when they did the harbor. I wonder how much it would cost for some depth charges to turn this into a bathing beach?"

"I'll ask Damon, he was in charge of the Ponto Lucido job," Chris said casually. "That's where he lost his foot."

"Lost his *foot?*"

"That's why he won't come swimming with us, he says it'd make you sick. Even if he wore a sock over the artificial one, he says you'd know it was there and probably be nauseated. I told him you weren't squeamish, you worked for the crippled children in New York," Chris said with detachment, "but he thinks he'd rather not chance it."

"Good heavens, how silly!"

"Yeah, but his wife vomited, and how does he know you're different?"

"*Wife?* He said he didn't have one!"

"He doesn't, now. She was American, a WAC, I think—it was in London during the war, and when he came back with only one foot, she left him and got a divorce in Reno." Chris sounded troubled. "Just because he couldn't dance, Nell . . . is that enough reason?"

"For some people, sweetie," I said slowly, choosing words with care because Chris was explaining everything to me, even though he didn't quite realize it. Damon's wife let him down—he went sour, went to Portugal, hunted up his wartime pal Dom Sansao, and became a smuggler?

Chris's eyes were on me, I pulled myself together. "In wartime, everything goes overboard, hon. People need someone to cling to," I told him, "not just men, but women. It's eat, drink and be merry, because it's only a twenty-four-hour pass and all too possible they'll die tomorrow.

"Comes the dawn—meaning armistice and demob—and they aren't dead, but stuck with completely the wrong person," I said impersonally. "The handsome major turns out to be a truck driver, and the cuddley armful in a WAVE uniform belongs behind a Woolworth counter, with a mind to match. I'm sorry that happened to Damon, I expect it'd be a terrible shock to find it wasn't you, but your dancing feet, that got a girl to marry you."

He nodded absently, brushing sand from his toes and stubbing them into the sneakers. "You mean his rigging got fouled because of the war, and that he wouldn't have looked at her twice if he'd had time?" Chris interpreted.

"Something like that." I zipped up the denims, and looked up at the cliff behind us. There was a definite path going upward to a jutting rock. "Let's try that for a view." When we reached it, there were the remains of a picnic fire with a delightful sheltered nook into the hill. It was the right size for two. Tactfully I averted my eyes and looked over the shimmering water.

"Let's go up to the next rock, I can see ashes there, too," Chris spoke up. The path narrowed a bit after that, but it was still firm packed leading from rock to rock, with evidence of campfires on all of them. "I think we hit Lover's Lane," Chris remarked drily when we were nearly at the top.

I looked back to the shore and wasn't happy at the thought of getting down again! "Does the path go any farther, hon? Perhaps we could scramble up the bank to our garden."

There was a big round rock; we went to the right of it and ended in a stymie with a five-foot overhang of bluff. "Let me have a cigarette, and we'll start back."

"Okay," he said agreeably. "Must be safe, there's a candle end up here." He held it up: a four-inch lopsided square of wax, like the things people make in old milk cartons. After he casually tossed it down to the sea, we couldn't hear a *plop!* in the midst of the waves beating around the rocks. I sat back against the bank contentedly, communing with the water. Demonio shimmered wickedly in the distance, but today it didn't bother me. "Nell, why didn't dad like Costa Demonio?"

"I—don't know, darling. He never told me."

Chris sighed. "He wouldn't tell me either. He said he didn't want me confused by adult matters until I was older. It must have been something about my mother, but all I know is that she died and there was a court case. Don't you know *anything*, Nell?"

"Only bald facts," I said impersonally. "Do you want them?"

"Yes, please."

"She became an alcoholic. She'd been in and

out of sanatariums from the time she was in high school. It was all hushed up, nobody told your father, so he married her. For a while it was all right. One thing: she was *thrilled* at having a baby, you. She wanted you *very* much, Chris; she was utterly happy all the way through," I told him, "and she had an extremely easy time, so it wasn't you at all . . . but, later, something sent her back to the bottle.

"Your father blamed her parents; they wouldn't take it seriously. He couldn't even keep her in an institution for a complete cure. The Drummonds always got her out and took her home, where she'd start drinking again. Finally she—died. Then her parents wanted to bring you up, and your father wouldn't permit it. He felt they ruined your mother, and he was determined you shouldn't be overindulged. That was why," I finished, "he left your guardianship to me, Chris. He knew I'd follow through on what he wanted for you. I hope you don't mind?"

"Jeez, no," he said awkwardly, "except—I only thought of it recently—but it's a bit much for you to be saddled with me, isn't it? I mean you're a young woman, Nell. You'll marry again."

So he'd been talking it over with Damon, who saw a neat chance for unsettling? "Perhaps, but you wouldn't be the way. There's money to get you through college. I kept your father's share in Valentim & Co. on the chance you'll want it, and they hope you will, Chris." I held my voice to steady impersonality. "It's possible you may have to work summers, if you want to make the international scene and go to the debutante balls, but there's plenty of bread, enough for the best butter."

He nodded. "I earn the jam," he said, matter-of-factly. "Where d'you get your jam, Nell?" When I stared at him blankly, he met my eyes with unsmiling maturity. "Yes, I *know* you aren't broke, you've got things figured *somehow*—but I know you too well, Nell." He scowled down at the water, tossing pebbles aimlessly over the cliff. "There was a lot of land in Vermont, and the Adirondack cabin . . . you kept it all, didn't you?" I nodded helplessly when he glanced at me. "Do you get anything out of the Valentim partnership?"

"I don't know, hon. I expect it'll depend on the year end." I shut my mouth firmly, but inwardly I raged. Damon wasn't content with simply insinuating Chris was a burden on a stepmother who was bound to marry again—although she'd only been a widow for two months. Damon Lord had needled Chris into consideration of our finances!

"What have you got to live on?" Chris asked bluntly.

"Insurance, dividends, the sale of the apartment," I said lightly, "and a rent-free castle. What more could you want?"

"Just want to be certain you aren't doing so much for me that you don't do enough for yourself," he said after a moment. "Dad wouldn't like that, Nell. He'd want you to be going to the opera and the ballet, to first nights and dinner parties, like always."

I closed my eyes against the sun on the water.

"With whom, Chris?" I asked, and couldn't control my voice. "WITH WHOM?"

"Well, gee—I don't know. But you had loads of friends," he said uncertainly. "I'm sorry, Nell—I just thought . . ."

"That it doesn't matter who's in the next seat so long as you can make the scene?" I snarled. "That's what your pal Damon married! I'm different. I've heard *Bohème* and seen Fonteyn a dozen times, listened to Brahms First a hundred times—and they were all new and fresh and—and unexplored, when your father sat next to me." I couldn't hold back the tears.

Then I found a handkerchief thrust into my hand, an awkward arm about my shoulders. "Nell, it's okay—*anything's* okay. I never meant you to fall apart, *minha mae*. I just wanted to be sure . . . I mean, if you're having to sell things," his voice cracked disastrously, "maybe I should stay here instead of going back to school."

"No, darling, don't be silly; the money's there, and *only* for school, so make the most because it only sits until you do," I pulled myself together. "Just don't try to marry me off right away. And don't fuss if I sell that horrid vermeil piece for a bit of ready cash. The thing is that there's plenty, but it may take time to realize it. That's all. You said the other night that your father relied on me—please, won't you, Chris?"

"Yeah, sure—I do, but I only wondered . . ."

"Well, don't!"

The sun danced warmly on the water, the view was soporific. From the deadly whirlpool swirling in hypnotic circles, my eyes moved to the thrusting outcrops scattered in the cove, following automatically from one to another until my gaze ended at the cliff beneath the castle.

Peculiar. . . .

Why had my eyes led so inevitably to that spot as though guided?

I opened my eyes and concentrated. Begin at the eddy . . . but once more my eyes went mechanically from one spot to another and ended at the sheer rocks of the headland. Why? I took off the sunglasses and picked up the binoculars, wincing slightly at the sun glare on the water, but it was quite clear: there were unobtrusive markings on certain rocks, a small cairn here or there, a splash of whiteness that could pass for gull guano but was more probably white paint, and a few sticks emerging from the water between the rocks.

Channel markings! They could be nothing else, and they were a way to the shore through the one cove considered impassable. Furthermore, this wasn't Lover's Lane; those ashes were from signal fires to guide a boat safely to . . . where? The headland was apparently sheer crags; I wouldn't have thought you could get anything bigger than a row boat within forty feet of it, or avoid breaking an oar going from cruiser to landing. Wherever it was . . .

Involuntarily I leaned forward slightly, trying to glimpse something that might be significant, and beneath me the loose pebbles scattered unnervingly. Chris grabbed my arm. "Watch it, Nell!"

"Yes," I said a bit breathlessly. "Alexi was right;

the place is dangerous. Maybe we'd better start back; I don't fancy being out here after sundown."

"Yeah, it's one strike against renting this place, unless we put up barricades. There's bound to be some jerk who'll get himself killed trying to scramble around."

"Cynical—but right, and I don't know what ever possessed us to try it!"

"Oh, we're intelligent," Chris grinned down at me as I backed carefully down the makeshift trail. "One more step and you'll be at the rock; put your hand to the left and you'll have it." I grasped the jagged edges of the outcrop and felt limp with relief. "Now if you'll sidle around out of my way, I'll join you."

I peered around the edge, my heart in my throat, while Chris calmly came down on his backside, a few inches at a time with loose shale shifting in his passage, but eventually he made it. "We do NOT do this again," I exhaled. "Understand? This is completely off limits, *verboten*, taboo!"

"Don't worry, I'm not about to get myself killed. I've got a lot of living to do," he said cockily. "Come on, we work over to the left, away from the shore, and haul up onto the verge behind the hedge."

It was rough going, we were both puffing a bit, but we made it—to face the high hedge of the topiary garden. "Now what? I'll never hurdle that!"

Chris reached up experimentally, testing. Suddenly he grasped, heaved, and was lying atop the privet. "You didn't eat enough pablum or something," he said snootily. "Wait there. I'll get a ladder."

I sat in the shade of the hedge, and inevitably I got out the binoculars again. From this angle you couldn't see a thing! I studied the cove incredulously. Could it be pure imagination, born of my nerves? I thought there was a smuggling operation going on, and fancied everything I saw related to it? Ought I to tell Mr. Plakidon? If I were right, it might be exactly what they needed . . . but wouldn't it take a complicated arrangement of grapnels to get down the headland from the castle to investigate the landing? Any such maneuver couldn't fail to be observed, would give away the show . . . but if I were right, there was some perfectly simple route to be used by whoever knew it.

The secret passage, of course—it might have been built by the Valentim who added the second section of the castle, but it must lead to the sea, or it would be useless for piracy. Someone knew where it was, too. That was why the light I'd seen last night had vanished. From my bedroom I couldn't see down the cliff face; the prowler had gone out the tunnel, and calmly walked home along the beach.

"Hi, here we are!" A ladder landed with a thud on my side of the hedge. It was secured by a stout rope, to be retrieved when I was rescued. Two rungs up and I could see Chris's twinkling black eyes. "Rapunzel!" he said dramatically, hanging onto the rope. "Come out, come out, wherever you are."

"Silly! My hair isn't long enough." I went up another rung, and beside Chris was Damon Lord. His eyes weren't twinkling at all; they were ice cold. I stopped abruptly, somewhat frightened by the controlled fury in his face.

"Come on, if you please, Mrs. Valentim," he said. "You may be a feather brain, but you are not without weight—which *we* are holding." I scrambled hastily from ladder to hedge top. It was hellish prickly on the backside, even through my denim pants; I'd be a mass of scratches, and how was I to get down on this side? They got the ladder back to the garden, when Damon calmly said, "Chris, take it back to Jorge."

"Aye, aye, sir!" Chris was lost around the first turn before I could find my voice.

"You wonder how you will get down, Mrs. Valentim?"

The odious formaliy of *Mrs.* Valentim wasn't lost on me! "I suppose I shall jump, Mr. Lord."

"And break your ankle on the stone bench?"

I peered down cautiously, and he was right; there was one. I looked right and left. Could I move along the hedge until I was beyond the bench? Never mind if I were lacerated beyond help.

"I shall assist you," he stated, "but first you will explain to me why all this is necessary. You have been explicitly told by everyone that the cliffs are dangerous. Huberto, Mariana, Jorge, Alexi, I myself—we have all warned you, yet you choose to practice mountain climbing on the most dangerous section of all. Not merely that, you take Dom Christo with you!

"One wonders what you have in mind, Mrs. Valentim. Is this some Freudian desire to be rid of your husband's son? You would like to inherit a castle, perhaps? I fear you will be disappointed, but minors cannot make wills. Costa Demonio will go to Chris's nearest blood relatives if he dies before his majority."

"Oh, no, it won't," I retorted. "Costa Demonio belongs to *me*, Mr. Lord. *In toto*, lock, stock and barrel—and I may or may not renew your lease at Quinta Choupo. Put that in your pipe and smoke it!" I moved gingerly along by inches, suppressing squeaks at the sharp privet twigs, and prepared for a spring to the ground, but I was picked off like a fly, set on my feet with firm hands on my shoulders.

"Is that true: *you* own the place? You could sell it?"

"Yes."

"Does Alexandre Valentim know this?"

"I don't know what he knows," I said coldly. "And do you mind removing your hands? I bruise easily."

His grip slackened, but was not withdrawn. His expression was inscrutable, sardonic, on the edge of a wicked grin of satisfaction. The pale blue eyes held mine compellingly, and he gave me a slight shake, "You're not to do this again, understand? If you want to explore, ask me first, d'you understand? I'll find time to come with you. Huberto's too old, except for telephoning when you're getting yourself into trouble." He snorted at my widened eyes. "Why do you think I was to hand, girl?"

"That," I twitched away from him, "is something I have wondered before. I may say that no acceptable explanation occurs to me, Mr. Lord. I may look like the blonde preferred by gentlemen, but, I assure you, my husband was under no delusions about my competence."

"Oh, neither am I," he stated. "You couldn't be as brainless as your general appearance, and Bartolomeu Valentim was reputed to be extremely shrewd. Mind the stone!" His hand lightly caught my elbow, steering me down the center of the allée, away from the border of small rocks outlining the paths. I raised my chin and stalked along without looking at him, but I could smell amusement. Damn the man, always catching me off balance. Chris could perfectly well have got me over the hedge, not the slightest need for Damon Lord to poke his nose in, making snide remarks, issuing orders . . .

We'd reached the rear door to the kitchen. "Thank you so much for your help, Mr. Lord," I said dulcetly. "I'm sorry you were troubled; I'm sure you have many more important things to do."

"Tchk! Temper, chipmunk, temper!" he reproached.

"Oh, stop sounding like a nannie! I haven't asked, nor needed, your chaperonage."

"That," his voice was oddly grim, "is what you think. There are dangers at Costa Demonio aside from falling stones, girl. Be advised! Don't allow your passion for exploration of your ruins to create a problem, or the adventure will be very serious indeed—for the boy as well as yourself. Good day to you."

He turned abruptly and went toward the stable, while I stared after him. I was in no doubt of his meaning, he'd warned me to stay out of his way, or—or something would happen to Chris. With a shiver I realized I was right: it *was* Damon, with Huberto helping. How had the old man known we were on the cliff? From one of the lookout towers, they probably all gave a complete view in every direction. He could see us poking about the harbor, tying up and going swimming—and the moment we started *up* instead of turning back to the lane from the dock, Huberto had alerted Damon . . . who came galloping over, but not for our rescue, for his own.

Had Huberto got back to his vantage post in time to observe me surveying the channel with binoculars? If not, it was okay; they'd be wary, but uncertain I could have spotted it. Chris hadn't. All he'd noticed were the campfires and nooks; he thought it was Lover's Lane.

I was tempted to drive into Caldarém and telephone Mr. Plakidon, ask police protection or something. Nearly dinner time, though; what excuse could I give for dashing to town at this hour—and I wouldn't get him anyway. He'd have gone for the day, home for his own dinner in Paris. Damned if I'd be stampeded, I decided grimly; I'd already stupidly let myself be stung into telling Damon Lord that I owned the castle. I would *not* give away anything more by agitated fluttering about.

Tomorrow, or the next day, without undue haste, giving every indication of complete calm and business as usual—I would look for the secret tunnel. I might be lucky enough to find it, or something helpful, at least. I felt sure I knew where to look.

CHAPTER VI

Alexi had returned from Lisbon. When I came downstairs, dressed for dinner, I found him chatting easily with Chris in the small salon. He sprang to his feet and kissed my hand gracefully, "Nell, *cara prima*, it is good to see you again—and looking so well!" He surveyed me seriously and suddenly decided, "Yes, you are rested. The eyes are not tired, that tiny wrinkle is gone from the forehead, *muito bem!*" He released my hand with a pat of approval, settled me in an armchair and hesitated. "You permit me to remain for a moment, Nell? I should have telephoned, but I arrived later than anticipated. There was just time to bring you the wine I promised."

His gesture indicated a large wicker basket on the floor beside Chris. "Goodness, what a lot! I thought you were only giving me a bottle of the new muscatel," I exclaimed. "Of course, sit down, Alexi. Won't you stay for dinner? Americans are dreadfully informal, you know, but I'm sure there's enough; there always is." I was unexpectedly glad to see him. Alexi was a relative, after all, as well as *commisário*. It was—comfortable to have the police at hand.

"That is kind, Nell. I should be delighted to join you."

"Chris, tell Mariana, would you?"

"Sure, but there'll be plenty, I already invited Damon," he said casually. "His peas are all gone, but Huberto plants ours two weeks apart so we'll have them all summer."

"Oh? well, that's nice," I murmured blankly, while Alexi pulled the basket across to me and gently picked up a bottle.

"Here is the muscatel. The others are a sampling of what we offer, and, as I warned, they are merely drinkable," He said ruefully, setting them out in a row. "I thought to make a courtesy present to Dom Christo from a lesser member of the family," he smiled as Chris came back. "It will do for the table, perhaps, or Mariana will use it for cooking, but this," he picked up the final bottle, "is more special. It is a Maderia from a small vineyard my mother owns near Funchal, and we do not really sell it, aside from a few dozens for our select list." He whipped out a folding corkscrew as he spoke, expertly opened the bottle in a minimum of smooth motions—to my deep admiration. (I am death on corks, it seems a peculiarly masculine talent.)

"Now," Alexi filled the glasses on the bar tray, "I shall ask your opinion of this. Nell?" he extended a glass to me. "Chris?"

"No, thanks, Alexi. I wouldn't know if it were good, bad, or indifferent," Chris said disarmingly. "Don't waste it on me."

"But the more reason to start training your palate," Alexi protested. "I am surprised Bart . . .

but I remember wine is not so customary in America. *Assim*, we begin!"

"Okay," Chris said good-naturedly, "but save that for Damon. I'll take a swig from Nell's glass. You don't mind?"

"Of course not." I handed it over, but taking it back from him I caught Alexi's expression. He wasn't looking at me; he was looking at Chris . . . with such sadness that I nearly cried out!

It was gone so quickly I scarcely recognized it, couldn't think about it because Damon was coming through the side hall, followed by Mariana with cocktail accompaniments. "Good evening all," he said cheerfully. "Hello, Alexi—when did you get in?" He shook hands briefly, eyed the wine bottles. "What have we here? How are you, Nell?" *Very* casual! an easy smiling nod, no handshake, no formality . . . already helping himself to Chris's rejected glass of Madeira . . . taking a canapé from Mariana's tray . . . chatting sociably with Alexi . . . sitting down in the larger armchair.

He was trying, I thought, to give the impression of family friend on first-name basis allowed to run tame at Costa Demonio—to convince the *commisário* that Damon Lord was on an inside track, approved by the Dom and his stepmother, constantly running in and out.

"Nice to see you at long last, Damon," I said lightly. "Afraid it's only pot luck. If I'd known you were coming, I'd have baked a cake."

"With Paris green frosting, no doubt." His lips twitched. "But you know I'd never put you to so much trouble, when you're practicially only just out of bed." He turned easily to Alexi. "We've been averting a nervous breakdown for the poor girl—everyone tiptoeing around, complete rest and quiet—but it's paid off, don't you think? She looks almost human." Damon sipped, rolling the wine on his tongue critically, and observed, "A very tolerable Madeira, Alexi. Very tolerable, indeed. You don't sell this, I suppose—or does an old acquaintance rate a few bottles on the private list?"

Alexi laughed. "I can give you a dozen this year, Damon—but no promise for next." He leaned forward to pick up the muscatel. "This is the new item, I'll want your opinion later. By the way, had you heard Fernandao is retiring?"

"No! One wonders what will happen . . ."

They were engrossed in local gossip, Chris listening and able to follow most of it. On the surface, a normal evening: three men, one woman; a private informal dinner with conversation general; food delicious, service unhurried. For once Chris did not fold up in a series of cavernous yawns; I was the one suppressing yawns. Wasn't anyone EVER going to leave? I suspected Alexi was merely simulating interest in the horse-conversation, but he wouldn't go. In fact, they all settled back when Huberto produced nightcaps and a large Coke for Chris.

And *that* was part of the oddness. Considering Huberto's tirade, how come he was serving dinner, and bringing a drink tray, correct to a shade, without a hint of distaste at waiting on his cousin's bastard grandson?

Then there was Chris, ingenuously but ingeniously avoiding questions about Costa Demonio, giving the impression he spent all his time at Quinta Choupo. When Alexi asked whether he'd found the *História,* Chris said (truthfully) that he hadn't. He never mentioned Dom Sansao's study, and when he finally went to bed, he went up the main stairs even though he'd been using his private ladder every night and morning since I'd showed it to him.

Midnight, and I strongly suspected the men were sitting each other out, like high school boys calling on the same girl. It was amusing, but the final touch of oddness: Alexi, turning everything into flowery compliments, and Damon, smiling into my eyes and calling me chipmunk caressingly! He knew I wasn't fooled, but evidently my puzzlement enhanced his enjoyment of the situation.

The back of my mind worked away busily under cover of their conversation. Chris had invited Damon before Alexi showed up, but why had Damon accepted? Fence-mending, of course: I owned Costa Demonio, and I'd threatened to cancel his lease; damned inconvenient to move his stables, let alone find another good site for smuggling operations. I could bet he'd wheedled the invitation from poor innocent Chris, too, all that guff about fresh peas!

It explained Huberto, as well: Damon told him to mind his manners. They hadn't expected Alexi, but had no choice. Now Damon didn't want to leave me alone with the local constabulary, and Alexi wasn't going to leave me alone with grandpa's crony, although he found it rough going. His command of English couldn't keep up with ours, particularly when I decided to play.

"What is this 'chipmunk'?" he asked.

"It's a very small, rather harebrained variety of American squirrel," I said. "Damon thinks I resemble one."

Alexi huffed with the insult to me, but Damon laughed. "Only in size," he remarked, "and no squirrel could be harebrained."

"Anybody can see there are no stripes on my back."

"I'd expect them lower down," he said judicially, "but with mutations there's no knowing what you'll get."

"Isn't it sad? Just one perfect specimen," I sighed, "and never enough to make a coat."

He broke apart at that, but we'd completely bewildered Alexi. "Tell me about Lisbon, I'm thinking of taking Chris for a jaunt," I smiled apologetically, and Alexi brightened.

"A superb idea! You will do my mother the honor of staying with her," he exclaimed. "No, I insist. She would be deeply hurt that Dom Christo goes to a hotel. Surely it is time to heal old wounds, which have nothing to do with you or Chris."

I could tell Damon thought poorly of the suggestion. So did I. Evasively, I said no date was set, "It depends on the foal. Chris wants to be here—can't blame him with the best teacher in Europe willing to give a cram course. There's no rush about Lisbon. What I want is an antique dealer."

"Rua Garrett, by cable car to Largo do Carmo," he said mechanically, "and down from the Vista

Alegre toward Rossio—but what do you wish to buy, Nell?"

"Not buy, sell," I told them gently.

"SELL?" they chorused, and both talked at once. Vehemently! "Are you planning to sell the treasures in this place? Dammit, girl, you can't be such a barbarian!"

That was Damon; Alexi was protesting, "No, you cannot, you have not the right to destroy Dom Christo's heritage. I have told you, Nell, I repeat: if there is a problem, it is *my* right to assist. Costa Demonio must be maintained for Chris."

"Shh! Wait till you see what I want to be rid of." I went to the pantry and toted back the vermeil centerpiece. When I'd set it up on the top of the piano, there was silence. "You see? Who needs this? Chris says he couldn't eat a bite if it were on the table. He can't believe anyone would buy it, but I imagine a dealer could get a thousand dollars from a collector."

"I see your point—and I wouldn't want it on my dinner table, either. Would you, Alexi?"

"*Por Deus*, no!"

"What else have you got?" Damon asked inscrutably.

"Sixty-eight irons," I told him promptly. "I think one is Elizabethan, for crimping those stupid ruffs—but something says not even St. Laurent could being them back into fashion."

"Irons?"

I nodded. "They're rather sweet. I expect they'll make charming lamps, but do admit: who needs them in a pantry closet? You didn't think," I widened my eyes, "I'd dream of selling the Fragonard, or the family portraits, or even the etchings in the game room? No, no—but I don't think we *need* the darling little Victorian rocking horse, do you? Or some of the oddments of Waterford crystal and Spode, the cunning old pony trap in the stable, the japanned bird-cage, Majolica cookie jars, unused sugar and flour bins, copper roasting pans big enough for a baron of beef—not that I know what anyone could do with them, but an interior decorator will think of something."

Damon's pale blue eyes narrowed sharply. "I expect you're right." Alexi was not so happy. "Nell, this is absurd! Dom Christo Valentim cannot be selling—household goods."

"He won't. I will," I said calmly. "And don't tell me I should give it to the Salvation Army, because we may be aristocrats, but we need the money, and I won't offer to lend it, Alexi, because why in heaven's name should Costa Demonio be stuffed with junk?" I waved my hand at the vermeil. "Get me a dealer, if possible with a contact in America, there must be one, or," I turned to Damon, "give me the address of Christie's."

Alexi continued to splutter, but Damon was intent. "Are you really in such poor case, Nell?" he asked abruptly. "I'll make you a firm offer to buy Quinta Choupo on the spot, and I'm certain Pintos could buy his farm."

"Out of the question, Damon. Nell has no right to separate or encumber Dom Christo's inheritance."

"The crisis is temporary," I avoided Damon's quick glance. "Very simply, we're land-poor on both sides of the Atlantic. You've both kept trying to push me out of Costa Demonio, but at least I can live off this land. The American end is unimproved acreage for a future ski resort. I don't say I expected what I found here, but it's still the obvious solution. We can't rent the place."

"But I have said I will deal with Revalhao."

"Useless," I shook my head calmly. "Mariana can't get anyone from the village to work here; they've been scared into fits with ghosts stories."

"What? *Por Deus*, I'll see about this!"

"Don't bother. I told Revalhao's office to take Costa Demonio off their lists—and that's an odd thing," I commented. "It turns out it hasn't *been* on their lists for the last four years, and they couldn't find any written instruction from Bart."

Damon slowly settled back into his chair, his eyes on me. "How did you learn this?"

"Went to the office in Caldarém with Mariana." I shrugged. "It doesn't matter. I've decided I don't want to be a landlady, anyway, falling over strangers who'll burn the furniture or spill drinks on the rugs."

Alexi sighed with relief. "Now *that* is sensible, I have not liked for you to be exposed to rudeness from *turistas*, if nothing worse. You are far too young and attractive, *cara prima*, and Chris is not of an age to protect you."

"So you will live off the land, sell some junk for extra cash," Damon's voice was dry. "I'm afraid you won't get much from old irons and a rocking horse."

I dropped the bomb. "I don't need much; I've only to get through the summer until investment income is coming in regularly, so I'm going to offer Costa Demonio for a photographic background in the fashion magazines," I said sunnily. "Don't you think it's a superb idea? I don't know why I didn't think of it before. I used to be a model, you see, and I still know everyone in the business."

That got a reaction! Damon was shocked speechless, his lips tight with control, but Alexi reluctantly approved, and the more he considered, the better it seemed. He believed a great many notable houses had been used in this way; I would not, of course, appear personally.

"On the contrary. I'm the bait. I'm not forgotten in the trade, I assure you."

"No, you'd be long remembered anywhere," Damon muttered grimly. "I should have guessed you modeled. For the record, why didn't you stay in New York? Why must you dash off to Portugal, to have this brilliant inspiration of filling Costa Demonio with a crew of beautiful dimwits who'll fall off the cliffs and sue for broken legs?"

"They won't break anything," I informed him serenely. "You'd be surprised how agile wc are for crawling about ruins, we're much more apt to get run over by a taxi in midtown—and I didn't stay in New York because I thought it better for Chris to be completely away.

"He's only fifteen, he—loved his father," I finished evenly. "Life changed for him as well as for me. I thought the adjustment would be easier here; I think I'm proved right."

"As you say," he shrugged curtly.

"I cannot like this, Nell. Photographs of the castle maybe, but *not* of you. Bart would never allow this!" Alexi fussed.

"You're quite wrong," I laughed lightly. "Every time Valentim had a special promotion, he asked me to do it, and he was odiously conceited that Avedon or Penn or Shaw always yelled for me the instant there was a bind. If he were here, he'd think it the lark of all time to dress in native costume and be photographed on a horse or holding a guitar," my voice trembled slightly. "You knew him, Alexi. You know he'd have been all over the place, hanging off turrets and making dramatic love poses with me," like that perfume ad, I thought . . . "if he were here . . ."

Damon stood up abruptly. "One o'clock, time to make our bows and retreat in good order, Alexi. Nell," he bent over my hand, "thank you for a — delightful evening. My Luisa can't equal Mariana, but will you judge for yourself tomorrow night? Alexi, would you be free to join us?"

"A pleasure! And the following night may I be the host? Would it amuse you to come out on the *Fortuna*, Nell? Damon? We must make some gaiety for summer vacation."

I could scarcely plead a prior engagement, I said I was certain Chris would be agreeable, and what time? "Five o'clock, we'll exercise the horses along the back roads you haven't seen? What about you, Alexi?"

"Excellent! It will give me a chance to examine the vineyard, I suspect it must be restocked, but if I can not spare enough sets," he shrugged, "everyone in Ponto Lucido will help . . . and on Thursday, we will view Demonio himself, eh? Four-thirty, to give us time for a run along the coast and return to Ponto Lucido for dinner. Chris will enjoy this?"

"Very much. If you give him a fishing rod, he'll probably catch our dinner!"

"*Assim?* One thought he had no idea aside from horses."

"No, no, Bart taught him to fish and hunt at our Adirondack cabin. I'm fond of fishing, too. Chris says there's all sorts of rods somewhere, but I haven't had time to investigate."

"You won't get any fly casting here," Damon told me. "It's either trawling nets or drooping a hook into the harbor, wiggle-wiggle and hope for the best—but you'll like the *Fortuna*. Coming, Alexi?"

Perforce, Alexi kissed my hand with a gentle squeeze. "*Amanha, cara prima.* Ah, it is what we have needed: a lovely woman to stir us out of our bachelor habits!"

I stood in the doorway and raised a hand in farewell as Alexi gunned the Porsche out to the road, turning left for Ponto Lucido. I was unsurprised to see Huberto leading Damon's chestnut from the stable, it figured. I called "*Até à vista,*" switched off the patio lights and loitered behind the closed door, while Damon pulled lithely into the saddle. I thought you'd never have known he had only one foot, aside from the faint careful placement in walking. He glanced back once, must have been satisfied by the darkened hall, and sat easily erect talking to Huberto while the mare sidled impatiently.

More orders for espionage? Chris was simple:

Damon had him under his eye practically all the time at Quinta Choupo. Senhora Valentim was the problem; no knowing what she'd do when! Now Huberto was talking earnestly, with quick interjections from Damon. Telling him—what? That I had the key to the safe, but presumably hadn't located it? That I had studied the water through binoculars?

But if I had uneased Damon and Huberto by intransigence—exposing Revalhao, who would certainly affirm where he'd had his instructions as soon as Alexi or I got our hands on him—planning to fill Costa Demonio with people, enlisting the aid of the local *commisário* to procure servants—they had given me plenty to think about, too. I went over it mentally while I undressed, and all reactions were expectable but one.

Why should Alexi be *saddened* by Chris?

Unless it was regret for something, I thought next morning. Had Alexi inadvertently caused that breach fifteen years past? He could have met Cecily easily enough, on the beach where he'd originally met Bart, suggested a drive, some mild diversion for Bart's wife, but if he'd offered alcohol to Cecily, as last night to Chris, *she'd* have taken it. How could Alexi have known? Bart himself was unaware.

Yet how could the acquaintance have ripened without Dom Sansao's knowledge? Alexi couldn't come calling at Costa Demonio. Had Cecily slipped out to meet him after dinner? No roadhouses in the vicinity, but there was his mother's home in Ponto Lucido. Had Alexi perhaps not realized how serious it was until it was too late—or even fallen in love with Bart's wife? Did that explain the faint underlying melancholy, his sadness when he looked at Chris, who was not his son, but the child of a woman he'd loved?

Vesuvius, Mauna Loa, Pele, would have paled in comparison to the Valentim row when Bart arrived at summer's end! Bart blaming his great-uncle for failure to be on top of the situation, and Sansao arrogantly disclaiming any responsibility; the girl was of age; he was not a nursemaid; and so on. If Cecily's family had left her alone, allowed her the chance for a cure—but they hadn't. By the time Sansao backed down, Bart was probably having such real hell as the result of that summer that he was implacable.

I thought it might have been that way . . . and perhaps Alexi had never even known, for who would have told him?

I went down to breakfast, and found Mariana throwing her weight around with two slaveys! "*Bon diá, senhora,*" she said regally. "As you see, Rosalia and Anita have come to assist; they decide perhaps the talk of ghosts has been exaggerated." She tossed a string of Portuguese over her shoulder that set them scurrying. "Eh, you were right: Ponto Lucido arrives!"

"Alexandre Valentim promised to attend to it, but I didn't expect such quick results."

"He calls himself Valentim?"

"Says he has his mother's marriage lines to prove it."

Mariana snorted. "If Alexandre Valentim the first, had ever married Maria Revalhao, that one would have stood in the plaza of Caldarém shouting it at the top of her lungs!"

I chuckled at her vehemence. "He's invited Chris and myself to stay with her in Lisbon," I said experimentally.

Her eyes widened. "*No!*" she said unhesitatingly. "This you cannot do, senhora. It is long ago, but it is not finished. Here, *com efeito,* you are clever to receive him, although not too often, *comprendido?* Already it impresses that he has dined informally at Costa Demonio, but Lisbon—no!"

"Why? Oh, I've no intention of visiting," I assured her, "but why did Dom Sansao disinherit his son?"

"He did not consider him fit to be Dom," she said matter-of-factly. "Alexandre Valentim was wild—always in trouble, expelled from schools an clubs, gambling debts, women. Eh, he was bad, a terrible embarrassment for Dom Sansao who was ambassador. Finally there was a major scandal, and Dom Sansao sent him here until it should blow over . . . and when he returned for a vacation, he found Alexandre had joined the smugglers of Ponto Lucido!

"Not merely that," Mariana warmed to the gossip. "the daughter of Luiz Revalhao, Maria, who was well known to be *chefe,* was pregnant. No question the father is Alexandre—and that was the last straw. Dom Sansao disinherited his son and chose his nephew as heir. Alexandre's name was never mentioned again."

"East Lynne in Portugal," I murmured. "Then what?"

"Oh, Alexandre moved down to Ponto Lucido.

When Luiz died, he became *chefe*," she said calmly, refilling my coffee cup.

"Good heavens, how humiliating for Dom Sansao!"

She nodded. "Worse, senhora, for at last the government made an effort to end the smuggling, and Alexandre Valentim was killed on the very shores of Costa Demonio. One supposes he knew these waters well, had often used them for escape—but the last time the agents were hiding in the old castle waiting for him," she said sombrely. "Dom Sansao had made it open to the government men—how could he do less, when he had been ambassador?"

"I suppose he couldn't, but what a horrible predicament."

"*Sim, sim,*" she agreed sadly. "I remember the lights and shots. It was the night before we were leaving for America, September 10th, 1938. I can be exact because we did not return until after the war.

"*Assim,* there was a massive interchange in the early hours, and someone came to ask Dom Sansao to telephone for a doctor because his son had been wounded—and Dom Sansao said 'I have no son!' *Porém,* it did not matter, for Alexandre was already dead," she shuddered dramatically, "at the foot of the cliffs. Dom Sansao would not even permit burial in the family crypt, senhora!" From her stricken expression it was obvious that Mariana considered this the absolute end. "Next day, when Senhor Bart asked about the shooting, Dom Sansao said only that a smuggler had been caught. It was months before we knew in a roundabout way, by a letter from my cousin, that it was Alexandre Valentim. As I have said, senhora, the Valentims are a hard family."

I was appalled. "Sansao could have said he had no son, but he should still have called the doctor."

"*Porém,* he would not," she said with finality, "and perhaps he was right, for in the middle of the night after Alexandre was buried in the village cemetery. Maria Revalhao took Alexi and whatever she could lay hands on, and vanished."

"Goodness, how intriguing! Alex said they lived in Lisbon."

"Yes, but it was some years before this emerged. Then it became known that Alexandre had all along established Maria in Lisbon as Senhora Revalhao, with a house of her own in the best section of town, and a business," Mariana snorted. "Revalhao & Filho, wine exporters. One hears it does well to this day, but one supposes it did even better as a cloak for Alexandre Valentim, and that it was not merely wine he exported."

I laughed. "I expect Maria did equally nicely as a rich widow in wartime Lisbon. I'm surprised she didn't get a second husband."

"Undoubtedy she did—but it would have been someone else's," Mariana said scornfully. "When do you go to Lisbon, senhora?"

"I haven't decided, I think," I looked at her innocently, "that it will be spur of the moment, a business trip only; there are other matters to set in order first."

"*Sim, sim,* you will wish to supervise the cleaning," she agreed blandly, "For today, we begin with pantries and kitchen. Tomorrow we move on to the salon, and through the other rooms in turn. Who knows what else we may find—like the irons?"

It was a solid ten days before I could get into the old castle unobserved! Every blessed day *something* prevented me. I went ahead with the photographic idea—and was tied up with transatlantic calls during siesta. Chris was underfoot, looking through the fishing and gun equipment. I tried weeding a few flower beds, cannily working my way closer and closer to the end of the topiary garden nearest the cellar staircase, when Jorge helpfully joined me, with about three words of English, but plenty of smiling sign language to indicate he *loved* gardens, this could be beautiful, leave all to him.

After watching him with the clippers shaping the old yew, I was happy to leave it to him; it was going to be a marvelous photo background, but he elected to do this on his own time, meaning siesta. I ventured to protest to Mariana that the boy ought not to be working in the hottest part of the day. It got me nowhere. Mariana said Jorge had been paid quite enough all these years that he could well afford to work during siesta; he should have done it before.

In between there was Mariana herself, driving her staff unmercifully. "It is not necessary that they have a siesta for sleep, senhora. Let them sit still and polish things in the shaded back room . . . and if you wish to sell, how about this? Or this which we have found in the lower store rooms?"

I'd written Mr. Plakidon of my discovery of the channel markings through the impassible cove, my deductions for the campfire ashes on the cliff, and where I thought the tunnel was located. Again I mailed it unobserved in Caldarém, but I'd had no answer. Perhaps he was busy with another job, but it was a bit nervous-making. I had Penn with two models arriving a week from Saturday to build an issue of *Vogue* around Costa Demonio and Eleanor Marchant—and the instant that leaked out, I had impassioned requests from two other crews for use of the pad. As it stood, there were going to be about sixteen people running wild over the castle within two weeks.

Meanwhile I had two beaux—or so they'd have me believe. I couldn't turn around but Damon or Alexi, or both were at my elbow. Alexi showed up at conventional calling hours; sometimes he telephoned first, sometimes he didn't, and apologized for dropping in without warning. It didn't escape my notice, however, that Alexi no sooner parked the Ferrari, and trot-trot: there was Damon about fifteen minutes later. Either Huberto or Jorge were johnny-on-the-spot at the estate phone! The excuses were various: Chris would be home for dinner; Chris would not be home for dinner; here was an interesting article in *The Economist*; Damon was going downstreet, had I anything to mail?

I couldn't tell whether Alexi realized the chaperonage or not; he was always smilingly happy to greet Damon, in spite of the original oblique warning against sociability. Alexi did not presume, exactly; nevertheless, there was a distinct impression that he was my unofficial protector, standing in the place of husband-father-brother. He was inclined to make slightly florid compliments, which is always a hazard with European men, but his behavior was unexceptionable.

There was still a certain strain. I didn't feel Damon wished to join us; it was something he *had* to do to be certain I didn't get too cozy with the *commisário*. Once he apparently couldn't make it on the alert—but Jorge was innocently trimming the hedge, and, when I deliberately led Alexi to the far end of the garden, Huberto turned up five seconds later to prune the dead roses. He was another strain, although he said no more about "receiving" Alexi and avoided me as much as possible. Huberto was less able than Damon to control his feelings, however, and his face wore a permanent glower.

It was amusing in a way—and also, it wasn't. If only I'd had some reply from Interpol because I really didn't *know* anything. I simply *thought* it was smuggling because of the Ponto Lucido reputation—and Damon's boat—and he was so damned anxious to get rid of me, so furious on the day I might have identified the channel past Demonio. Now he was either always on hand or Huberto took his place. But what the hell could Damon be smuggling, and *why*, when he seemed to have a very lucrative business in the horses?

In one of the few uninterrupted moments we had, I asked Alexi, "Off the record, is there still any smuggling? Chris says Bart told him fantastic stories about it years ago."

Alexi laughed. "Oh, the great days are gone completely; Tangier is a thing of the past, Nell." He grinned at me wickedly. "I don't say there aren't occasional encounters with the fishing fleet. If anyone in Ponto Lucido has ever paid full price for a bottle of wine, a cigar, a pair of nylons, I would be much surprised! But," he said seriously, "there is little profit in smuggling these days. Everything can be bought everywhere, and the price is not enough less in one place or another to be worth the risk of prison."

"What do people smuggle?" I asked curiously. "I mean, if they're making a career out of it. All I've ever heard of was wearing Paris frock off the plane or carrying a fur coat over your arm, that sort of thing."

"Today's smugglers are more sophisticated, I believe. Small objects easily secreted: jewels, of course, collectors' items like postage stamps, coins, a single rare book." Alexi smiled at me. "I don't really know much about it, Nell. It was my father who was the smuggler, you see, and he—died before he could train me."

I laughed involuntarily. "I expect he'd think you very dull for ending as a *commisário*."

"Perhaps," Alexi said after a moment, "and perhaps not. I think he would be pleased with what I have done for the small business he established for my mother."

"Does she handle it when you're away? I mean, how can you be *commisário* for Ponto Lucido when you have a business in Lisbon?"

"Oh, quite easily; there is not really any crime here."

I laughed again at his bland twinkle. "But then why do they need a *commisário* at all?"

"In a way they don't, but it is good to have one

head man to whom anyone may turn—someone to say 'Well, if you cannot agree, then I will tell you what you are to do.' It is not often needed, but that strength must be there. It was my grandfather until he died; it would have been Bart if he had been here—and in time it will be Chris." He shrugged. "I merely—bridge the gap, Nell."

"Yes, I see. I'm glad you can do it, Alexi," I said warmly.

We dined at Quinta Choupo, following a tour of the stables and a leisurely ride to the vineyards. Alexi was no gaucho, he sat his horse, while Damon and Chris were fluidly blended with theirs, but when he dismounted and inspected the vines, Alexi obviously knew what he was talking about. Damon looked sardonic, while Chris was walking along with Alexi and absorbing a short lecture. From where I sat (on a frisky mare named Medora), I couldn't see anything disastrously wrong, and when Alexi finally remounted (he had a handsome but sedate gelding named Manfred), he was enthusiastic.

"It is far far better than I thought, Nell! Here and there a replacement, but I shall be able to spare whatever sets you need. During the summer, as I have time, I will go through carefully with Chris and show him the fine points."

"Well, that's good news. How much do we get out of these vineyards? Is it drinking wine, sweet or dry, red or white? We won't use much for Costa Demonio aside from cooking," I said briskly. "Could the overage be sold?"

Alexi nodded. "Oh, yes, I would take it off your

hands, Nell. The price depends on the quality, but it used to be very good."

"It still is," Damon remarked impersonally. "Sansao got three pipes of red and two of white laid down each year. You'd better see how much Huberto has, Nell. There'll be anything up to ten or fifteen years by now. Sansao bottled and cleared out annually from five or six years previous, but of course it hasn't been done since his death. Alexi, I think you may have a find; 1955 was a particularly good year, if you remember—and 1960 was superb. In fact," he said thoughtfully, "I'll put in my bid for all that's left of the 1960, Nell. Let Alexi set the price, but you won't have to bottle; we can transfer the pipe to Quinta Choupo. Is it a deal?"

"Can't see anything wrong with it."

I couldn't see anything wrong with Luisa's cooking, either, nor with Quinta Choupo itself. It was a rambling old farmhouse, and compared to Costa Demonio the rooms were small, but there seemed to be plenty of them and the furnishings were as authentic as anything I had. Admittedly it was a man's home, but there was a casual warmth in the untidiness, and all the appointments were quality, whether antique or modern.

I couldn't say as much for Alexi's home in Ponto Lucido. The effect was good, but a contrast in every way. Somehow I suspected it had been done up by an interior decroator: things *matched*. The house itself was charming, situated on a bluff at the far end of the village, with a magnificent view of the water and a much nicer cove than ours, but the furniture was mostly modern. Where Damon's table silver was not particularly pretty in design, by its appearance and monogram it was inherited; Alexi's was probably from Georg Jensen. Damon's coffee cups were delicate Limoges, Alexi's were Swedish modern, and so were the ashtrays and wastebaskets, even the woodbox was new.

Call me a snob, but it was interesting. You couldn't say there was a thing wrong with Alexi's house. It was in perfect good taste, no expense spared, but it reminded me of that character in a Saroyan play who keep saying dolefully, "No foundation!"

The *Fortuna* was another matter. She was luxury in the nth degree, with a crew of six, and Alexi in a peaked yachting cap to welcome us aboard. "Luiz Belendo will take the wheel," he said with a dramatic wink, "so I can give my attention to my guests. You understand the crew is paid by the municipal funds for use by the *commisário*? And since we do not have any criminals at the moment, the crew scarcely works at all. It will be good practice!"

She was a bit bigger than Damon's *Thetis*, and she cut through the waves like a knife. We cast off, back away from the berth, and were out of the harbor in astonishingly short time. Rounding the bluff into open water, I could see the old castle on its headland and caught my breath. It was truly awesome from this angle! So was Demonio—and from any angle I didn't like it. Alexi took the wheel himself briefly and brought us close enough for a thorough examination.

The horrifying thing was that it looked so innocent—rather charming in its lazy circles, if you didn't know what would happen if you got into it. "Nell, would your nerves stand a small demonstration?" he asked quietly. "I can cut through Demonio a little way—on the outer edge only—and the *Fortuna* has the strength to pull free. There will be no danger, and I think you should experience the drag of the water."

Instinctively I looked at Damon, and he said, "Go ahead, Alexi. Let her go once around; there's no problem about getting out with a boat this size. You could probably do a second turn, but let's not experiment that much."

"Nell, you permit?"

"Why not?" I said valiantly . . . but it was terrifying! It was like one of those Coney Island rides where you jerk along on a level track and suddenly *whirl*, only to jolt along the other side and *whirl* again. You couldn't believe the inexorable strength of that circling water! Alexi edged the Fortuna slowly over to the outer rim—and with petrifying speed, you could feel the whirlpool grabbing us, sending us forward in a smooth lane curving with a sickening sidewise cant as we hit the inner end. Around we went—*and Alexi's hands were not on the wheel, we were moving with the water!* I clung to the rail, looking at the turbulent center of the maelstrom, hypnotized by the water pouring down and under—to what?

"It's really quite safe," Damon said quietly. "Don't look at it, chipmunk. We'll be out in a minute."

"Oh, I don't care about me, but Bart wouldn't like it if I lost Chris," I returned foolishly.

"You won't. Come over to the other side; we're starting to pull free."

I looked at the placidly rolling, rollicking waves outside the whirlpool, aware that Alexi had taken the wheel once more . . . but Demonio didn't want to let us go. You could feel the boat shuddering, fighting, until *finally* we were skimming along smoothly, with Demonio left behind. I drew a deep breath and fumbled for a cigarette in my tote bag.

"It's dangerous," Damon's lighter was waiting, "but I've done three turns in the *Thetis* and still pulled free. Both your boats could get out on the first turn; don't worry about Chris."

"No—he's very sensible. The castle looks quite different from here, doesn't it?" I said at random. "I never realized how much rock there was."

Chris insisted on trying the fishing rods. "In the afternoon? Don't be silly, hon."

"I just want to get the feel, Nell, and if we go down coast, there's a cove with enough overhang for shade. Jorge says it's where Ponto Lucido goes in off hours, we might catch something."

Amazingly we did! It was quite a fair-sized mullet, and Chris was in high fettle. "I can have it for breakfast, since Mariana has chicken for tonight. Let's go back and swim in the harbor."

We found Damon on the *Thetis*. "Come aboard." She was much older than the *Fortuna*, and must originally have cost a packet for the decorative details alone: solid mahogany everywhere; panels picked out in gilding; a luxurious bar of old-fashioned design. She was completely a gentleman's private yacht, intended for parties with pretty ladies. It seemed sad that she should have sunk to the rank of a smugglers' bark. I wondered where Damon stashed the swag, she didn't appear to have enough space for a worthwhile haul—but perhaps whatever he smuggled was small. . . like jewels? Or narcotics! I thought with a gulp; *that* would certainly draw Interpol!

The horrible thing was that when he wasn't trying to bully me, Damon was exactly the sort of man I like. When Alexi was at hand, Damon needled him by pretending an affectionate intimacy; when we were alone with Chris, he was simply courteous with casual friendliness . . . and he *was* good with the boy. Chris was learning from Damon all the small things he'd have learned from his father, although not by formal instruction. Bart would have *told* his son; Damon did not presume that far, not his place to teach another man's son. It was very subtle, very disarming. There was no question he liked Chris wholeheartedly, although he could never have expected to be saddled with a devoted teenager merely because the boy adored horses.

I'd suspected Damon of an ulterior motive in attaching Chris so firmly, but instinctively I knew that wasn't true. Whatever the outcome, Chris would come to no harm; the issue would rest between the smuggler, Interpol and myself. Still, I kept having to remind myself Damon *was* a smuggler, it seemed so unlikely . . . unless he was viewing it as some sort of Robin Hood operation?

Well educated, well bred, there was no denying he was far better company than Alexi—although some of that was due to the language barrier.

Even Damon didn't always immediately get a swift American humorous interchange between Chris and myself, although he did have his own special sense of humor, I realized suddenly.

"*Thetis!*" I exclaimed. "Of course! What a clever name!"

"Why?" Chris asked.

"She was Achilles's mother. Oh, come on, sweetie," when he still looked puzzled, "you *do* remember Achilles, or why am I sending you to school? She dipped him in the River Styx until he became invulnerable except for the heel she had to hold him by—and I always wondered why she didn't change hands and coat that heel, but maybe she was only allowed one dip. Silly, this is the *Thetis* because of Damon's foot that he hasn't got any more!"

Chris's face cleared. "Gosh, I never thought of that. Is Nell right?"

"Yes," Damon said with an effort. "Well, that's the end of the tour. If you're going swimming, there isn't much time." He turned his back and walked away to the prow. Chris was mercifully unaware; he called, "See you later, Damon," and trotted down the dock.

"With you in a minute," I said while he was stripping off his jeans. I went after Damon. "Sorry if I hit an exposed nerve," I told him. "I occasionally speak without thinking, Damon. Forgive me, please?"

"Nothing to forgive." He shrugged. "I'm not sensitive, if that's what you mean—I was just caught off balance for a moment; I didn't realize you knew."

"Chris told me. Did you think he wouldn't? I must say you handle the thing well! Did they take it off above or below the ankle?" He stared at me speechlessly. "One of my friends' husbands lost half a leg in Vietnam," I said steadily. "You should have seen us helping him get used to the artificial one when he got home! In the hospital it's all on the straightaway, but a home has traps, like furniture. It took a week to move things around until Bob couldn't run into a chair or table. Claire says actually it was the greatest relief to have a cast-iron excuse to get rid of the Victorian family stuff she'd always loathed—and Bob always was a lousy dancer."

Damon's face was pale. "You and your friend take—mutilation very lightly," he said. "How did the man take it?"

"He took it," I returned tersely. "He doesn't *like* giving up tennis and active sports, but they found other things he enjoys. He turns out to be a whizz at chess and bridge that he never had time to learn before. Claire says of course it's horrid for poor Bob, but on the other hand it's rather fun trying to see how much he can do, and at least she'll never be a golf widow." I smiled.

"She's a very exceptional woman . . . or did you invent her for some sort of well-meant feminine therapy?" he sneered.

"Oh, no," I shook my head. "Chris knows her . . . and I'm no Pollyanna; if anything I'm being bitchy. Do admit the loss of one foot isn't in the same league with a whole leg. Are you sure you don't still have your Achilles's heel?" I asked quietly. "Again, I'm really sorry if I pinched a sore spot. I'm going swimming. Care to join us?"

"Yes, I will," he said after a moment.

When he came down to the dock, I knew by his expression it was a test. He was daring me to ignore the sock strapped over his right ankle, he was expecting covert glances of suppressed revulsion at the very least. I fooled him; I never even looked at it! I'd seen all I needed while he walked down the steps: it was only the foot, he still had the ankle judging by the placement of the sock. Actually, I thought he probably could still do a sober foxtrot, if he practiced.

Chris shot a quick glance at me when Damon appeared, but all I said was, "C'm on in, the water's great!"

When we were alone on the way up the lane, Chris bearing his fish tenderly wrapped in a wet towel, "How'd you manage Damon, Nell?"

"Told him about Claire Treadway, you remember her?"

"Sort of. What about her?"

"Bob Treadway lost a leg in Vietnam. A single foot is nothing to fuss about."

Chris chuckled. "You're liking Damon better, aren't you?"

"I suppose so. He is here, and we do have to get along—and what's it to you?"

"Oh—I like the people I like to like each other."

Alexi showed up after dinner. "I have had the thought of an antique shop near Pria Rocha," he bent over my hand. "I came to bring the suggestion merely; I do not stay."

"Oh, why not? Won't you have coffee, or do you have an engagement?"

"No, but again, I should have telephoned," he shrugged ruefully. "*Porém,* if I shall not interrupt?"

"Of course not! We are working on a jigsaw puzzle. Do you like them? There are dozens in one of the nursery closets. I'm afraid we're addicts; we mean to do every one. Draw up a chair and join us. Chris, get another cup from Mariana?" I pounced on a piece tinged blue, fitted it in place, and sat back cockily. "I knew that had to be somewhere. Tell me about the shop, Alexi? We've found all sorts of ther things, with Rosalia and Anita turning out cupboards. Thanks for lending them," I said. "Mariana really couldn't do it all by herself, but I never expected you to give up your own servants, Alexi!"

He shrugged. "*De nada.* They are trustworthy and better trained than some of the others, but for a bachelor establishment anyone will suffice. Easier for me to send the reliables to Costa Demonio and replace with the village women, no matter who. Someone comes each day. I think they decide who has least to do tomorrow," he chuckled, "and that one comes to me—but it is good enough. As for the dealer, it is a distant cousin of my mother, Lazaro Revalhao." He raised his eyebrows meaningly. "One supposes there will be a slight extra effort to gain the maximum price."

"I depend upon it," I laughed, "but will he get as much as might be had in Lisbon, Alexi?"

"More, I should think. There is a little competition and many more tourists with idle hours to be filled, *comprendido?*"

I did, thinking of the deceptively modest shops in Long Island summer resorts. Pria de Rocha had the advantage of being no more than a hundred-mile drive; we could transport everything in the Rolls. The disadvantage was Alexi's certain knowledge of exactly how much I reaped from the sales. It was still a good idca to carry through at once on my plans as outlined. "Have you spoken to your cousin?"

"I have explored the possibility, without mentioning names. Lazaro is extremely excited; it appears difficult for him to procure enough items to maintain a stock that will appeal to his customers," Alexi winked at me and laughed, "who demand specialties. The rocking horse, for instance would not be found in every shop, after all?"

"Lazaro sounds worthy of Easthampton," I remarked. "That's an American resort somewhat similar to Pria de Rocha. Come see what else there is and have your coffee when we finish; I suspect Mariana's making fresh, Chris is taking so long to bring a cup." I led the way across the hall. "I'm stacking everything in the grand salon; we never use it, and it's better to keep everything segregated until we're ready to ship."

Somehow I was not surprised to find Damon in the sitting room, and Huberto presenting a tray of assorted liqueurs to accompany the fresh coffee—but was it Chris or Huberto who'd alerted him? Chris was constantly checking by phone on Allegra's health, he'd be certain to say Alexi was here. I thought it was Huberto, though, because Chris was eagerly inquiring about Allegra. So he hadn't called—and what was Damon's excuse for this visit?

"Went out for a breath of air, remembered you wanted the polish for the bosses, Chris, so I brought it along." He tossed a small can to Chris and looked about casually, "Am I interrupting?"

"Of course not, we were just fiddling with a puzzle when Alexi came in with news of a relative in the antique business."

"Naturally. My dear Nell, haven't you realized Alexi is related to half of Portugal? Whatever you need, name it and he'll turn up and aunt or third cousin," Damon drawled, "but it's a good idea," he nodded approvingly at Alexi. "Wouldn't have thought of it, myself—but then I haven't any relatives here."

"What are you talking about?" I demanded suspiciously.

Alexi's lips tightened briefly, then he chuckled. "Damon, why must you interfere? Lazaro *is* a relative," he smiled at me ruefully, "but as Damon surmises, he will merely buy on behalf of his brother Joao, who has a much more exclusive shop on the Rua Garrett in Lisbon. *Assim*, it will never be known that anything has been sold from Costa Demonio—and you will get the best possible price, Nell. I assure you of that," he added earnestly. "Lazaro will sell a few items in Pria de Rocha, for five percent commission only, and send the remainder to Joao, who will charge ten percent but who has the good fortune to be one of the European dealers authorized to buy for several American concerns. There," he shrugged, "I have confessed. But is it not exactly what you wanted, Nell?"

"Yes, but why couldn't you have said this in the first place?"

"*Cara prima,*" he said affectionately, "what would you know of business? For this one needs a man; you are not to be bothered, *queridinha.* Leave it to me, eh?"

"Yes, but I think I'll go along for the ride," I smiled sweetly, ignoring Damon's suppressed chuckle. "I'd like to see Lazaro's store, Alexi, and know what he thinks he could sell there . . . and they'll have to be a list of the consignment for Lisbon. You don't mine, do you?"

"*O contrario!*" he exclaimed. "We will make a day of it! Chris, it would amuse you." Alexi frowned faintly, "Damon, there would not be room in the Rolls, but why do you not drive Chris in your car with whatever cannot be packed into Nell's?"

"An excellent idea! And we will lunch at Porfario, dine at Cordeiro Crias. Make it Friday, and we can drive home by moonlight!"

So that disposed of another day, and Jorge spent Saturday and Sunday ecstatically trimming up the garden, informing me via Mariana that he would have it in fine shape for *la senhora's* guests. The advent of visitors caused Huberto to fix up the beach cabins with a coat of fresh paint, but the gaily striped awnings had cracked at the folds in six years of storage. Huberto appeared to take this disaster as a personal humiliation and was not comforted by my assurance that it was the natural fate of awnings. Costa Demonio had always had awnings, the beach could not be said to be properly dressed without them. He became, for Huberto, positively loquacious in describing the way they were placed, and when he'd indicated the iron stays to which they should be fixed, I could see he had a point.

Awnings would turn the dull cabanas into an approximation of an Arab desert tent. I'd realized about five hundred dollars from the small items, leaving the rocking horse and the centerpiece with Lazaro on consignment. Huberto drove me to Calderém, where I gladdened his heart by purchasing not merely awnings, but some beach cushions and basket chairs; they wouldn't stand up against sand and salt air, of course, but they'd make a photographic background.

In the middle of everything, Allegra foaled. Naturally. Not even animal mothers drop their babies at a convenient moment—although I suppose what I mean is "convenient for other people," as I understand it, any time is desirable for mother, and the sooner the better.

This was an occasion for great rejoicing, and in fact I was happy to have it over too. Now I could probably pry Chris loose if Interpol said "Get out of town." By good luck, he was at Quinta Choupo when the stableman alerted Damon that the accouchement had begun and was able to observe all the obstetrical details. The birth was normal, presenting no challenge to Damon's veterinary skill. "How nice for Allegra!"

"Yes, but I didn't learn very much. It's a filly. Damon says you're to name her."

Perforce I deferred hunting for the secret passage yet another day, and paid a visit of congratulation. Mother and child were doing well. "What shall we call her, Nell? I thought of Brava, or Jovanna because dad once had a mare called that."

"What does Damon suggest?"

"Why not, chipmunk?" Damon grinned.

"She hasn't any stripes on her back either," I said absently because it was suddenly shaping in my mind. Chris had Conrad; I had Medora. Alexi had ridden Manfred; Damon's chestnut was Anne. Via Chris, I knew Caro had recently been bred, and the sire was Sansoa's Corsair. I looked at Damon, "Call her Bread-and-Butter. I think you've used everything else."

His eyes flickered, and he stopped smiling. "I might have known," he murmured resignedly, "but it really started with Sansao. He was very fond of poetry."

For once, Chris looked faintly resentful. "Will you quit making adult gags? How can you call Allegra's foal Bread-and-Butter? What's it *mean?*"

"Sorry, hon. I expect you haven't hit Lord Byron yet," I said apologetically. "I think you'll get him in college, he wasn't considered respectable enough for high school."

Damon laughed helplessly. "He wasn't respectable enough for anyone! Maybe that's why Sansao liked him."

Chris was still fixing me with a compelling eye. "All the horses are named for characters in Byron's life or poems," I explained, gently. "Anne was his wife, Allegra was his daughter, Caro was his mistress, and all the others were poems. I forget where 'they always smell of bread and butter' comes from, but it fits a very young girl."

"Who was this Byron?" Chris frowned. "I remember there were some things of his in the study."

"He was a poet in England, around 1800," I dredged around in my memory. "He was a best-seller, and all the girls fell in love with him, because he was terribly handsome, in spite of his limp." I could feel Damon stiffening beside me; I ignored it. "There were a number of scandals, and finally he had to leave England. I forgot if he really was going to prison or if it was just that nobody would speak to him any more, but he caught something and died in Greece."

"Yeah, but Bread-and-Butter's a peculiar sort of name," Chris objected.

"You can shorten it to B and B, if you like—or call her A Piece of Cake," I shrugged, beginning to feel impatient. "If Damon would stop fussing about his silly old foot, you could move on to another poet."

"If you're implying I think I'm Lord Byron—" Damon began explosively.

"No, no. You're not nearly handsome enough, if I'm remembering the right picture," I said pensively. "Anyway, he had both his feet. I forgot if the limp was a club foot or a disease of the hip joint, but whichever, I distinctly recall both his feet always pointed to the nearest bed."

For a second I thought he was going to slap me, I could see his fingers twitching. Then suddenly he relaxed, "Dammit, chipmunk, *pas devant!*"

"Oh, Chris knows all about irregular relationships . . . and the better the family, the more there are," I said sunnily. "It's only the bourgeoisie who obey laws, don't you think?"

For some reason, that restored him to good humor. "Yes, I do—and we're none of us bourgeois, are we? Well, Chris, shall we settle for Bread-and-Butter?"

"I was only fooling," I said quickly. "Chris's names are better—which would you rather, hon?"

"I kind of like Jovanna."

The following day, miraculously, Costa Demonio was deserted! Mariana had decreed uniforms, and Huberto drove everyone to Caldarém directly after lunch. Chris was at Quinta Choupo as usual. Jorge was occupied in one of the upper fields. Alexi had said yesterday he was going on a routine check of the sea coast—meaning Damon wouldn't be turning up to chaperone. I was alone.

I wasted no time in getting out to the castle, where I attached the twine securely to an iron door handle and began prowling. Reason said that the passage was in the section with those horrible cages, but the light I'd seen was much farther in. Why—unless the cache was in that direction? I tried to be systematic, but it was nearly impossible; I kept coming up against a warped door that obviously hadn't been disturbed for a hundred years. Then I had to retrace, balling the twine until I reached the main passage and could start in a different direction. It was dreadfully confusing, once or twice I was sure I'd inadvertently got back where I'd already been, but at last I thought it was always the *same* door that shut off progress.

Furthermore, when I looked at it closely, I felt certain that door was merely locked, not warped shut. The wood might be filthy with cobwebby panels, but the hinges weren't rusted and the great iron handle was free of dust—as though a hand turned it and prevented any accumulation. That keyhole would require a large ancient key, nothing like the ones Huberto had given me, although some of them were fairly big, such as those for the stable and the outer door to the disused estate room. Huberto wouldn't have handed over his key in any case, and it would take more than a hairpin to pick a lock of this size. Leave it for Interpol; at least I had *something* for them to work on.

The cages were not quite so unnerving today, I was too intent on my search—not that I had the faintest idea how one went about finding secret passages. Logically, it would be at the far end, coming directly up from the sea, but the wall semmed nothing but solid stone blocks. I tried pressing the corners singly and in various combinations, working methodically from the bottom block to as high as I could reach, which left two top rows. But somehow I couldn't envision old Basilio standing on a ladder with a devilish leer in order to open his tunnel for whoever was shoving the hostages up from the boat.

No, the combination would be within easy reach because not all the Valentims were tall, I remembered. Some were small like Alexi. That was encouraging. I went on pressing one block after another, moving slowly from one row to the next, but when I'd got completely across the wall I'd found no slightest quiver anywhere. I sat down cross-legged on the dirty stone floor, lit a cigarette and pondered. I was tired enough to give up, but also stubborn enough to keep going.

Could the passage be a one-way arrangement, only to be opened from inside? No, or where had the visitor with the flashlight gone the other night? I was positive the last glimmer I'd seen was in here, beyond the transverse hall to the opposite stairway. Could it be not a passage but a trapdoor somewhere in the floor blocks? Briefly I felt excited by that idea—until it occurred to me the opening device must still be elsewhere. Otherwise anyone stepping on the crucial spot would learn the secret with startling rapidity. It was still a damn good possibility, better than the wall, in fact. The floor blocks were large single squares, any one of which was big enough easily to admit a man coming up a flight of steps, while the wall was uneven. That is, the blocks supported each other; they were fairly random. I couldn't see any section that might be a door.

How dumb could you be? I thought disgustedly. All that tiresome pressing and pushing, and one glance said there *couldn't* be a door. Oh, well, forget it. Now, where would be the opener for a trapdoor? Right next to the appropriate block, of course; they didn't have electric switches in those days. It would be some sort of iron bar or handle that would unlatch at the top of the stairs beneath, so the block could be pushed up, and logically that block would be somewhere at this end. However old Basilio had managed a tunnel *anywhere* under the wall of the original castle, it must have been a considerable job—not likely he'd pay for an inch more than required.

I finished my cigarette, scrambled up with renewed determination, and began inspecting the iron bars of the cages nearest the far wall. No, no, it couldn't be anywhere within reach, or the prisoners would be amusing themselves by opening it all the time.

It couldn't be anywhere that any prisoner could *see*, either! Otherwise the instant they were ransomed they'd have broadcast the secret. It took a bit of intestinal fortitude, but I went into each of the end cages and lay flat on the stone floor next to the end bars.

After that it was simple. There was just one section of the ceiling that couldn't be seen from any position. I went out, dusting myself off, and looked.

There was an unobstrusive circle of iron, looking utterly innocent, as though it were a sort of decoration. And when I looked again, there were similar twiddles next to every cage, but *this* was the only one no prisoner could see. I reached up and yanked.

A jagged section of the wall silently swung open about three inches!

When my heartbeat settled down, I pulled it back with no more than two fingers. Beyond was a flight of steps and Stygian blackness. I got out my flashlight, and I could see there was a sloping passage curving away from the bottom of the stairway. Did I dare examine to the end? Suppose I couldn't get out again? I had another cigarette and forced myself to *think*.

I had the passage; it was in use; every device for operating exit and entrance must be working smoothly—but would I be able to find them? There'd be another door at the lower sea end, of course, but suppose it only opened onto water and required a boat? Cautiously I stood at the edge of the jagged door and inspected with the flashlight. There was another iron circle hanging naked and unashamed directly to the left at the bottom of the steps. I was still not minded to investigate without somehow propping open that door. Just in case . . .

I went back and prospected about. There were some old andirons in the original kitchen, they weighed a ton, but I finally dragged one back to set across the opening. And how right I was. The instant I set my foot on the second step, the stone door silently swung back to crash against the andiron! I swung around at the noise, and nearly fell down the rest of the steps, but the andiron had held; the door was still open a few inches. When I could manage my legs for walking once more, I grasped the lower circle, and the door ceased straining against the iron, hung docile and motionless.

So that was all right, I could open the door even if someone sneaked in to remove the andiron. I tested it out, going back up the steps and finding I could avoid the device in that second tread. The stairs were shallow, so it took a bit of care to omit the switch-step coming down, but I could manage that too, If I sat on the top tread and extended my legs, then pulled slowly along the rough side walls.

The passage below was a dark hollow, stone-faced with iron cressets set along the sides. It was fairly clean (I had a frivolous mental picture of Huberto sweeping it out every week) but I wasn't sure I cared to follow it to the other end. I'd found the thing, who not leave exploration for Interpol along with the storage door? I ventured as far as the curve, to find another five steps and another curve at the bottom. Too irresistible not to go down and take a peek.

There were three sets of shallow steps connected by curving stone slopes, and ending at another huge stone door with the iron circle handles both inside and out. Then I was standing on a natural outcrop, looking down at the swirling water. To the left was the last small curve of the headland, but it was enough to form an unsuspected cove. Beyond lay Demonio, paralyzingly close to the land; a very small boat *might* be able to slide past it at this end, but I thought I wouldn't care to try it! No, I was more than ever convinced a smuggler went the other way, threading through the channel between the rocks, and by the looks of this cove, it would take the *Thetis* with no difficulty. To the right were rough rock steps; I thought some were natural, some had been cut, but all were worn smooth, very easy to negotiate.

When I got down to the bottom, there were a number of iron spikes driven into the granite for tying up a boat. I couldn't see the place Chris and I had reached, there was an immense jut of rock cutting off any view of the cliff except the first beacon nook we'd encountered . . . but there was a sort of path skirting around above the water. I didn't dare try it; it was slippery from the wave spray, but I didn't doubt someone *could* get past the outcrop and down to the sandy shore. That was where our visitor had gone when I lost his light. It would be about a half mile, and he'd come out at our dock.

I needn't say how immensely pleased I was with myself! I was practically chirruping with pride when I closed the sea door and trotted back to the upper end. Hah! let Interpol do the rest—if they ever condescended to answer my letter. I reconnoitered before stepping out to the cage room, but there was no sound—aside from my dragging the andiron back to the kitchen. Couldn't leave it out of place or it would be spotted at once—my heart was beating fast by now, wanting only to make good my escape. I'd no idea how long I'd been out here, Huberto might be back by now—or someone else could be about: Jorge, in the toolroom, Chris wanting something from the stables, *not* Damon; he knew Alexi was out in the *Fortuna.* But the cream of my discovery was to get completely away, so that no one knew I'd even been near the castle.

With my foot on the steps to the garden, I remembered: cigarette stubs—Good God, I'd never make a spy if I left such positive traces! I dashed back into the cage room and was picking them up when I heard a faint sound behind me. Startled, I reared up to whirl about—and something connected painfully with my head. . . .

CHAPTER VII

I opened my eyes slightly, and I was lying on a couch in the grand salon, with Mariana waving the ammonia bottle under my nose and a ring of concerned faces behind her. "What am I doing here?" I asked faintly, pushing the ammonia away.

"Huberto found you in the garden," Damon said evenly. "We thought you must have tripped and fallen against one of the edge stones. Can't your remember, Nell?"

That I could, and I wasn't about to tell, quite apart from the throbbing pain in my head that made me disinclined to conversation. I knew perfectly well I'd been knocked out in the cage room *by someone coming up the tunnel.* He must have had the shock of his life when he stepped out and saw *me* bending over to pick up the cigarette butts. No time to duck back and get the door closed, I was beginning to turn, so he bashed me efficiently. Later he'd artistically arranged the appearance of an accident by laying me in the garden. I supposed I should be grateful he'd fixed it for me to found fairly easily—but if he hoped I might conveniently have forgotten the sequence of events, I hadn't!

"No, I can't remember a thing," I murmured. "I think I did go out to the garden—or was that yesterday? How long have I been here?"

"The best part of an hour. We don't know how long you were lying in the garden. Huberto saw something, your foot or hand, when he brought the maids back from Caldarém." Damon was still impersonal, but now that I was beginning to focus, I saw his expression was grim. "He phoned Quinta Choupo at once, of course; I wasn't home, but Chris came over and carried you in here while Huberto called the doctor. He should be here shortly."

I *bet* Damon wasn't home! He was busily knocking me out in the cellar! "Where were you? How'd you get here then?"

"I went to Caldarém to meet a friend at the airport. Chris heard the car and flagged me on my return."

Then *who* hit me? Not Huberto, he was in Caldarém too, with the maids. Jorge? Or was there someone I hadn't suspected, one of the Quinta Choupo stablehands perhaps? Dimly I heard flurried motion in the hall, and Alexi hastened in with a strange man carrying the usual black bag. "Nell, what has happened? Here is Doutor Mercia. I saw him passing as I came from the *Fortuna*, and he tells me has been summoned for you."

Fortunately the doctor stuck a thermometer in my mouth at that point and picked up my wrist efficiently. Chris gave the official explanation, while I peeked through slitted eyes at Damon and

Huberto—not that Huberto looked any more surly than always, but there was no doubt Damon was controlling fury. His pale eyes were two cold stones, his lips were tightly pressed, and his expression boded no good. In spite of myself, I was scared by that face. How far would this man go to prevent interference in his racket? He'd warned me, both in words and by actions of surveillance—I already had a hit on the head. Whether or not he already knew which of his pals had clobbered me, he'd be in no doubt of my reason for being in the cage room, and correspondingly worried that I might have found the tunnel.

While Doutor Mercia was, most painfully, inspecting my head, I made up my mind to *butt out.* I would telephone Interpol, demand someone to protect me and Chris; they'd begun this, let them get on with finishing it. "Oooooh!" I couldn't restrain a whimper, which only made me angrier and more frightened.

"*Desculpe,*" the doctor murmured sympathetically. "It is soon finished. A little minute more, senhora. There, it is done." He laid me back on the couch and smiled encouragingly. "*Sim, sim,* it aches badly, but there is no serious damage, no break in the skin, no fever. The pulse is correct. We place you in your bed now, senhora, with a small sedative," I felt a tiny sting in my arm, "and tomorrow it will be no more than an uncomfortable bruise. Rest, move slowly for a few days, and all will take care of itself." He stepped back and added, "Can someone carry her, please?"

"Of course." Damon and Alexi moved forward but Chris pushed them aside, quietly authoritative. "I can manage, thanks." He swung me up as easily and as strongly as ever Bart had carried me, turned to the door and was halfway up the stairs before I realized I was weeping silently. "Shhh, it's all right, *minha mae*," he said softly. "Here's Mariana to get you into bed, and I'll be downstairs if you want me." He laid me on the coverlet, and kissed my forehead awkwardly, trying to smile. "You'll be okay, rolling with Royce before you know it," he assured me—but his eyes were troubled.

The damned sedative worked far too quickly, I was almost asleep before Mariana went away, so it was broad daylight next morning when I could organize my mind. Mercia was right that I'd have an uncomfortable bruise, but I also had a dull skull. I couldn't do anything *but* move slowly. Eventually I pulled around sufficiently to get washed and into a housecoat. Then I sat quietly and thought—principally of what would happen to Chris if anything happened to me. I hadn't been thinking of that while I was gaily sticking my nose into Damon's business. I hadn't taken anything seriously enough. It was all just a game: to find the tunnel—and pinpoint the probable storeroom behind that locked passage door. But it was no game to Damon, so much was now evident. I was a definite threat! Leave it to the experts!

I got through to the phone number on the letter-head and demanded M. Plakidon. He wasn't there. Well, that figured; in the past few months nobody was ever there when I wanted them. "Has he an assistant?"

"*Mais oui, madame.*" Shortly I was talking to a soothing voice who appeared to be up to date on *l'affaire Ponto Lucido,* whatever it was, which was the first thing I asked.

"Is it smuggling?"

"We believe so, madame."

"What? Or is it better if I don't know?"

"MUCH better not to know, madame," Monsieur Aigullon said firmly. "If I may explain?"

"Please do!"

"It is that Monsieur Plakidon has the matter well in hand, your information has just reached him. He had been concerned in another affair, but on his return he wrote to thank you for your cooperation yesterday, I believe . . . yes, it is here," scrabblings among papers. "However, it need not concern you further, madame."

"That," I informed him, "is what you think. Yesterday I found the smuggler's tunnel and got bashed on the head for it. No, I didn't see the man; he hit me too quickly."

Aigullon was shocked into muttering, "Ah, *merde alors!*" and was even more shocked when I said, "You can call it shit, if you wish, but I call it a lump on my skull, and I don't like it. WHERE is Monsieur Plakidon, WHO is in charge of this, and HOW fast can you clean it up because I've got a houseful of people arriving in two days, and if they're in the way it's his fault for not writing me. I can't put them off now, you understand, but if there's going to be a gun battle around here, I don't have the insurance to cover it."

"*Mais oui, madame,*" he stuttered. "This tunnel, where is it, please? Monsieur Plakidon may be aware, but I had not heard . . . that is, could you describe?"

"It's at the sea end of the cage room." I gave him a succinct rundown on the circular handles, the second step closing mechanism, bottom exit. "It's obviously in constant use. And there's a locked door at the opposite end of the cellar hall that is either a passthrough to the next section of the castle or the storeroom."

Aigullon sucked in his breath and sputtered more than ever. "Madame, all will be transmitted to Monsieur Plakidon at once—but please to stay completely away! *Soyez tranquille*; arrangements will be made!"

"Well, please let me know what they are, or you run the risk that we'll innocently louse you up," I stated severely, and ran off feeling much restored at having told Interpol the WHAT.

I stayed in bed all day, aware of the lump on my head but not in active discomfort so long as I didn't move too much. The phone rang constantly, requiring Mariana to toil upstairs each time, but I wouldn't speak to anyone . . . until she announced that Professor Eugéne Crillaud of the *Societé Nationale Géographique* wished to talk with me. "What about?" Obediently Mariana inquired on my extension.

"I am not sure, but it appears to be photography, senhora."

"All right, I'll take it."

Professor Crillaud was overjoyed to have reached me. "It is that I have learned through a friend connected with *Elle* that shortly you are permitting photographs at Costa Demonio," he said, "and it occurs to me that if you will agree, madame, I might be allowed to send two photographers at the same time. We are anxious, in cooperation with the American National Geographic Society, to arrange a documentary film of the coasts in that area as part of a larger documentary concerning Henry the Navigator.

"Much can be done from boats or public beaches, but it is not complete, you understand? So I have presumed to approach you directly for this permission, it is an opportunity not to be missed," he said earnestly, "when already there will be the disturbance of photographers at your home. My men would not interfere in any way! They would wish only to film the coast and the birds—there is a subsidiary program of ornithology that interests the Audubon Society. It would be a *great* privilege, Madame Valentim."

"Well, I don't mind—but how long would they be here, and where will they stay? There isn't a pousada, you know."

"*N'importe,* they will have a trailer. If you would allow them to place it in a field, perhaps, or in a corner of the stableyard where they would have access to water," he said eagerly. "It will be no inconvenience to you, madame, *je vous assure.*"

"Yes, but I can't think of any suitable spot for a trailer, Professor Crillaud. They'd better stay here," I decided. "There's plenty of space, and two more for meals won't make any difference." I cut short his polite demurrals, "No, no, it's quite all right—in return for one set of their photographs?"

"But of course, madame! Ah, *vous etes bien*

gentille. One had not hoped for such cooperation."

"Oh, well, my father's subscribed to the National Geographic for forty years, it's a household word," I told him. "What are their names, please, and when will they arrive?"

"Messieurs Gerson and Kranski, and if I can reach them—they are near Faró—they would arrive tomorrow, if that is convenient?"

I said it was and rang off rather brusquely in the middle of his fulsome thanks. I thought it'd be excellent to have a couple of people crawling around the cliffs to photograph birds. That should get beautifully in the way of Damon-Huberto-Jorge et al! I was feeling better and better, aside from the slight stiffness at the back of my head. I crawled back into bed, renewing acquaintance with *Pride and Prejudice* which I'd abstracted from the study a few nights past, but not getting very far, because I was thinking.

Point One: Huberto, who would know every inch of Costa Demonio, and was fanatically devoted to Dom Sansao . . . leading to Point Two: the old man had known what was going on; it had begun before his death, and he had condoned it—Otherwise Huberto wouldn't have touched it with a ten-foot pole, no matter how friendly Damon and Sansao had been.

It came to me suddenly: What would Dom Sansao have condoned? Why, *people*, of course! It might have started during the war, with full-scale continuation afterwards for refugees from the Iron Curtain. Twenty bedrooms, ample food on the estate, and elderly autocrat who'd been all over the world. No one in Ponto Lucido would have been surprised that Dom Sansao was entertaining foreigners. I'd buy that, I decided, and if that's all it was, I'd go along with it myself . . . but obviously that was NOT what it was today.

Somewhere following Sansao's death, the pattern had altered, become dangerous, a serious moneymaking scheme. Possibly Huberto was not aware of that aspect, was simply angry that my arrival was interfering with Sansao's helping hand, free room and board.

But why hadn't Interpol contacted Alexi, the local *commisário*? Or had they, and he wasn't telling me? He mightn't know I was aware of correspondence between Plakidon and Bart. He certainly hadn't wanted me to stay at Costa Demonio, and when I wouldn't leave, he was constantly, protectively at hand. I thought I'd buy that, too . . . but better to say nothing. Let Interpol play it their own way; *they* knew I was inadvertently in the middle; if they thought wise, let them tell Alexi to speak to me. Anyway, I hadn't really found anything, now that I thought of it. How dumb could you be, I thought disgustedly! Of all people, Alexi knew the tunnel: his father was the heir until Sansao kicked him out.

Throughout the day I became more and more convinced that Alexi did know the whole setup, was in a quandary about me. Even if Plakidon had briefed him on my active cooperation, his European idea of women as fragile little flowers would prevent any exchange of news. Both he and Damon had called repeatedly during the day; I had sent word that I was fine but didn't feel like talking. Around five o'clock, Mariana came in with a huge vase of lovely roses, "Alexi brought them," she said impersonally. "He is waiting to learn whether you feel able to see him."

Perhaps he had something to tell me. "Bring him up in five minutes." I splashed water on my face, combed my hair gingerly avoiding the back, and neatly spread up the bed. A bit of powder, a touch of lipstick, I was sitting in the chaise longue at the end of the room. "Alexi, it is good of you to come. The roses are beautiful!"

He chuckled. "As if you had not far-better specimens at Costa Demonio." He bent over my hand, continued to hold it and surveyed me critically. "I will not stay more than a minute, but I had to see for myself that you were really recovered. *Cara prima*, tell me the truth: how do you feel?"

"Not good, but better than expected," I shrugged. "Do sit down, Alexi. Mariana, bring a bar tray?"

"*Sim, sim, senhora.*"

"Nell," Alexi said abruptly, when she'd gone, "what really happened?"

It was on the tip of my tongue to tell him—but still better to let Interpol play it. "I don't know, Alexi," I said carefully. "I think I remember going out through the garden to look at the shrubs, and I think I stepped on a stone in order to see the top of a rose tree . . . I'm not sure, but my left ankle aches, so perhaps the stone turned, and I lost my balance, fell back against one of the others. It must have been that way, but I've no memory of it."

For a moment I thought he was going to say

"That isn't what you told Interpol." but he only sighed. "Jorge should check all the stones, Nell. There may be others that are loose."

"No one but silly me would ever try to stand on one, and I assure you I shan't do it again!"

"Please do not!" Alexi reached for my hand with a smile, stroking it gently. "You do look better," he said relieved. "When do your friends arrive? Will you be able to endure so much commotion?"

"She'll lap it up," Chris was coming forward, smiling at me soberly. "I came back before, but you were snoozing. Damon wants to see how you are." He called over his shoulder, "She's okay, Damon. C'mon in, Alexi's here."

"Hello, chipmunk. How d'you feel?"

"Oh, tol-lol, thanks. I'll live," I said vaguely, looking at the two men standing side by side. Damon's face was oddly colorless and strained, as though he'd had a sleepless night. Alexi was smiling down at me faintly—but quite suddenly I recognized that despite the resemblance, he *wasn't* Bart.

Furthermore, I had a blinding flash of certainty that Alexi would like to kill me!

I've no clear memory of how I got through that cocktail hour. Huberto brought the tray and prepared the glasses; Mariana followed with plates of tidbits. The men talked of local matters, with Chris putting in a word now and then. I sipped my highball and pretended to listen, but of course everything had fallen into place.

Alexi was working *with* Damon. They were working the psychology both ways: Damon growled and warned me of danger; Huberto scowled and stormed over Alexi's presence at Costa Demonio; and when I couldn't be scared off, Alexi did a *volte face* and presented himself as Bart's intimate childhood friend. Damon and Huberto had first tried to make me uncomfortable; Alexi followed up with full assistance, sending his own servants, offering every help—and I had nearly fallen for it!

As near as nothing I'd unburdened myself of the whole bit, confirmed every suspicion they had. Hah! I'd see them in Demonio first! I drained my glass, and said, "Darlings, it's been lovely to see you, but this is enough. Finish your drinks and trot along, see you again sometime."

"Ah, we have tired you!" Alexi sprang to his feet. "Nell, forgive me? I must be in Lisbon for a few days; I should have gone this morning but I had to see for myself that you were all right."

"*Caro primo*," I murmured, holding out my hand and fluttering the eyelashes, "never worry about me. I'm indestructible! Thank you for the roses, and let us know when you get back."

Alexi's hand tightened like an automatic reflex about mine. "Be sure that I shall," he smiled.

And I thought, "He knows I own Costa Demonio, he will not kill me until he has tried to marry me."

I went downstairs later for dinner, even with the extra help it wasn't fair to expect Mariana to carry trays approximately a quarter mile to my bedroom. "Mmmm, this is delicious! What is it?"

"*Polvo*, baby octopus. Alexi brought them for you, and the *lagosta*," she deftly exchanged plates, and I was surveying succulent baby lobsters. "Senhor Lord sends the wine, and Luisa has made *suspiros* for your dessert. She does them very nicely," Mariana conceded, setting a dish of asparagus beside the *lagosta.* "Huberto has found the last spears until the next growth. For tomorrow there is an eel." Her eyes sparkled with satisfaction. "Alexi has brought this also."

If I hadn't known better, I'd have been touched by the small gourmet gifts. . . , but if Huberto was actually culling asparagus for ME, it was the most frightening thing yet! When I'd gone to bed, I lay staring into the darkness and felt desperate. I could literally NOT think what best to do—and I hadn't really any choice until I'd got rid of the photographic sessions. I still thought that might have been a good idea to load Costa Demonio with people wandering about in all directions. Damon hadn't been happy about it; Alexi hadn't cared—which meant nothing was going on, right now. Perhaps I gould get Chris away before it started.

As I was falling asleep, I thought vaguely that crime certainly makes strange bedfellows. You'd never expect a coalition between Damon Lord, Huberto, and Alexi; I could believe Damon and Huberto might get along, but Alexi didn't really fit. He's a bit of a bounder, I said mentally—and was asleep.

Gerson and Kranski were two pleasant American boys of about my own age. They showed up, with trailer, about noon next day, and inside of an hour they were *at home*, in that special easy way of American men. "Wow, what a place!" they said respectfully. "Is it okay if we ramble around, just to look?" I said it was, but not to come upon any accidents unless they had insurance. They were first-name pals with Chris in five minutes, had stuck the trailer among the olive trees across the road, unhitched the car and whizzed off to Quinta Choupo to view the horses almost before I could blink.

Professor Crillaud was right, they were no trouble at all. Glancing from my window later, I saw them ambling about the garden, and later still they were coming away from the castle. "Gosh, Mrs. Valentim, it's super! There's a whole colony of *Pedicans suturii*, nesting in the base of the headland . . . and we saw some *Merulas*, and Bob's certain there are *Ratigo superbus*. Is it okay if we hitch some ropes to swing down the cliffs? You needn't to worry; we'd give you a release form but we never have accidents—and it'd almost be worth an accident to get those *Pedicans* and *Ratigos*." (Those aren't the right names, but that's what they sounded like.)

I said I didn't care what they did, provided they didn't kill themselves, and it was five P.M.—how about a drink before dinner. They said they didn't mind if they did—and in about five more minutes they were Bob and Ted, and I was Nell. Chris came back for dinner, and we were very, very American. Gosh, it felt good to talk without wondering if it'd be understood!

The following day Costa Demonio was overflowing with people to the point that a few dancing bears would scarcely have been noticed. Cars crowded the stableyard, overflowed into the olive orchard, and there were twice too many people, because everyone had brought a husband or wife, or a "friend". One of the secondary groups showed up a week too early. "You said there were twenty bedrooms, sweetie—and we have this unexpected assignment in Majorca for next week. Does it matter? There's such heaps of good spots we can't possibly get in each other's way."

"No, it doesn't matter at all—*But,*" I said impressively, "*nobody* is to take unsupervised rambles, understand? Some parts of the cliff aren't safe, and if you swim in the rocky cove you'll be scrapes all over, which is not photographable. The castle won't fall down, but it's terribly confusing, you could get lost for hours until we began searching. *Please* stay outside, and don't go anywhere without telling somebody?"

"Like the ski resorts?" they nodded. "We stay in pairs, and ask first. Right! Gotcha!"

They'd brought quantities of fabulous clothes, but as anyone knows, high-fashion modeling is hard work. Just dressing and undressing is damned exhausting, to say nothing of the exotic makeups and hairdos. Chris was mercifully preoccupied with Jovanna's daily progress, the National Geographic boys were on their own but appeared to meld nicely with the fashion photogs. Mariana produced food at suitable moments, my head bruise had absorbed itself. Life was copacetic. I had locked the study. "You don't mind to use the main stairs, hon? I don't want people pawing over the books, even if they have washed their hands first."

"Gee, no!"

"Tell Huberto to go down the inside stairs to air and dust."

Otherwise, Costa Demonio was alive and fully in use. I could imagine what it must have been like years ago when the guests were elegant cosmopolites. My people were no barbarians, they *recognized* the paintings, old rugs, valuables; they'd just never seen such a lot of everything under one roof, and were correspondingly enchanted. All, but ALL, must be sampled, to see what it felt like. Nightly they broke out the poker chips and distributed evenly, "Here's a million for you, George," "Lou, get the birdcage." "I'd rather play poker." "All right, call the blue chips a thousand bucks?" Impossible sums changed hands on paper. "I never hoped to be able to stake a hundred grand on one dice throw, it's pure Regency!" "Yes, but what you made was what I lost, Dickie. I shall need one of those Greeks to bail me out!"

Gay butterfly people, the sort I'd known before I married Bart—but when I had him, I hadn't missed them. Now it was good to slip back to the casual endearments, the nonsensical non sequiturs and naughty gossip. Damon was what the girls wanted, the instant they saw him. "Ooooh, that sleepy Burton smile, those weird pale eyes." "I *die* for the way he looks at you sideways, don't you?" "You simply KNOW he detests you, *loathes* himself for wanting you . . . mmmmmm, all that controlled passion—and a title!" "What title?" "Younger brother of the Earl of Matcham, he's an

Honorable. I think there's an heir," regretfully, "but Divine Damon's next in line."

In the midst of the photo sessions, I'd had no time to think. Damon was not around much; he had a house guest. But why not bring the man with him?

Perhaps the guest was not a man? Maybe the head of the smuggling ring was a female? No more absurd than any of the rest of it, and now I thought of it, Damon had been in suspiciously good spirits recently. "Is this *true*, you have a title?"

"I'm afraid so. I'm sorry, chipmunk," he said anxiously, "but need it come between us?"

"Nothing *is* between us," I said crossly, "so let this fill the gap. I just think you might have told me, is all."

"Why?"

"I would have been calling you honorable Sir, of course."

"Ah-so," he murmured irrepressibly. When I chuckled helpless, he said, "You're looking better every day. This is your sort of life really, isn't it: dozens of people, chit-chat, couturier gowns, hostessing parties?"

"Not really—it's—something I know how to do. Bart and I were rather quiet, actually." We were sitting out in the end garden, and I looked absently at the sea. "We went to the opera and the symphony, ballet—anything musical, Bart played the piano very well. We invited one or two couples to dinner occasionally, or visited for an evening. He worked hard, weekends often—and there were foreign businessmen to be entertained, sometimes with wives, but I tried for him to have four quiet evenings a week. We'd play chess or Scrabble, once in a while there'd be something on TV.

"We did more things on holidays when Chris was home, to expose him to—I suppose you'd call it culture—and summers we went wherever Bart decided: the Adirondack camp, or a dude ranch." I shrugged. "It's fun to see a bit of my former life, but there's not one of these girls who wouldn't gladly exchange. The only difference between models and other young women is facial beauty, which doesn't make for an easy life. You have to cash in on it rapidly, which leads to the overwork causing wrinkles, which leads to no work."

"Doesn't appear to affect you."

"No? You should see the careful makeup," I said dryly.

Alexi returned on Wednesday and was an instant success! "How *fantastic* that family resemblance! But if they *all* look so much alike, darling, how can you be sure you're sleeping with the right one?"

"Well, personally, I'd switch on the light."

"But what good would that do? They say all cats are gray in the night, but apparently all Valentims are the same in any light."

"Don't be vulgar, sweeties," I said austerely. "I'm sorry, Alexi, we're being American again. Please pay no attention. It doesn't really mean what it sounds."

"*Que penal!*" Alexi sighed. "I had a faint hope, and you dash it to the ground!"

Alexi's reappearance brought back my fears, although he threw himself heartily into the work and actually was responsible for extending it. "Nell, darling, d'you mind if we stay on for a bit? All this space. We're not really in the way, are we? And Alexi's found us some villagers to stand about with fishing nets. He says there's some marvelous coves, and we can have the *Fortuna* for backgrounds."

"I don't mind, but I thought you were due in Majorca?"

"We've put it off; this is too good to miss. Alexi's got a Lisbon designer flying down a load of new clothes."

"Oh? Well, if you like to publicize an unknown—I only hope you can sell the shots, is all."

"*Nichevo*, sweetie—the thing is, we're having *such* a good time. You don't really mind?"

"Not at all, Stay as long as you like," I said recklessly. "You've only scratched the surface. There's all sorts of interiors, or the fields, vineyards, kitchen garden, horses and livestock, an ancient Rolls, and there's a pony trap in the stable. Make yourselves at home—but don't crawl around cliffs or castle without asking!"

"Don't worry, darling. Alexi's coming with us, so we'll be quite safe. He's got some marvelous old native costumes, *perfect* for posing at the courtyard entrance or on a gallery."

"How—nice."

"But it is Dom Christo who should be photographed," Alexi inserted smoothly. "I am only the family bastard."

"You *are*? Oh, I do call that unfair! Nell has all the luck: this huge castle, with family retainers, a

Rolls, her own wine, and now there's even a bastard to go with it. It is unfair!"

And you can say that again! I'd got the picture slow but sure, and Alexi was shrewder than I'd realized. Of course Damon had told him my unwary disclosure of the true ownership. Alexi was playing it close to the belt because I wasn't at all his taste in women. When I thought of it, I knew instinctively he'd prefer plump breasts and a sultry brunette perfume. He didn't really want a wife anyway.

Neither did he really *want* Costa Demonio; Alexi would rather use it for his cover, staying officially outside as the *commisário* of Ponto Lucido. I had forced his hand; since he couldn't beat it, he'd joined it. He announced loudly that he was the family bastard, but by the time those pictures appeared, everyone would be so confused that the captions would read Dom Alexandre Valentim!

Amazingly Huberto came to the rescue. He produced an ancient suit of ruby red velvet, embellished with tarnished gold lace and real pearls! "For formal occasions, senhora, Dom Oliveiro has worn this, Dom Sansao also."

"It's gorgeous! Wherever did you find it, Huberto?"

"In the attic," he grunted, stumping off.

"An *attic?*" As if I didn't already have too much of everything! "*Sim, sim, senhora.* There are stairs at the end of the passage," Mariana said briskly, "but it is merely a small storage space for luggage. We had not reached this as yet, but as you see," she threw open the door, "there is nothing of importance."

Old trunks: stuffed with clothes, furs, crumbling leather gloves. Hmmm, turn the models loose in here, they'd clear it out for me!

"Oooh, Christmas in July!" "Nell, darling, what *marvelous* fun we're having!" "Oh, the *sweet* little bed jacket, all maribou and frills; say you don't want it, may I have?" They disinterred everything, but I was right they knew what was what. "*Letters,* Nell! Where to put until you examine the stamps?" "Oh, there are coins in this purse; someone get a box." "Nell, these shoes are *gone* but the buckles are real diamonds, I think; look how they flash colors in the sunlight!"

We ended principally with Victorian and Edwardian wardrobes, but there was one formal dress of deep sapphire velvet that resembled an Infanta's. It was a perfect match for the suit—and the suit had been made for a tall Valentim. Chris couldn't resist trying it on that night. A few strategic pins restrained the slight fullness allowed for adult embonpoint, and the boy was suddenly the epitome of a Portuguese aristocrat. "D'you mind being photographed, hon? Call me a witch, but I don't want Alexi taking center stage," I said evenly.

"I feel kind of foolish, like a fancy-dress party," he shifted awkwardly, looking at himself in the long mirror. "Anyway, I'm not the Dom. You own the place, Nell."

"Never mind that. Until this is finished, you ARE Dom Christo, understand?"

"Why? What's going on that I don't know about?"

"Nothing—except Alexi trying to cut himself

in," but, although he agreed to join the session, I knew Chris didn't quite believe me.

I didn't believe Interpol. It had reached a point where I called Monsieur Aigullon every morning and said "WELL?" He was obviously unhappy, but had nothing to reassure me. Plakidon, he insisted, had the matter in hand, there was no need for alarm; all would arrange itself. "WHEN?"

"We believe it may be only a week or two, madame."

"Two WEEKS? I could be dead by then! I tell you I'm positive it's a gang: Damon Lord, Alexi Revalhao, Huberto, Jorge Pintos . . . heaven knows how many others there are, perhaps all of Ponto Lucido. I'm *surrounded,* don't you understand? I can't leave because of these photographic sessions," I said desperately, "and now Mr. Big has arrived to visit Damon."

"I—beg your pardon?"

"I *told* you: there's somebody under wraps at Quinta Choupo. I don't know who it is, even Chris hasn't met the man. Damon says it's the younger brother of a college friend, and he's supposedly on a walking tour, but I don't believe a word of it," I stated firmly. "I think he's the mastermind, particularly if you say it's only a few weeks off, but I'm scared to death. Don't you SEE, they've got Chris! He's there every day, I can't keep him away," I was sobbing under my breath, "and I don't dare tell him anything; he's too young! Please, can't you hurry?"

"*Mais non, madame,* these things must flower of themselves," he said earnestly, "but I *assure* you there is no danger, neither to yourself nor to the boy. Monsieur Plakidon has arranged everything." He coughed slightly, "I comprehend your distress, madame, but it is unnecessary. Merely continue as you are. In that way you will help us best."

So we did the major costumed shots, all of which featured Dom Christo Valentim in the family heirloom suit, towering tall over his bastard cousin, Senhor Alexandre Revalhao. After initial shyness, Chris got as thoroughly into his part as ever Bart could have done! Alexi was completely overshadowed. At Quinta Choupo, where Dom Christo was a photographer's dream in his natural element among the horses, Alexi faded into insignificance—and when the Honorable Damon Lord appeared in hunting pink with the insignia of the most ancient English club, I felt confident there'd be no mistake in magazine captions!

Whether or not his plans were going as hoped, Alexi was still with us, a veritable bundle of joy and helpfulness. He flirted lightly with the models, produced photographic supplies by special messenger from Lisbon together with the designer's clothes, which proved unexpectedly original, and arrived daily at breakfast armed with fresh suggestions. All Ponto Lucido was at our command, in an endless stream of assistants to Mariana as well as whatever extra food was needed.

We ate in the banquet hall, seated anywhere—but Chris was always at the head of the table in the great carved chair. Alexi arranged an evening of *fada* and flamenco in the ballroom—and asked Chris to give the signal to commence the entertainment. In the game room, Alexi was croupier, with an elderly Ponto Lucidan who'd been employed by Sansao. "The Dom does not run his own game, Christo, even if we do not play for money."

At every turn, Alexi deferred to Chris with tiny sotto voce instructions on the formal behavior of a Dom, keeping Chris in the forefront and only stepping forward as though a mere representative of the Dom when the boy had gone to bed. I had to admit Alexi never put a foot wrong, although he was inclined to overemphasize the importance of being Dom of Costa Demonio. Chris went along with it good-naturedly, but he had Bart's twinkle in the eye, and I could tell he wasn't losing perspective. Still, it wouldn't hurt Chris to practice some stuffy aristocratic veneer. Bart had used it once in a while; Chris might find it handy sometimes.

Similarly, Alexi consulted me seriously about each project, as though he were allied with me in the training and development of Bart's son. The impression was that he asked nothing more than to be my unofficial aide, since it was all too much for a woman to handle alone. There was an immense amount of hand-patting, gentle unsexy hugs, admiring words for my gallantry in facing tragedy—but be of good cheer, *cara prima,* for after the storm returns the sun, and *I* am here to help.

He was acting like a bachelor brother-in-law, and what in hell was he getting at? I knew he was deliberately keeping everyone at Costa Demonio;

they were really completely through, but every time they mentioned leaving, Alexi came up with a reason to stay one more day. Damon, too.

Half of me wondered why a smuggling ring wanted the place overrun with people; the other half grew impatient with Interpol. Dammit, weren't they ever going to DO anything, send someone to check the tunnel and that locked passage door? This was a perfect opportunity, with so many people around already, but Aigullon remained evasive. Finally I made up my mind I'd see for myself. The more I thought of it, the more that door seemed possible if I had a pair of long-nose pliers, and if I picked a moment when they were photographing at that section of the castle, I ought to be able to try under cover of the confusion.

I found the pliers in the toolroom; Alexi took a few of the crowd into Caldarém, the others were easily persuaded to work at the far end of Costa Demonio . . . and shortly I faded backward to the shadows of the passage. In two twiddles the lock was turned. Far behind me I could hear the photographic session in full swing; nobody'd be able to sneak up and clobber me this time. Very quietly I grasped the handle and pulled open the door . . . and inside stood Damon Lord and a strange man in a brown gabardine suit. . . .

CHAPTER VIII

For an interminable moment, nobody said anything. We just stared at each other like fools, until I was ready to collapse from the shivers sweeping over me. Then Damon drew a long breath. "Mr. Plakidon, this is Senhora Valentim," he said resignedly. "I warned you not to try to keep her out of it."

"Mister—Plakidon?"

"Of Interpol. My house guest. The head of my smuggling ring," Damon amplified politely, "and will you kindly come in and shut the door behind you?"

"I—don't think I can."

"Why not?"

"Because it's only the door that's holding me up," I said simply. "I may faint, please stand ready to catch me. One hit on the head is enough."

Mr. Plakidon stepped forward hastily. "Lean on me! Damon, get the door shut. How in the world did you get it open, senhora?"

"Long-nose pliers," I held them out while he was lowering me onto something firm. "Are you really from Interpol?"

Damon chuckled irrepressibly. "Yes, *really*. What a fertile imagination you have, chipmunk, those daily *communiques* to Aigullon! When you reached the point of assuring Paris that their own man was the mastermind and the whole village was in it," he laughed helplessly, "oh, chipmunk! All that saddens me is how could you suppose I'd ever stoop to working with Alexi!"

"Well, it did surprise me," I admitted, "but I didn't realize he might be in it until I found the tunnel. I thought it was all you and Huberto, and then I didn't know what to think when I was hit on the head and none of you was around. Alexi was on the *Fortuna*, Huberto was in Caldarém with the maids, Jorge was in the upper fields, and you'd gone to the airport. So who bashed me?"

"Did you really think I would?"

"Of course," I said, surprised. "You've been perfectly *odious*, except when you were fun because things were going well."

Plakidon cleared his throat loudly. "Why should you think it was smuggling, senhora? My letter never mentioned this."

"Don't be silly! Given Costa Demonio, what else could it be?"

"But why pick on me?" Damon asked plaintively. "You couldn't get even half a horse on the *Thetis*."

"You could get people," I countered simply. "I thought it was the sort of thing you would do, after the war—or maybe Sansao started it. But he and Huberto were too old, so you took the boat and did the active work." Damon's eyes were a clear blue, intent on my face, waiting. "When San-

sao died and Bart didn't take over, I thought perhaps you continued, but you wouldn't take money from frightened people, so you might—might be making a bit on the side from jewels or paintings," I finished shakily.

"A modern Robin Hood?"

"Yes, and don't be snide, dammit, it's exactly the sort of thing you *would* do," I flared indignantly. "I never really thought it was dope or guns. But if it's all Alexi, that's different, and you have to tell me in detail because of Chris."

There was a long pause. "Thank you for the vote of confidence, Nell," Damon said quietly. "I'm sorry . . . but it is dope."

"Did Bart know?"

"Yes," said Plakidon. "He wrote that he knew there was only one person who would enjoy contributing to degradation for Costa Demonio, that he could and would deal with him this summer. Senhora, he signed that letter Dom Bartolomeu Valentim."

"I see," I said calmly—and I did; it was adding to a hundred. "You should have told me all this before." I stood up. "Can you lock that door, or shall I? Damon, hold the torch, please." A few twiddles and it clicked over. I took back the torch and flashed it about the space, but there seemed to be nothing more than kegs. "Come on, let's get out of here and talk later."

"About what?" Damon's voice was casual.

"Alexi." I looked at Plakidon militantly. "You are in charge of Chris," I said. "If it's dope, Alexi'd chance doing a mischief to Bart's son—just for the hell of it, understand?"

"Later," Damon said in an undertone, pushing Plakidon out into a dark jog. "I don't know what's on her mind, but she's probably right; I never met a woman with more ESP! Hurry up, Homer—not that I think he'd be back yet, but you never know."

We made it up to fresh air via a narrow flight of steps that brought us out next to the courtyard opening for the second section of the castle. The models and photographers were still busy toward the sea end—and Alexi was coming through the topiary garden with the group that had gone to Calderém! I gripped an arm each and turned the men swiftly forward, around the hedge toward the house. "Get lost temporarily; when you come back, I'm Nell and you're Homer. We'll have a council in the study when it's safe."

A woman can do anything she has to do.

I picked a couple of late roses and rambled back to the group. "Alexi! I have been thinking about an American clambake, Portuguese style. It might be rather fun. Would you help, *caro primo?*" I asked dulcetly. "We'll need bushels of clams, and the largest *lagosta.* Jorge can fix the pits, Huberto can give us chickens. There ought to be a spit threaded with pork ribs, and corn roasted in the husk, but this'll do well enough."

"It sounds like a magnificent feast!" he exclaimed, peering over my shoulder. "You are alone, Nell? I had the impression I saw—"

"Damon, with his house guest," I nodded casually. "A nice lad, they were going through the arcade toward the beach. You'll help with the clams and *lagosta*, Alexi?"

"Of course," he smiled affectionately. "Ah, you see I was right! This is the life you should be living, *querida*; you are more beautiful than ever, how happy Bart would be to see you!"

"And how happy we would be to see him," I murmured sadly, letting my fingers rest artistically on Alexi's arm, bending my forehead to his shoulder for a brief moment—but even while he was tenderly agreeing, I felt the involuntary tightening of his muscles.

I left everyone gaming for Federal Reserve stakes and let myself into the study, locking the door behind me. Absently I got out the decanter and glasses, pondering. Now that I knew, I felt ashamed of all the wild stuff I'd dreamed up. My cheeks were hot at the memory, although Damon had taken it well. There was still a piece missing from the puzzle. I'd nearly got it when there was a faint tap-tap on the far shutters by the desk. "Nell?"

"Yes, come in and have some wine. I'm thinking." I latched the shutters again and sat on one of the footstools while Damon filled glasses, handed one to Homer and one to me.

"What are you thinking, chipmunk?"

"That it's more than money," I said slowly. "Sansao thought Alexi deliberately caused the breach with Bart—Bart told you there was one person who'd enjoy degradation—Alexi tells us of his intimate childhood memories with Bart, yet Bart never mentioned Alexi to either Chris or me. Alexi lived in Libson, apparently has a thriving business there. But as soon as Sansao died, he began moving back until he was firmly entrenched in the village.

"Bart didn't want to come here this summer; it was purely his duty, and he never shirked that. I don't think he had the faintest idea Alexi was back in Ponto Lucido." I went on working it out. "He never wanted to hear of Costa Demonio again, I understand that now. Even when Bart became Dom, who would have told him?"

"Huberto tried," Damon remarked tersely. "The letter was returned unopened, like every other."

I nodded. "Yes, but the real pity is that you weren't here that summer, Damon. You wouldn't have let it happen; I don't know why Sansao did."

"Let *what* happen?" Damon asked, bewildered.

"Cecily—Bart's first wife, Chris's mother—was an alcoholic," I said simply. "What was it that Alexi did deliberately? I thought perhaps it was unwitting—even Bart hadn't known she was in and out of sanitariums ever since high school. But that has to be it, Damon. If *only* you'd been here . . . although I suppose if you had been, I wouldn't be."

Damon leaned to refill my glass. "That," he murmured, "would be my grave loss, chipmunk. Homer?"

Plakidon extended his glass with a slight frown. "I do not understand what you are getting at, Nell."

"Why did he deliberately transfer his operation to Costa Demonio as soon as it had an absentee landlord?" I countered. "You may only have caught up with him here, but don't tell me he hasn't been using Revalhao y Filho for years!"

Homer nodded. "Untaxed wines principally,

and some suspicion of fencing for robberies—a purely local problem, nothing to concern us, but you are right that the expansion began about five years ago. We supposed it was merely the tempting availability of a deserted castle."

"Oh, no, it's a private vendetta, and Bart knew it existed, but I wonder if he knew why."

"Do you?"

"I think so, and it's much the most important and dangerous part," I said evenly. "You'll have to ask Huberto, he'll know *exactly* what happened on September 10, 1938, when Alexi's father was killed by waiting government agents on the shore of the Demonio cove. I expect Bart repeated something Alexi had told him, don't you?" I heard a sharply indrawn breath, but I was still thinking. "So you see, Chris is in very real danger."

"My God!" Homer muttered.

"Exactly," I agreed. "The well-known eye for an eye, tooth for a tooth. I'm not sure Alexi's round the bend to that extent, but I can't chance it. I brought the boy here to get him out of the country, in case his mother's parents tried to get custody, and that's the main reason you couldn't dislodge me," I glanced at Damon's intent face and he nodded brusquely.

"Send him over to Quinta Choupo."

"For what reason?" I asked levelly. "He's a big boy, Damon; he has to have reasons, but if he knew *anything* it'd be too much, because he still is a boy. He doesn't think highly of Alexi in the first place, and wouldn't, if he knew that his father, whom he loved and deeply respected, didn't like the man." I shrugged. "You see? Caution is not expectable from true Valentims, Damon, and Alexi's already on the *qui vive*. No, leave it as is—but watch him!"

"What about watching you?" Damon said grimly.

I debated. "I think I'm relatively unimportant, and Bart's already dead. Anyway, you could never destroy me with alcohol—nor even with dope. I'm older than Cecily. If I woke up feeling *peculiar* after an evening with Alexi, I wouldn't go back—that's if I'd ever gone in the first place, which probably I wouldn't have," I said thoughtfully. "No, I'm sure I'm right. What he really wants is to destroy the Dom of Costa Demonio in reprisal for the death of his father.

"In a way," I smiled mirthlessly, "it's backfired: Bart died before (so far as Alexi knows) he could be humbled. Destroying Chris won't be the same, nor me. Bart isn't here, do you see? It'll be a Pyrrhic victory. All that will trouble him is whether or not Bart ever told me where the tunnel was. It was bad luck he found me down in the cage room when I'd been so upset over it the first day, but I gave the impression I'd been concussed briefly, didn't remember, so Alexi would never expect any brains from me.

"You can see for yourselves." I widened my eyes and looked from one to the other. "You couldn't possibly think I knew enough to pull the chain, let alone be the daughter of a nuclear physicist and a computer programmer, now could you?"

Homer shook his head speechlessly, while Damon blinked. "Good God—and *you* had the consummate gall to complain because I didn't tell you I had connections with the nobility?"

We laughed.

And the ball continued: Alexi took everyone on the *Fortuna* to accompany the Ponto Lucido fishing fleet. Following the village smacks out to sea in the predawn grayness, seeing them more and more clearly as the sun rose in fingers of light, until at last it was curving up behind the distant shores and we were drifting lazily among the smaller boats—the photographers were enthralled! I suspected they might actually *get* a piece for the National Geographic. The rest of us fished. We'd apparently hit a school, and you had only to throw over a hook for a catch, most rewarding compared to some expeditions I've accompanied. We left the fleet to its job and turned back about eight; Alexi had provided a champagne breakfast, and said, "Let us go on around the cape to Faró? There will be shops for more film. We will order lunch set aboard to eat on our return, and reach Costa Demonio in time to swim before dinner."

The Portuguese clambake took place the next night. That morning Chris led the way to a cove reputedly teeming with *lagosta*, from which both boats returned loaded to the gunwhales. Faced with fish, Chris is never able to restrain himself to a suitable amount. I kept Alexi busy, supervising construction of a sand pit lined with flat stones; Jorge made a sturdy barbecue spit, and Huberto provided a slaughtered kid in place of ribs, plus ten chickens and immense baskets of fresh fruit.

Damon organized a horseback safari to lunch

and bathe in the farthest cove of the estate. "With all these chances, why can't you manage to find the real swag?" I asked Homer.

"A good question, to which I have no answer," he replied grimly. "We managed once to get a telephone man into Alexi's house; he found nothing. Gerson and Kranski did the *Fortuna* as best they could during the photographic sessions, but aside from spotting potential storage, it can't be checked out. The crew is around all day, and Belendo sleeps aboard."

"It wouldn't be there anyway, don't waste your time," I said absently. "He'd never chance anything that could be connected to him for longer than transportation time. No, there's a secret room in Costa Demonio, but the book doesn't say where—and there's probably any number of hideyholes too. That door we came out of, where does it go, aside from the outer steps?"

"Into the scullery and kitchen of the next section of the castle."

"There you are then."

"If you say so, chipmunk—but if I may say so, where are we now?"

"At the foot of a staircase leading up to Dom Basilio's study, among other rooms," I said, surprised. "He built the tunnel; he probably built other things too. If you can find his personal room, there'll be a medieval safe."

"Hmmm. Where?"

"Aren't hidden closets and stairs generally near the fireplace? Something like a baking oven, only secreted behind carving or set around to the side. Wherever it is, it'll be easy for Alexi to trot downstairs and use that locked room as a pass-through on a direct line to the tunnel," I said. The men looked at each other. "Sounds logical, but why didn't you or Huberto find it when you were looking for the tunnel?"

"I don't know," Damon shrugged. "Perhaps because we were concentrating on the seaward walls; we thought the tunnel must lead into the farther cove because we didn't know there was a channel past Demonio. Oh, well," he sighed, "up and at 'em again. Forward the Buffs!"

But they couldn't find anything, although they worked over the rooms intensively while I was keeping Alexi busy playing host as far as possible from the castle. Then, completely out of the air, Chris requested a square dance!

Going into Caldarém just for the ride, he killed time in the record shop while Mariana marketed. On a rear shelf of unsaleables, he disinterred half a dozen American disks with a famed caller. The manager was so glad to be rid of them that he gave them to Chris for nothing! "And they're collector's items, Nell. The boys will flip when I bring 'em back to school, but couldn't we try 'em out some evening?"

My guests flipped at the mere mention of square dance. "Could we have a social? Nell, sweetie, let's make cake and ice cream; clear out the kitchen help; we'll do it ourselves."

It was a fun evening for everyone but Damon. Chris was in charge, since no one knew the calls as well, not even I—although I could follow him better than the others to demonstrate the steps. Homer picked it up quickly; Alexi had two left feet.

The others varied from good down to fair-to-middling, with rueful laughter and tiny shrieks of dismay at mistakes. I'd spread the word that Damon had a wonky ankle that prevented dancing. "Oh, *good!* Maybe I can get him to myself for a change. Oooooh, that sultry smile!" "Courteous boredom is more like it, lovie. Just leave enough for the rest of us?"

Somebody sat out with Damon every dance, but by intermission he'd evidently had it. As the record ended, I saw him going out to the garden blackness. "Sit out time, serve up the ice cream and cake!" I fixed two plates, and slid unnoticed through the end window. He was all the way along to the farthest bench. "Here's the refreshments, and I hope you like coconut cake. Lou *would* make one, she says you can't have a social without."

"I'm not hungry, thanks." Damon drew a long breath. "I gather by the solicitude that you told everyone I'm a cripple?"

"I said you had a bum ankle for this kind of dancing. You aren't a cripple," I said calmly licking icing from my fingers, "except in your own mind."

"More therapy?" he snorted. "Dammit, can't you get it through your scat-brain that I'm not a whole man, I'll *never* be a whole man again. Leave me alone!"

"Of course. Sorry I hit another nerve; I didn't realize you meant to be a Nureyev."

He stood up abruptly. "Stop needling! I'm a man who doesn't care for sidelines."

"I shouldn't think you had many, except things

that require instant balance," I reflected. "Tennis, mountain climbing, figure skating and skiing. Did you like to do those things?"

"No."

"Only dancing?" Dimly the music began once more, a rhumba, and anyone knows the man simply stands still, shuffling from one foot to the other (and usually looking fatuous) while the woman prances around him as voluptuously as possible! I put down my plate and got up with decision. "Come on, Damon, dance with me. *I dare you!*"

"How can you be so cruel?" he choked. "D'you want to see me fall flat on my face?"

"How do you know you will until you try?" I stepped forward, arms raised, waiting. Automatically, Damon put his arms about me and we caught the rhythm, moving gently back and forth, not trying for more than keeping time until I sensed he was feeling steadier, gaining confidence enough for me to twirl away and circle. I danced on my own, placing no strain on his hand as I went around and back to face him. It was quite simple. He must have been a superb partner originally; he had instinctive tempo in shoulders and hips. "You see? So you can't frug or Watusi, who wants to? Maybe it'll take practice for a waltz, but you can *still* dance if the rhythm is slow enough for you to be able to set your foot firmly."

The music started again: "The Shadow of Your Smile." He stumbled once. "We oughtn't to be practicing on this uneven patio. You'd be all right on a floor, but I think better not tonight—all the girls will dash for you madly. We'd better have a few solo sessions first."

"I suppose your husband was a good dancer?"

"Yes, if it was quiet romantic music, and no, if it was anything where he'd have to exert himself. He had natural rhythm, like you," I said deliberately. "Chris has it too, but Bart preferred small evenings, I told you that. He'd go to a few charity balls for business reasons, and he'd come with us to summer square dances, but usually he drifted off with the older men after one reel, and left me to partner Chris."

"Hmmm. How's Alexi?"

"He hops!"

Damon laughed so heartily that he stumbled again. "This is enough for the first lesson," he said, his arms still lightly about me. "Thank you, chipmunk. I should have met you twenty years ago."

"You wouldn't have looked at me twice," I said mischievously, stepping away to pick up our plates. "I was a ten-year-old brat, with missing teeth! Come on back, and for heavens' sake eat a piece of Lou's coconut cake."

Within two days there were enough fulminating phone calls from the world's fashion capitals to melt the cables: Why was everyone still at Costa Demonio? I bore the brunt. Everyone said Nell's castle was utterly *divine*; the menu was too, too slimming with fresh vegetables and fish; the photographs were *sensational*; the little designer in Lisbon was a major discovery . . . after which the callers got hold of *me* and screamed. When the editor of *Vogue* addressed me as Mrs. Pharoah, and sang me a chorus of "Go down, Moses!" at transatlantic phone rates, I went out to the roulette table (it was after dinner due to the time difference) and said, "Now hear this: it's been Utopia, but you will pack and leave soonest, before I am blacklisted!"

What with straightening out who was due to go where, and arranging transportation, complicated by a weekend, it was still going to be some days before the place was cleared out. "Your boys will have to go too, I think," I told Homer. "Haven't you found the strong room yet?"

He shook his head. "Couldn't get in for an intensive search, we've done what seemed most likely—which isn't to say we didn't miss it, what with having to work fast. It may be easier when the place is empty."

I thought it would be easier while there was milling about, but who was I to tell Interpol its job? The next afternoon was blessedly peaceful for the first time in the past weeks. Alexi took Rog and Dickie to Caldarém to fix up air tickets for everyone; Chris took a final fishing party around to the shaded cove, and everyone else was down on the beach. I went out to the central section of the castle and wandered about, trying to visualize what all these rooms were ever intended for.

It wasn't easy. The place was a square arranged like a mirror image. That is, the right and left sides each contained an immense salon, flanked by anterooms—and the connecting sections contained a string of small rooms, broken only by the entrance archway. It seemed a peculiar architectural design. Logically, the big room over the kitchens must be the banquet hall, but why was the other large room across the courtyard? It was an awfully long walk to supper, although there was a covered gallery with narrow Moorish arches evenly spaced along it that ran completely around the ground floor.

Perhaps Dom Basilia's wife had finicked about cooking odors. Logically, you'd expect his private study to be near the grand salon, but if he was a real Valentim, and his wife had a weak stomach or was subject to the vapors, Dom Basilio would have put his room as far away from her as possible. I chuckled to myself. I knew the Valentims; they could never have been any different from Bart and Chris!

Anyway, I was convinced the hidey-hole had to be close to Alexi's locked pass-through. He wouldn't chance trotting around the gallery to a room on the other side; it was too long a trip. No, the secret was somewhere in the righthand section. It might not even be Dom Basilio's personal lair, but a real strong-room . . . which could be anywhere among the cellars around the kitchen, and *that* was a discouraging thought. You could hunt about for months, and time was of the essence.

I might as well have a look now I was here, see if I could find the rear door to Alexi's storeroom, and where it might point. I went around the gallery and through the gaping door into the banquet hall. At either end was a stairway leading down to a wide lower landing, thence to the kitchens, probably routed one side up, one side down, when the servants were serving dinner. There were a dozen kitchens below, leading from one to another and evidently meant for specialties. Two were bakeries, one was probably for fish with a crumbling iron swimming tank in the corner. The main kitchen contained four fireplaces, equipped with all those mysterious chains and hooks.

In, around, and about was a maze of small storerooms and passages, and the locked door that must lead to Alexi's storeroom was so unobtrusive that I nearly missed it entirely—except that I knew it had to be there, and kept looking. It was around a corner in total blackness, like an afterthought.

Starting from there, I went back through the kitchen and faced the double stairway—but which one did Alexi use? Instinct would send anyone to the right. I went left, and at the far end of the passage from the dining hall there was a square room with a huge carved fireplace. Through its two broken windows I could faintly hear the voices of the swim party. I stepped carefully over the debris of glass and dead leaves that littered every room, and I could see the beach clearly, as well as the smaller headland beyond. Involuntarily I lingered, chuckling at Lou trying a somersault and collapsing in the middle.

And then, behind me, there were rapid pattering footsteps on the stone steps. . . .

CHAPTER IX

Hopeless to try to duck out the one door, I'd only run straight into Alexi. *Stay where you are and brazen it out. He may not be heading for this room. Then you'll know where the swag really is.*

It was here.

The steps stopped abruptly. I looked innocently over my shoulder, "Alexi! Where'd you spring from? I was just about to go down to the beach," I nodded to the window. "I never knew you could see it from here. We should have got some angle shots."

If I'd had any doubt it was gone. Alexi's face was incarnate fury, then suddenly he relaxed. "Nell, how could you do this to me? I thought it was agreed you would not walk about in here alone. I come back from Caldarém and someone says you have gone to the castle," he closed his eyes faintly. "They do not understand the danger, the way I do." He opened his eyes and came forward to clasp my arms gently. "The heart stops still," he said simply, and pulled me against him.

"I went through the old cellars first, searching for you, calling your name," he was a broken man, shattered by the dread of fatality. "*Why* did you not answer, *cara prima?*"

"I didn't hear you," I said truthfully, *and that's a bad slip, duckie: how the hell did you get through to this section? What would you say if I asked?* "I'm so sorry you worried, Alexi, but I was only looking out the window at the bathing party."

"But why are you here at all?" he demanded, holding me away from him and staring at me with anguished eyes. "It was agreed no one would be alone in these parts, Nell."

"I didn't go anywhere that we hadn't been photographing, that you said was safe," I widened my eyes pathetically. "I was looking for something that hadn't been done. Costa Demonio is so fresh and unspoiled for the photographers, Alexi. There'll be other crews wanting to come, and I have to have something to suggest. Please don't be angry with me."

"*Never!*" he declared passionately. "It would be impossible that I should be angry with you, *queridinha.* Anxious, yes, how could it be other wise? You are so little, so unprotected against the world and the responsibilities here," he smiled ruefully. "Oh, I undertand the tiny white lie that Bart's son is Dom Christo—you think to make matters easier with the village loyalty, eh? But it was unimportant who owns Costa Demonio, you had only to be here to gain your own loyalty. Simply—I am a little hurt that you could not turn to me, trust me, *namorada!*"

"H-how did you find out?" I managed tremulously.

"Bart's lawyer sent a copy of the will to Revalhao for the business details, and last week we have encountered each other in Caldarém. He told me." Alexi stroked my hair gently. "But why could you not tell me this, Nell? How have I failed, *querida*?"

I'd suspected that if Alexi knew I owned the castle, he'd try to marry me. *Here it comes!* "You've *never* failed me, Alexi," I murmured, leaning my forehead against his shoulder. "You never will. Don't you suppose I knew that after these past weeks? How would I ever have survived without you! And you do understand—you must understand—why I said nothing about Bart's will?" I drew back slightly and looked up at him wistfully. "It was only meant to protect Chris. Of course he must have the Valentim heritage! As soon as he's of age, I shall turn Costa Demonio over to him; it's what Bart would have wanted, don't you agree?"

"Yes . . . shsh, *querida*, do not weep!" Alexi smiled fondly at me. "Ah, you must know what is in my heart, *meu coraçao*, what has been in my mind day and night from the first moment I found you here at Costa Demonio, like a tiny buttercup against all these grim walls." He sighed. "It is too soon, I know it is too soon, *namorada*, and only God knows whether I shall ever have my heart's desire, but it will be something if I can be with you, help you, comfort you."

I must say he was nearly as expert as Bart at cuddling! There was no comparison for enjoyment, however, although I played up as best I could. I didn't think Alexi's heart was really in it either. He stroked the nape of my neck and kissed my temple softly, but I knew he was *thinking* all the while he was murmuring sweet nothings. All I didn't know was just exactly what he was thinking.

Had I slipped by so much as a word, an inflection that would make him wonder? Or was he, I thought coldly, planning how to kill Chris and marry me? Involuntarily I shivered, and Alexi was all solicitude. "I am a villain to keep you here in this damp place," he exclaimed, turning me quickly toward the door. "Only—it is so sweet to have you to myself for a few moments, *querida.* Forgive me, please."

Go for broke . . . "I expect I'll always forgive you anything," I murmured seductively, "but—give me a little time, Alexi? So much to think of, to plan: what's best to do here, with the land, how much could be grown, you'll know. But how can we talk while there are so many people around?"

"Do not worry about it, *queridinha.* Leave all to me," he said tenderly, "I will take all the burdens from you, I promise." He'd got me propelled forward to the passsage, was unobtrusively pulling the door firmly shut behind us. We walked like lovers, my head against his shoulder, his arm gently about me, matching our steps to pace along the gallery like a pair of supernumeraries in *Romeo and Juliet.* Alexi murmured broken phrases, "Ah, this is so sweet. I had not dared hope it might stir in you, hadn't dared say a word, *querida . . . meu namorada.*"

And I rubbed my cheek against his jacket, catlike and sighed. I make no apologies: it was what had to be done; I did it. All women have a dash of

Delilah when required. We reached the courtyard exit, and Alexi's hand turned my chin gently upward—but I thought better... *not.* Only three months a widow; far too soon for kisses; don't appear too willing to be off with the old and on with the new. Besides, I didn't like the odor of his after-shave lotion.

"Not—yet, please," I murmured, sliding strategically so his lips hit my temple, and pulling free to look shyly at the stone floor of the corridor.

It was the right maneuver. Instantly Alexi was completely correct, straightening up, drawing my hand to his lips, breathing deeply in and out, the picture of a man mastering passion, prepared to wait forever for the favor of the one woman in the world. "Forgive me, Nell?" he asked quietly. "For a moment I forgot myself. From the beginning it has seemed so inevitable that you belonged to me already. There is no doubt in my mind, but perhaps—perhaps you will never be able to feel this. God knows I am no substitute." He sighed, holding my hand against his cheek for a second. "Now we will say no more of it, but see how it will come about naturally, eh?"

"Yes, please. Thank you for understanding!"

"*De nada!*" He smiled at me affectionately, we went out to the garden, along to the arcade leading through to the beach side of the castle . . . and I wondered who was fooling whom.

Certainly not Damon—he was standing on the cabana porch as Alexi carefully led me down the beach stairs, and his pale eyes were bleak gray pebbles. "Oh, there you are. Where've you been?

I came over to suggest a final cocktail party on the *Thetis*."

"What a good idea! Is Chris back, or shall we just go along and catch him when he docks? Come on, everybody. Last chance for partying," I called gaily, but Damon's expression was far from hospitable.

"Your lipstick is smeared," he observed coldly, while the others were collecting their beach stuff. "Where have you been?"

"That's not lipstick, it's canary feathers," I told him in an undertone. "I've been in the castle, of course. And if you want to know where's the hidey-hole, it's in the far corner room at the left end of the passage from the dining hall." I moved away from him, casually mixing with the group who were starting to straggle up the steps. They were carrying Alexi along with them, laughing and chattering, but when I looked back, Damon was standing rooted to this spot. "A fine host you are," I said warningly.

He shook himself alive at that, and came after me. "Did you *find* it?"

I shook my head, "Hadn't time," I muttered, "but that's where it is. Alexi made straight for that room. Tell Homer."

Damon's face was ashen, "He caught you there? My God, girl, will you keep out of this?"

"With pleasure," I said politely, "and will you kindly cheer up for your party? If he sees your expression, he won't think it's jealousy over my turning up with him, you know."

That brought back some color. "So help me, one

of these days I will be able to smack you as you deserve!"

"Pow! Right in the kisser," I murmured involuntarily. "Never mind. I'll explain some other time—if there ever is one. Hasn't Homer any idea when this thing is going to blow up?" I was keeping an eye on Alexi, but he seemed not to be looking back, was still surrounded by people, going into the house. "I'm beginning not to like the situation," I told Damon hurriedly. "Alexi's found out that I own Costa Demonio through Revalhao. I'm thinking I'll take Chris away, but for how long?"

"I don't know. Homer's sent for more men; they must think it'll be fairly soon," Damon said, catching my arm urgently. "Nell—did that bastard try to make love to you?"

"Of course," I nodded. "Didn't you know he would? Don't worry, his heart isn't in it. *Ouch!* Let go, will you? I bruise easily."

"God, we'll have to get you out of here, you can't be exposed to that sort of thing! It's—it's indecent," he muttered. "Sansao—and your husband! they'd never forgive me!"

"I'm not so sure," I said after a moment. "I don't know about Sansao, but Bart would back me to settle things with Alexi, no matter what I had to do. It won't require rape, you know; I'm not at all his type. I shouldn't wonder if he's got a plump little pigeon stashed in Lisbon. I'm not even sure he wants Costa Demonio enough to marry me," I debated briefly, "or that Chris is in any real danger. I have a hunch he'd prefer status quo, let Chris go back to school and perhaps I'll go home, too—or if I don't, he can diddle me. He doesn't think I have any brains, you see. He was flummoxed to find me in that room, but I'm fairly certain he never dreamed it anything but an unlucky accident. I wonder how he's going to explain not having his car here," I added suddenly.

"I'm positive he came through the tunnel and the locked room. He said someone told him I'd been seen going into the castle, and he was searching for me. I wonder if he locked the door behind him?" I chuckled. "I didn't ask how he'd got from the old section to the next—and for heaven's sake don't comment on the whereabouts of his car!"

Damon drew a long breath. "I won't comment on anything, but I'll have to get hold of Plakidon." He glanced at his watch, "There's time enough. My party begins at five; everyone meets at the boat."

It was a lovely party. The next day we waved goodbye to everyone, and by the day after, Mariana had everything back in order. The extra help had returned to Ponto Lucido; Jorge and Huberto were back to their usual chores. The ball was over, and after so much cheerful noise, Costa Demonio was oddly desolate. Alexi showed up each day briefly. He said he'd let things pile up during the fiesta, must go to Lisbon for a few days. Homer was still visiting Damon, but I saw nothing of them. Damon telephoned once, succinctly: Homer thought better not to be seen at Costa Demonio now that the mob had dispersed. They had not been able to locate the hidey-hole in the short time between our leaving for the *Thetis* and the necessity for Gerson and Kranski to follow. Interpol anticipated rapid action, however; they were geared for Thursday, somewhat confirmed by Alexi's telling me he must go to Lisbon shortly.

"And you are to *stay away* from the castle, and lead a blameless life," Damon finished. "You understand, chipmunk? That's not my order, but direct from Interpol."

I said I asked nothing better than a blameless life, in which to work on a thousand-piece puzzle spread all over the banquet table. "It's turning into a florid scene from Shakespeare, I think, but we can't have anyone to dinner until I finish it."

Chris thought he would get up early next morning and go fishing. We were, he stated, out of fish in the freezer. "You mean we've actually eaten up all those boatloads you've been catching? Incredible!"

"Yeah, isn't it?" he agreed blandly. "Lucky we have an ocean in the backyard. I never saw anyone eat as much as those models."

"The men weren't far behind." I remarked. "All right, go fishing, but remember there's only us. Leave room in the freezer for something else, please. Where are you going?"

"Along the coast a piece, Jorge says there are baby octopus among the rocks, and I might find some *écrivisses* and *lagosta*."

That's what caused me to wake at dawn next morning. Dimly I heard Chris moving about, collecting equipment, and finally the door closed. The sun wasn't up as yet, the day lay on the garden, and mist obscured the water. I remembered I'd meant to weed out the end flower beds, this was a perfect moment. Fling on some old clothes, grub around for an hour or so, and come back for a bath before breakfast. Chris was ambling along toward the dock when I came out armed with trowel and trug. I was tempted to forget gardening, to yell "Wait for me!" and go fishing instead, but as I debated, he vanished around the last curve.

So I wandered over to the flowers and stood for a moment, breathing deep of damp cool air, idly admiring the outcrops softened by their scarves of mist . . . and suddenly I sensed motion. Jorge or Huberto, starting the day with the livestock? No. the byres were still closed. With my heart in my mouth, I wriggled cautiously around the end of the topiary hedge and peered down to the water.

Beneath me, in the inner cove by the tunnel entrance, rode the Fortuna.

All the while I was racing for the house, I was incredulous. Interpol had definitely expected, had practically guaranteed, Alexi would move at night. But here he was, loading up to slip out under cover of the mist! Damon answered the phone at once.

"It's now this minute," I babbled breathlessly. "The *Fortuna* is in the cove, Damon. She's not moving, he must still be packing up."

"Right," he said tersely. "Keep out of sight, Nell. We'll be on his heels. He can't risk too much speed coming out."

I relaxed limply and hung up—only to be struck by horror: *Chris!* He'd gone fishing, he'd be out in the small boat heading for Jorge's cove for the octopus. *But which way along the coast was it?* I didn't stop to consider, I knew in my soul it was to the left beyond Demonio. Chris would be cutting directly across Alexi's bow in a small slow motor boat. He could never pass around the headland before Alexi would be starting up and know the boy had seen the *Fortuna* where she'd no business to be.

Could the bigger motor boat overhaul Chris? I stopped just long enough to grab the gun Huberto kept loaded for farm vermin, and ran for the dock, praying Chris hadn't hurried about casting off—hopelessly, of course. He was leisurely but no dawdler. The boat was gone; I had a single glimpse of it passing beyond the outer rocks of the harbor—and I was right: he was turning toward Demonio! While I cast off and followed as rapidly as I dared, I began praying Alexi *hadn't* started. If he were still at the tunnel, he might hear the comfortable putt-putt drifting over the water, and he'd lie low, knowing the *Fortuna* couldn't be seen. Please, God, let Alexi still be loading until we get past the headland, *please?*

God was busy elsewhere this morning.

When I rounded from the harbor, the *Fortuna* was gracefully sliding forward at lowest speed and there was no sign of Chris . . . until I could maneuver my boat among the outcrops behind Alexi. Then I saw—and heard. That ominous *splat* of sound: the *Fortuna* edging sideways. A shrewd shot had put the putt-putt out of commission, and Alexi's wake had forced Chris into Demonio! The boy was frantically trying to repair the damage, to start up sufficiently to get out, and already halfway around the first rim of the whirlpool! Alexi hadn't seen me, he was holding the *Fortuna* only long enough to be sure Chris was inextricably caught.

"You murdering devil! I'll kill you with my bare hands for this!" I said it aloud, quite calm with rage. I knew exactly what I was going to do, one way or another I could get Chris out of the eddy. *Just keep your head, girl. Time it right.*

I brought my boat out of the sheltering rocks carefully, idling outside Demonio exactly as Chris was swept around beside me. "Chris!" I called placidly. "Stay cool, darling—I shall toss you my anchor. Hold it, don't fasten it, understand? We'll either pull your boat free, or you'll leap for mine and the anchor will reel you in. Got it?"

"Right," he steadied himself waiting. For a few seconds, we were synchronized to his drifting speed.

"Here you are!" I tossed. Chris caught and held. I gunned my engine and shot at a tangent. For a moment I thought we couldn't make it, he'd have to jump. Then, very slowly, Demonio let him go. I cut speed until Chris was roped in. "Change over," I said tersely. "Forget the putt-putt and keep cool, Chris. We aren't out of this yet."

He was ghastly white with shock, but Bart had trained him for instant obedience in emergency. He held together and sat down beside me, waiting for instructions. "Take the wheel, hon, and steer us in among the rocks as best you can to cover us."

He nodded dumbly. "Nell, he shot at me!"

"I know. I'll explain later, dear. Keep going."

Automatically he concentrated to avoid the hidden rocks, heading toward the harbor headland shore. We didn't quite make it. I hadn't thought we could before Alexi would realize Chris was no longer in Demonio. I was ready and waiting for him, when he was suddenly leaning over the railing of the *Fortuna*, his face contorted with fury. "Keep going, Chris. Don't look back. Don't be thrown off course," I said quietly. "Crouch down as low as possible to be out of my way. Just keep going—while I shoot him."

I aimed for Alexi's head, but with the motion of both boats, I couldn't get him. He couldn't get me, either, and we were nearly to shelter. But that wouldn't be the end of it. Alexi would bring the *Fortuna* about for pot shots to drive us into moving, with every likelihood we'd stave in our boat, which would leave us marooned on an outcrop for him to pick us off. I *had* to get him.

On the third shot, I did. At least I could see that he rocked back, his gun wavering, while we scooted behind an outcrop. The trouble was, he'd also gotten me; when I looked, there was a nasty line of welling blood up my left arm, and the short sleeve of my blouse was torn at the shoulder. Dazedly I felt from the neck downward, while Chris was sobbing under his breath. "Hold everything, hon. The bullet just grazed me and ripped out at the top. I can't feel any actual wound."

"But you're bleeding, Nell!"

"Get hold of yourself!" I said sharply. "Tie up to that jut behind you, and give me the bath towel beside you."

I soaked the towel in sea water and wrapped it around my arm. It stung so badly I thought it must be a good antisepsis.

Chris had spent a few moments being sick. "Sorry 'bout that, chief," he said forlornly. "What do we do now?"

"Relax, and when you can stand, take a peek? He'll come after us, hon. He can't afford to let us go. Be ready to move us around opposite the *Fortuna*, but *not* into the channel where he could push us back into Demonio." I was feeling a bit sick, myself, but I fought it down. "Try to get us toward the shore and duck behind one rock after another, if you can. If worst comes to worst, we'll have to swim for it, and hope we can find cover."

It didn't get that far, thank God, but I never want to relive those next minutes, hearing the *Fortuna's* engines purring softly, stalking us, while we huddled beside the rock, with Chris holding us off by the boat hook. "Nell, can you hold for a minute, while I look?" Carefully, he pulled himself erect until he could peer toward the channel. "She's backing up," he said shakily. "I think I better move us."

"Pull us by the anchor rope, while I hold us off." Slowly we slithered around until once more we were hidden, but a disastrous scraping noise said we were blocked by an underwater extension of rock . . . and we were still exposed for a direct hit if Alexi went down channel far enough. "Oh, where are they?" I cried involuntarily. "What's taking them so *long?*"

"Who?"

"Damon and the Interpol men," I said distractedly. "He said they were coming, why aren't they *here?*"

Chris stared at me. "So that's it," he said finally

and picked up the gun. "Change places with me, Nell. You hold us off. Maybe I can get him for good." Now it was I who silently obeyed Bart's son, while he crouched in the center of the boat, the gun to his shoulder, waiting . . . waiting . . . as the *Fortuna* slid slowly into view stern first. Alexi was in the wheel cabin, protected by glass that might shatter but would certainly deflect a bullet. Chris held his fire, adjusting to the sway of our boat, still waiting until Alexi would think he had us.

Then everything happened at once: sirens, searchlights, two boats racing around the harbor headland. I could see them passing beyond the string of outcrops along the shore, but Chris was not deflected. "There they are," he said calmly and fired exactly as Alexi turned frantically back to the wheel. "I got his arm, but he's still going to run for it," Chris stated. "Hold the gun until I get up to the top, Nell . . . I'll get a better shot." He was scrambling out, searching footholds on the slippery granite, reaching back for the gun.

"Please, God, if you're free for a moment now, let Chris avenge his mother?

Bart's son stood tall and steady atop the rock, he set the gun to his shoulder, aimed with deliberation and fired. Then there was a furious spatter of gunfire farther off, and Chris came sliding down into the boat, his hands and legs badly scraped from the jagged granite. "He's out of range. The others'll have to get him, If I missed—but I don't think I did," he said impersonally, dashing water over the scratches. "C'm on, let's get you back to a doctor, Nell."

It took careful maneuvering to get us free of the underwater rocks and back into the channel to see that the *Fortuna* was not out of range. She was caught in Demonio, with the *Thetis* and a very businesslike revenue cutter going after her. I remembered Damon had said the *Thetis* got out after three turns—now it was happening before my eyes. I couldn't believe it. Alone, perhaps, but she wasn't heavy enough to rescue the *Fortuna*, not even with the cutter to help.

I can remember the three of them spinning around in narrowing circles. I can remember crying hysterically, "Damon! Let her go! Don't! Don't! *Please* don't! Oh, PLEASE!"

And finally they cut the grapples, laboriously pulled themselves free, while the *Fortuna* went on—and on—an on . . . until at last she spun like a top, and with a sickening jolt, upended to plunge bow first as though diving into the water. Then there was only Demonio, circling about lazily . . . and for the first time in my life, I fainted.

CHAPTER X

When I opened my eyes, I was in my own bed and the room was full of people, or so it seemed. The sun was slanting low through shuttered windows. *What could have happened to me,* I thought dazedly. Did I fall down the cliff? Never mind, it'll come back to me in a while.

Beside me, Chris was cross-legged on the floor, his head resting against the bed frame. His face was gaunt, but with a strange maturity, as he turned the pages of a magazine desultorily. Huberto sat beyond him, and Mariana was bolt upright in a straight chair on the other side of me, her black eyes fixed unwaveringly on my face. "*La dona* is awake," she stated, and a man brushed past her to stick a thermometer in my mouth and pick up my wrist. I lay docilely, wondering if I'd been ill, vaguely recognizing the doctor . . . what was his name?

"There is no fever; the pulse is normal," he said.

"It always is. I'm offensively healthy. Chris?"

"Yes," he was scrambling to his feet, bending to kiss my cheek awkwardly, "I'm okay except for rock scratches, and Doutor Mercia says your arm will be all right. You probably won't even have a scar."

"Doutor Mercia? Yes, of course. I thought you looked familiar."

"I could wish that I did not," he said austerely. "However, we will hope that you refrain from damaging yourself in future. I gave you an injection this morning to ensure rest during the day. The arm will be painful for a while, but I anticipate no infection. You are, as you say," he smiled, "offensively healthy—but," he added soberly, "this has been an horrifying experience, coming directly after the original mental strain that you have complicated by this photographic work, Dona Eleanor." He turned away, counting pills into a small envelope. "One of these every three hours for the next two days. One of these at bedtime until the arm has healed. Stay in bed as much as possible for at least a week, *rest* is imperative!" He closed the medical bag briskly and bowed. "If there should be any extraordinary discomfort, Mariana will send for me. *Adeus*, Dona Eleanor."

"Why does he call me that? I'm Mrs. Bartholomeu Valentim. No," it was beginning to come back, "I'm Mrs. Eleanor Marchant Valentim, if you believe in Emily Post," I murmured groggily.

"*Non vous êtes la Dona de Costa Demonio*. This is now known, but why should you not have said this, madame?" Huberto demanded.

"I was scared of you."

There was a long pause, while he looked at the floor. "*Oui, vous avez raison*," he admitted gruffly. "I am an old man, Dona Eleanor. For me, time does not change as it should, perhaps. I think only to preserve what has been. *Alors*, it will be different in future." He stumped forward, picked up my hand and kissed it conventionally. "*A votre service*, Dona Eleanor."

I was suddenly wide awake, remembering everything. "Chris!" I said wildly. "Oh, *Chris!*"

"Shhh, you're not to think yet . . . or me, either." he said shakily.

Yes, don't give way and upset the boy with hysterics; he's been through a lot, too. I hauled myself up in the bed, gingerly favoring the bandaged arm, and made an effort for normalcy. "I should like a cigarette, a rather stiff scotch highball, a bath, and something to eat—in that order," I managed a smile for Chris.

"*Oui, madame.*" Huberto departed, while Chris stuck a cigarette between my lips and lit it, with a deep sigh of relief. "That sounds more like you, Nell."

"Of course." I tossed aside the bedcovers and started to crawl out, at which Mariana uttered a faint shriek and dashed forward with a robe. "Why do I need this just to go to the bathroom?"

"*Sim, sim,*" she insisted, thrusting it around me, and, from the shadows at the far end of the room, Damon loomed up with Homer beside him. So they were safe, I hadn't had time to imagine it—it was only Alexi and the *Fortuna*. . . . Don't *think*. *Pull the robe around, girl!*

"Oh, them," I said disgustedly. "If they've never seen a woman in a nightgown before, they won't know what I am, and if they have, I won't surprise them." But when I saw myself in the mirror over the hand basin, I *was* surprised. I looked like a Vietnamese war atrocity, like Quasimodo's second cousin twice removed! I splashed cold water on my face, dragged a comb through my hair, but results were far from favorable.

Oddly enough, it was rather cheering to discover I could be so repulsive. I felt like a woman, instead of a magazine cover. I put on the robe properly and came out. "Good God, chipmunk, is that YOU?" Damon muttered, incredulously.

"Mhmmm, this is the way I look every morning," I told him sunnily, ignoring Chris's choke of laughter, "and what are *you* doing in my bedroom, gentlemen?"

Homer stepped forward hastily, "I had to be certain you were all right, Nell. I should have left three hours ago, there is nothing more to be done here and I must be in Copenhagen tomorrow. Lisbon will finish this. You will have the formal thanks of Interpol for your help." He peered at me earnestly. "Now, you are sure you are all right? Doutor Mercia is very competent."

"I'm perfectly all right, thanks, Homer . . . never mind how I look."

"Then I think I should leave at once." He consulted his watch. "There may still be time to make a plane at Caldarém. Damon, do you mind trying?" He shook my hand impersonally, "I trust we'll meet again under happier circumstances, goodbye. Goodbye, Chris." Homer clapped him on the shoulder with a smile. "Your father would be proud of you. Come on, Damon. You can talk to her when you get back." Homer strode purposefully toward the stairs, with a nod for Huberto coming forward majestically with my highball on a small silver tray.

I crawled back into bed and eyed Damon—who was eyeing me. His eyes were pale gray pebbles, his fingers were twitching with the urge to shake me, although I couldn't think what in hell I'd done this time. "Chris, sweetie, flop over the other pillow? Ah, *merci mille fois*, Huberto!" I took a delicate sip of the drink and remarked, "I don't like to seem inhospitable, but isn't Homer waiting for you?"

"Yes. I'll see you when I get back."

"Not if I see you first."

Damon paused at the hall door. "That's what you said in the beginning," he observed. "May I depend on it this time?"

"You may," I assured him graciously. "Good night, goodbye, and God bless."

His eyes flickered briefly, but his face was expressionless. "As you say," he murmured after a moment, and was gone with Chris beside him. I could hear their steps moving along to the stairs, descending, fading into the distance.

Those next weeks were peculiar. They were both obscure, and illumined. Perhaps I should simply state everything baldly.

Chris had grown up. Just like that! His voice never cracked again; his body moved with assurance. He was no longer a boy, he was a young man; he no longed asked, he told. Servants, villagers, stablehands obeyed him unquestioningly. It took all summer for this to emerge fully, but I knew it had begun when he came back after I'd had my bath. "We'll eat here. Huberto, put the table there, please. Nell, sit in the big chair and prop your feet up until dinner's served."

He lit the fire, set cigarettes and highball beside my chair, took the platter of canapés from Mariana. "Thanks, we'll serve ourselves." He spread a napkin on my lap, gave me a plate and filled it with a selection, "Keep your arm quiet, Nell." Huberto set the table. When he'd stumped away, Chris poured a small glass of wine and held it up like a toast. "Thanks for saving my life, *minha mae,*" he said quietly.

It was the sort of moment that must be taken lightly, or all the strings will come unstrung in a welter of overemotionalism. "*De nada,*" I snapped my fingers nonchalantly. "Any time, kid."

Chris choked on his wine. "Oh, Nell! I only hope I find a girl like you."

"Luckily for civilization, there aren't too many of us around."

"Yeah, Homer says you're unique. Damon says you're frightening," He chuckled, sampling the canapés. "They explained everything while you were asleep. We went through the tunnel; the storeroom's empty, of course, and we still couldn't find anything upstairs. Homer's going to send an expert." He stared at the fire for a moment. "I understand why you didn't tell me. Probably you were right—but don't try to shoulder everything again, Nell. Dad wouldn't like it."

"All right, darling. As soon as I'm up to it, we'll go over things together, so you'll know how we stand."

He nodded dismissingly. "I think I'll sell Allegra, d'you mind? You'll have Medora. I can use Conrad to breed, and I'd kind of like to keep Jovanna."

"Whatever you say, sweetie—you're in charge of horses . . ."

However, I was still in charge of finances, and while the heat was off, so to speak, I was thinking of permanency. I'd got a couple of thousand from the vermeil centerpiece and the other oddments sold in Pria de Rocha, which was ample walkabout money in Portugal with no loss on exchange. The money from the photographic session was to be paid in New York. I thought it better to use the tax-devil I knew than a Portuguese one, but it was still income and fully taxable. Better leave it in dollars until I knew how much I'd net. If nothing else, it'd pay taxes on Bart's land and provide emergency backing for Chris.

There was the trust money for school and college; I hadn't to worry about that—but in a way, I had. What had been set up originally wouldn't begin to cover the cost of college today due to inflation. I didn't doubt Dom Sansao's "investments" were valuable—but how to sell 'em without losing half the money in inheritance taxes? On the other hand, did it matter? I was certain to realize something, and if it wasn't what Sansao had paid, the more fool he for buying things instead of AT&T or IBM.

Daily I felt stronger physically and mentally. With the removal of Alexi and cessation of mystery over Costa Demonio, the place was increasingly pleasant. I was further cheered by a letter from mother who'd investigated what to do with the valuables and had a number of sensible suggestions. If I sold just a few each year, I should end with some capital without losing too much in tax.

Eventually I recalled the big key from Sansao's desk. It *had* to fit something, logically an ancient safe, because the major question was what had become of Sansao's cash? Everyone including my husband had thought he was rich. Rented farms and pipes of wine . . . did they produce only enough now to pay laborers, repairs, taxes? Now that I could think again, I didn't believe it—or whence had come the money for Sansao's investments?

Furthermore, what had happened to it in the five years since his death? It might have been some sort of annuity that died with Sansao, but I doubted it.

With determination, I locked myself into the study at siesta time and concentrated. Any safe had to be on the main floor. I couldn't see Dom Sansao trotting up stairs every time he wanted an important paper. It could not require moving books from a shelf, or standing on a ladder. Not a hidden space in the desk, or why need a key? Not in the farther cubby with files and typewriter; there wasn't enough free wall space. No, it would have to be fairly large, built in and concealed by paneling, and no more than five feet from the ground, because not all the Valentims were tall.

There was only the staircase hall, although I'd gone all over it when I'd first found the key. Perhaps in one of the stair treads? At a glance that was out; they were carpeted with brass rods on each riser, and an exploratory tug showed none was movable. So it had to be under the stairs—or did it? When I really looked, I had it at once. The study was a Bullfinch oval—the tiny hall was straight-sided, which left enough space for a safe to be sunk into the far end behind the curve in the study.

It still took time. I pressed and pushed, tried to swivel, broke a fingernail rather painfully, and just as I was hot enough and mad enough to go in search of a hatchet, I found it. It was a double section of paneling. I pressed evenly on both sides of the top. Then a spring released the wood about an inch, and when I felt inside, there was another catch to lift and the whole thing swung open. Behind was a two foot square metal door with a keyhole, and with a tiny *screeeck*, my key turned in the lock.

With a deep breath, I squared my shoulders and pulled open the door. Dom Sansao's safe was in two parts, and both were filled. At the bottom were large boxes, bags, and what appeared to be ledgers. A small shelf above held chamois bags and an unmistakable three-inch wad of currency. For a few moments I contemplated the trove and felt tired all over. If those chamois bags contained what I suspected they did, it'd be the outside of ENOUGH!

Eventually I dragged everything out to the desk, and it was both better and worse than I'd feared. The items in the bottom of the safe were Valentim heritage: la Dona's jewels, stamp albums dating back to Oliveiro, and a large bag of gold coins. Aside from a charming delicate diamond tiara, the jewelry was Victorian-Edwardian hideosity, but the stones could be reset for Chris's wife. The coins would always be worth face value, but after rubbing against each other for years, I doubted they were up to numismatic standards.

The stamp albums were different. They were almost entirely filled, first by Oliveiro and up to five years ago, by Sansao. I'd a hunch they were incredibly valuable, but aside from total cataclysm, definitely not for sale. Let Chris carry on . . .

The bothersome part was that upper shelf. The packet of money was simple, but those chamois bags? One after another I untied the strings and contemplated—rubies, emeralds, sapphires, diamonds, pearls. In each group, some large, some medium, some smaller. The largest bag contained all sorts of stones, I thought they were semiprecious and frankly liked them better than the gems.

And looking at the haul spread over the desk, I thought, "All this legally belongs to me . . ."

In the distance there was a stirring of sound, siesta was ending. Rapidly I returned the Valentim heritage to its place, retied the chamois bags and stashed them away . . . but I kept the money and the sack of all-sorts. I wasn't sure what I'd do with them, but by now I felt I deserved *something.*

It took time, even with a pocket calculator, to convert escudos to dollars, but apparently I had about ten thousand bucks. *Dear Lord, I thank Thee* . . . I bundled it into the morning room desk together with the bag of stones, and collapsed on the chaise longue in a state of euphoria. I must have dozed briefly, and heaven knows what I was dreaming, but when I was roused by a tiny noise, I sat bolt upright and said hollowly, "Taxes!"

It was Marianna, quietly setting a vase of flowers on the desk. "*Desculpe,* Dona?" she said, startled.

"Taxes—who is paying them?"

Her face cleared. "My father, as always, Dona. Please not to trouble yourself until the weariness is gone."

"How can it be gone until I have all the facts?" I cried wildly. "Was my husband paying them from America? Who collects the farm rents? Do we have an agent somewhere?"

"No, no—do not distress yourself, Dona. Only let me call my father to explain." She scurried out and I could hear her calling "*Pai, Pai*—Huberto?" Shortly they returned, carrying a huge ledger and a large metal cash box. I hoped it contained receipted bills, but didn't depend upon it—and how right I was.

In that box were the five year profits of Costa Demonio—in cash.

It was quite simple, given the personalities involved, although it took time to sort through the finely-minced mixture of English, Portuguese and French. Chris came in partway along, and stayed by my request. "You can't legally *do* anything yet, but you'd better know what lies ahead."

Huberto had always handled the estate business for Dom Sansao, merely turning over the net profit at year's end, and with no idea of what became of them. Well, of course I knew: Sansao bought gems and paintings; Huberto merely put away in cash, although it troubled him.

"I'll bet," Chris muttered with awe, glancing at the ledger. "If I'm right on the exchange, Nell, it's about seventy grand."

I suppressed a strong desire to *scream* . . .

In America and based on the reported inheritance, Bart never realized there were any profits. Nor could Huberto get through to him aside from Marianna. When asked for instructions, Bart said "Carry on and don't bother me," or words to that effect. Ergo, as the cash piled up, Huberto did not know what to do. I could see it clearly: *Never* would Huberto have divulged to a woman (Marianna) that there were monies. And when we came to Costa Demonio, he thought Chris too young for financial matters, but lacking a responsible male guardian, Huberto did not dream of telling *me*. With the revelation that I was La Dona, he knew it his duty to speak to me—but Marianna forbade.

"Perhaps I did wrong, Dona, but you are so little and so tired," she apologized. "I tell my father to wait until you recover."

I made an effort. "That was thoughtful of you, Marianna."

"Now what?" Chris asked.

"Now we ask Huberto to continue the management of Costa Demonio until you are of age," I said quietly. "He will have to refer all to me, but you are old enough to decide with me, and you will give our orders to him when you are here. You understand, Huberto? Legally, I must handle everything, but it is your responsibility to train Dom Christo for the position he will assume in six years."

For the first time, he beamed at me. "*Sim, sim,*" he agreed. "Eh, it will be good! There is much to learn, but already I know Dom Christo is worthy of his name, Dona . . . as yourself. Marianna explains to me," he shuffled his feet and hung his head. "La Dona is American and all is different there. Ladies take charge of their business matters. That is why Dom Bartolomeu leaves all to la Dona. I beg la Dona's pardon," he finished humbly, "but I am old and I do not know these things."

When they had gone, Chris eyed the cash box with a frown. "What the devil do we do with it, Nell?"

"Stick it in the safe with all the rest of it," I said, and led the way to the study. "You'd better know it all, while we're about it. Legally everything is mine, but if anything happens to me, Anderson has my will leaving all to you, Chris; he and Rafael Valentim are your guardians. Here," I said calmly, "is Dom Sansao's personal safe—just so you know the location. I have the key, but observe the pressure points?" I demonstrated, and stepped back. "Now you do it . . ."

Silently, Chris opened the paneling and goggled at the blank metal door—but I opened it. "For the moment I shall keep the key, because there's more than you'll know what to do with."

"Yeah," he muttered, stunned when I'd brought it out once more to Sansao's desk, "but it's all yours, Nell. What'll *you* do with it?"

"Keep the Valentim heritage, of course, unless you don't want it . . ."

Chris wanted it, but insisted that the jewelry was mine. "Dad would have wanted you to wear it," he stated in a voice as deep as Bart's. "Have it cleaned, have some of the stones reset modern, Nell—don't fuss about my future wife. Today's girls don't want tiaras . . . at least, not the sort I'd marry."

In the end it was decided: we would have the gold coins evaluated and then decide if we should sell . . . we would keep the chamois bags of gems and cautiously convert to cash . . . and we would definitely keep the Valentim stamp collection, to which Chris would add his own American collection begun by Bart. I could tell that this was a hobby to keep him out of mischief for years! As for Huberto's wad of cash, we would live on it until it vanished . . . and we would declare the annual profits for tax purposes thenceforth.

"Huberto will not approve," I told Chris, "so I think you will not tell him that we are buying stocks instead of jewels."

"Yeah, you're right," Chris agreed. "It'd only worry him."

For myself, I was unworried about anything. There was going to be *enough*. We could take time to convert Dom Sansao's goodies, and perhaps we'd want to keep a few. Brazenly I replaced the milkmaids in the morning room with two Renoirs and a Monet, and told Marianna to use the red-banded Meissen for our dinners. With Jorge's enthusiastic assistance, I worked out a new plan for the gardens, and sent him to select proper roses and flowering shrubs. One day we bought a putt-putt and a replacement for the motorboat that was lost in Demonio. (Chris was a bit grim-faced, but he threw up his chin and chose. We said nothing about it later, and he seemed oriented, happy to go fishing again.)

A couple of days later, Gerson and Kranski came back, accompanied by Interpol's expert on medieval castles. It didn't take him fifteen minutes to find Alexi's hidey-hole. It *was* the fireplace, rather than in it. He grasped the mantel carving, and the whole thing swivelled to reveal a walk-in chamber hollowed out of the rear wall blocks. It was almost disappointingly simple, and contained nothing but a half bottle of wine and some cigarette butts rushed on the stone floor, but the expert's eyes glistened with exploration lust when he looked at Costa Demonio. "If I may presume, Dona Eleanor, it would be a very real privilege to be permitted to examine . . ."

I said the privilege was mine, and it certainly was. Chris tagged along, fascinated by the speed with which Signor de Lucca located hidden store holes. At day's end he reported that nearly every fireplace contained a cavity of some sort, but de Lucca's triumph was finding the major strong-room behind the fireplace in the room at the other end of the hall from Alexi's. "It's a whacking great thing about ten-foot square, and guess what we found in it?"

"The skeletons of Rhadames and Aida?"

Chris chuckled. "Something more useful: Moorish gold and *jools!*" He set a small tray on my lap, and there were a dozen assorted coins, a small handful of glinting colors. "They were in a box eaten to bits with rust. I wonder whose ransom it was."

"Some one of no importance, if Dom Basilio thought it too paltry to bother coming back for it."

After the first shock, Ponto Lucido was rather relieved *not* to have to go on smuggling. "The older folk are past it, and the younger generation thinks it's pure camp." Kranski grinned. "They've been wanting out, but as *commisário*, Alexi cracked a whip: loss of a fishing license, cancellation of a farm lease, and so on. Your husband could have settled it in twenty-four hours, Chris was too young. But now that they know the situation, Ponto Lucido rather likes having a Dona. There hasn't been one for about fifty years."

"But Sansao was married."

"She deserted him," Kranski consulted a pocket notebook, "in 1913. She ran away with a Bulgarian prince, deserted that guy for a Turkish caliph in 1919, when she embraced Islam, got a Moslem divorce from Dom Sansao and married the Turk. She had two children by the Bulgar, another by the Turk, and died of natural causes in Ankara, in 1950."

"Of natural causes? Good heavens, how tame!"

Conscientiously, I rested as much as possible, but it was finally borne in on me that for several weeks there had been a great absence of Damon Lord. "Is he sulking in his tent?" I inquired. "Could you tell him, diplomatically, that I wasn't responsible for what I said that day?"

"Oh, he isn't here. He went to London the next

Saturday; I'm in charge of the stables until he comes back."

"When's that?"

"I don't know. He's thinking of selling out, going home to England."

I sat upright on the chaise longue and stared at Chris. "But he *can't!* I mean, he can sell the horses, but he can't sell the lease on Quinta Choupo. How do I know we'd like the new owner? What in hell has gotten into him?" I demanded wrathfully.

"You," Chris stated succinctly. "He's head over heels in love with you, Nell. He thinks you wouldn't look at him twice, he's too old and a cripple into the bargain."

"But he *isn't!*" I cried. "We even danced together on the terrace. What makes you say this? Have you been talking it over with him?"

Chris shook his head calmly. "Of course not. I just *know.* That's why he's so curt and fusses at you. Dad was the same way before he got up his nerve to propose. If you hadn't been overtired and worried, you'd have realized too." He stood up, stretching lazily, his back toward me. "I think you'd better marry him, Nell," he said authoritatively. "I mean, when you get around to it, of course. Dad would have liked Damon, and he wouldn't like you to be alone for too long."

I was so astounded that I was speechless, and before I could think of anything to say, Chris had departed, "Have to exercise the nags."

It was too much; it was the ultimate problem. I knew Chris was wrong, but it was infinitely bothersome if Damon were to give up Quinta Choupo because I'd invaded his privacy. He'd kept telling me to leave him alone, but I'd had to be the reformer, the helpful ray of sunshine, I thought bitterly, until he couldn't stand any more of it. Oh, damn—DAMN! Well, all right. I'd go back to New York when Chris returned to school and get a modest apartment somewhere, leave Mariana here to help Huberto, give Damon time to realize I wasn't trying to move in on him. Next summer we could come back. He had nothing against Chris, it was only me—but without the complication of Alexi and Interpol, he wouldn't need to see much of me.

I felt oddly desolate at leaving Costa Demonio. I'd got used to the place, to the leisurely pace of life, the fresh vegetables and fish, a bath in the sea, a short ride on Medora. I'd been planning a major renovation of the gardens, to Jorge's delight, and looking forward to browsing through the books, working all the puzzles, playing solitaire to music from new records I'd buy in Lisbon. Vaguely, I'd thought Damon might come to dinner once in a while—but I'd ruined everything.

We would fly home from Lisbon September 4th, allowing time for wardrobe requirements before Chris went back to school. "Why are you coming? I can get whatever I need by myself," he said bewildered, "and Cousin Rafael will put me up for a couple of weeks. It's silly for you to come too."

"I just think I will," I said evasively. "I'd probably have to sooner or later for business; better to have you for company."

"How long are you going to stay?"

"I don't know. I thought I might get an apartment in New York for the winter."

He looked at me suspiciously. "Why? Have you got some notion you have to look after me?" When I shook my head, he persisted. "Then what are you going to do with yourself all alone?"

"What I usually do. I've plenty of friends, or I could go West to visit mother."

"Why d'you need an apartment, then?"

"Sweetie, do stop the cross-examination? I'm not sure *what* I mean to do, I just think I'd like to go back with you—and what's it to you?"

"Is it something to do with Damon?" he asked bluntly.

"Yes—no, not in the way you think."

"Mhmmm. What *do* I think, Nell?"

I made an effort, "Darling, you've misinterpreted, and much as you've grown up, practically overnight, you haven't yet the experience to understand adult relationships. Can't you leave it there?"

"No! After living with you and dad, I know more about adult relationships than you think I do. Are you going away because you couldn't ever care enough for Damon?" His voice was troubled. "Maybe my timing was off, at that, but I thought you ought to know how he feels, Nell. You could be thinking about it for later on."

"Yes, but that's what you misinterpreted, Chris. That isn't what Damon feels, quite the contrary," I said carefully. "He never wanted to be bothered, but the mess with Alexi forced him to be involved—and very thoughtlessly, when he was more or less trapped, I was coming on strong about his foot. I'm sorry about it. Now the action's over, Damon could perfectly well retreat to life as he likes it, but he thinks I'll be in his hair. Can't you understand, hon? He doesn't know I won't be running to him every second minute, particularly after you've gone, and he's too much the gentleman to wash his hands of me. That's why he's so irritable, Chris, but I can't have him uprooted. Isn't it better for me to spend the winter in America," I asked seriously, "and by next summer, we'll all be in perspective again?"

Chris nodded. "I see. So you're just trying to make him comfortable—it isn't that you dislike him?"

"Heavens, no! When he isn't snapping at me, he's exactly the sort of man I like: well-educated, great good fun. He's a bit like your father—completely different, of course, but the same sort of unexpectedness," I said reminiscently. "Absolute bedrock character; you never know what they'll do or say spur of the moment. It's a pity I wasn't paying attention, but you *do* see how Damon isn't sure I'm not a designing widow?"

Chris stood up, "Yeah, I understand." He dismissed it, "Huberto's teaching me to play chess. Want to kibitz?"

My birthday is August 24th. By then I was feeling rested and fairly frisky. "Let's go to Lisbon for a jaunt and sight-see a bit before going home?"

"No," said Chris flatly.

"Sweetie," I protested, "managing Quinta Choupo can't be *that* vital! If the hands couldn't manage for a few days, what did Damon do before he had you?"

"It's not that—it's a special birthday present I've planned for you, you have to be here to get it," Chris said. "We can go to Lisbon the day after, if you still want to."

"Well, all right, if you say so," I felt disconcerted by his decisiveness. What on earth could he have gotten for me?

As it turned out, all of Ponto Lucido had something for me! Throughout the day there was a steady procession of small tributes: baskets of fruit, flowers, bottles of wine, two superb fish from the fleet, an embroidered apron from the equivalent of a Ladies' Aid group, and a small black kitten decorated with an immense red bow. It was very heartwarming, and at the same time saddening to have to be leaving Costa Demonio just as I was beginning to feel at home.

I'd almost forgotten the reason we were here and not in Lisbon, when Chris came out to the garden, "Nell? Oh, here you are. Your present's in the study. Jorge had to get it from the airport. Come see?"

Wonderingly I followed him into the house and along the rear hall, where he threw open the door. "Happy birthday, *minha mae*, and will you please stop being stupid!"

From the depths of the fireside chair a figure rose. Damon said, "Happy birthday, chipmunk." His face was strained, while I stood speechless. "Sorry, I'm late, missed connections in Lisbon. . . . Chris asked me to bring you this from London." His voice was casual; throwing it away, but the eyes were agonized by my silence. "Here you are—and this is a slight token of my esteem." He held out two gaily wrapped parcels.

I finally found my voice, while I went forward and put my arms about Damon. "What a marplot you are, Chris. But thank you! This is the one thing I was wanting for a perfect birthday!"

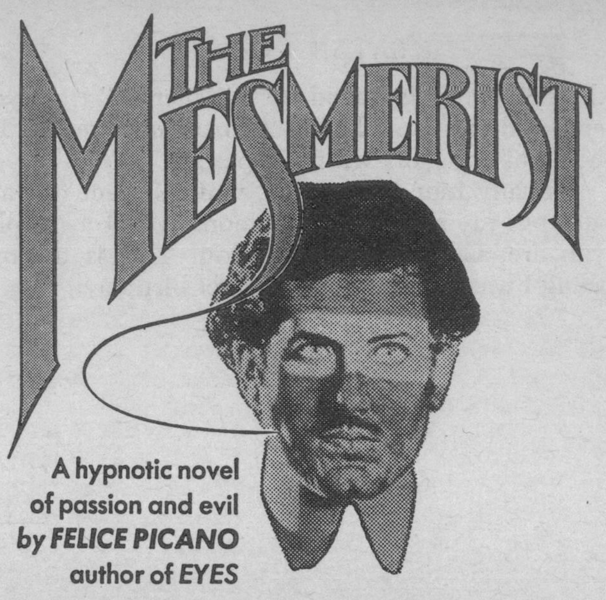

A hypnotic novel
of passion and evil
by *FELICE PICANO*
author of *EYES*

In the Spring of 1899, a stranger came to Center City. He was young and handsome—but his dazzling smile and diamond-hard stare concealed a dark and deadly power! Too soon, Center City was in his debt; too late, it was in his power. Terror gripped Center City like pain, and only the mesmerist knew how it all would end—and why . . .

"Compelling!"—*Chicago Tribune*

"The reader is pulled into the horror of minds in jeopardy. A gripping, well-written tale!"—Mary Higgins Clark, author of *Where Are The Children?*

A Dell Book $2.25

At your local bookstore or use this handy coupon for ordering:

Dell

DELL BOOKS
P.O. BOX 1000, PINEBROOK, N.J. 07058

The Mesmerist $2.25 (15213-5)

Please send me the above title. I am enclosing $__________
(please add 35¢ per copy to cover postage and handling). Send check or money order—no cash or C.O.D.'s. Please allow up to 8 weeks for shipment.

Mr/Mrs/Miss__________

Address__________

City__________ State/Zip__________

- ☐ **INVASION OF THE BODY SNATCHERS** by Jack Finney $1.95 (14317-9)
- ☐ **MY MOTHER/MY SELF** by Nancy Friday $2.50 (15663-7)
- ☐ **THE IMMIGRANTS** by Howard Fast $2.75 (14175-3)
- ☐ **BEGGARMAN, THIEF** by Irwin Shaw $2.75 (10701-6)
- ☐ **THE BLACK SWAN** by Day Taylor $2.25 (10611-7)
- ☐ **THE PROMISE** by Danielle Steele based on a screenplay by Garry Michael White $1.95 (17079-6)
- ☐ **MAGIC** by William Goldman $2.25 (15141-4)
- ☐ **THE BOYS FROM BRAZIL** by Ira Levin $2.25 (10760-1)
- ☐ **PEARL** by Stirling Silliphant $2.50 (16987-9)
- ☐ **BUCK ROGERS IN THE 25th CENTURY** by Richard A. Lupoff $1.95 (10843-8)
- ☐ **COMES A HORSEMAN** by Dennis Lynton Clark $1.95 (11509-4)
- ☐ **TARIFA** by Elizabeth Tebbets Taylor $2.25 (18546-7)
- ☐ **PUNISH THE SINNERS** by John Saul $1.95 (17084-2)
- ☐ **SCARLET SHADOWS** by Emma Drummond $2.25 (17812-6)
- ☐ **FLAMES OF DESIRE** by Vanessa Royall $1.95 (15077-9)
- ☐ **STOP RUNNING SCARED** by Herbert Fensterheim Ph.D. & Jean Baer $2.25 (17734-0)
- ☐ **THE REDBOOK REPORT ON FEMALE SEXUALITY** by Carol Tavris and Susan Sadd $1.95 (17342-6)
- ☐ **THE FAR CALL** by Gordon R. Dickson $1.95 (12284-8)

At your local bookstore or use this handy coupon for ordering:

Dell

DELL BOOKS
P.O. BOX 1000, PINEBROOK, N.J. 07058

Please send me the books I have checked above. I am enclosing $________ (please add 35¢ per copy to cover postage and handling). Send check or money order—no cash or C.O.D.'s. Please allow up to 8 weeks for shipment.

Mr/Mrs/Miss____________________

Address____________________

City________________ State/Zip________

Something is happening to the young girls of St. Francis Xavier High School—something evil.

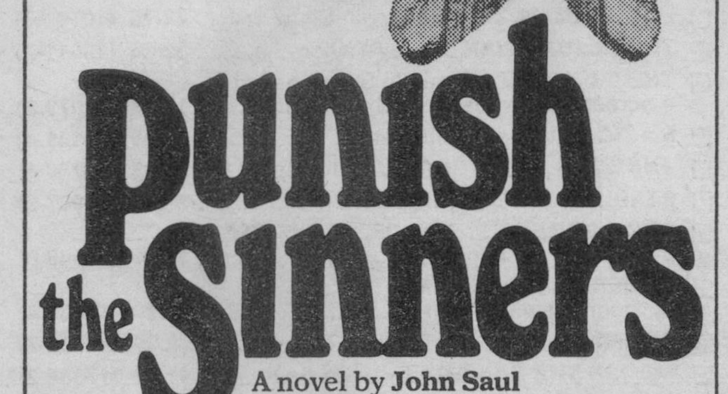

A novel by **John Saul**
author of *Suffer The Children*

As Peter Balsam arrives in a sleepy desert town to teach psychology at its only Catholic school, he finds a mystery of mounting horror. A "suicide contagion" has afflicted the young women of the town, while a dark order of holymen enacts a secret medieval ritual...

A Dell Book $2.25

At your local bookstore or use this handy coupon for ordering:

Dell

DELL BOOKS
P.O. BOX 1000, PINEBROOK, N.J. 07058

Punish the Sinners $2.25 (17084-2)

Please send me the above title. I am enclosing $________
(please add 35¢ per copy to cover postage and handling). Send check or money order—no cash or C.O.D.'s. Please allow up to 8 weeks for shipment.

Mr/Mrs/Miss________

Address________

City________ State/Zip________